To Curt,
On your fifty-fourth
birthday.
Love,
Mom

Growing Up on Route 66

by Michael Lund

BeachHouse Books
Chesterfield, Missouri

Copyright

Graphics Credits:

Cover by Dr. Bud Banis. The front cover is composited from an original photograph by Donna Lea of Riesel Texas (See her other work at http://mistyowl.com) and Photo Objects from Hemera Technologies (www.hemera.com) with text and enhancements by Dr. Bud Banis. The picture of the Chain-of-Rocks Bridge at the end of the book is courtesy of Jim Potts of St. Louis, Missouri
http://home.stlnet.com/~jimpotts/home.htm
and http://oldgas.com
Publication date September, 2000
ISBN 1-888725-31-1
First Printing, September, 2000

Library of Congress Cataloging-in-Publication Data

Lund, Michael, 1945-
  Growing up on Route 66 / by Michael Lund.
    p. cm.
  ISBN 1-888725-31-1
  1. United States Highway 66—Fiction. 2. Teenage boys—Fiction. 3. Missouri—Fiction. I. Title.
  PS3562.U486 G76 2000
  813'.54—dc21

                          00-011224

BeachHouse Books

an Imprint of
Science & Humanities Press
PO Box 7151
Chesterfield, MO 63006-7151
(636) 394-4950
www.beachhousebooks.com

Growing Up on Route 66

by Michael Lund

Michael Lund
7 January 2001

For my parents.

They, not alone, but more than anyone else, made
my growing up in the Circle magical.

Growing Up on Route 66

As we sat down to the table, it occurred to me that he liked to look at us, and that our faces were open books to him. When his deep-seeing eyes rested on me, I felt as if he were looking far ahead into the future for me, down the road I would have to travel.

Willa Cather,
My Àntonia

Prologue: The Open Book

At the next-to-the-last rehearsal for my high school's junior class play, Linda Roper struck Martin Pruitt in the groin. She did not do it on purpose, of course; and Martin was not seriously hurt. But for over thirty years I have carried a picture of that event around with me; and now, suddenly I understand what was involved.

Here is some more of the picture as it has reappeared recently in my memory: the play's cast, about a dozen eleventh graders from Fairfield (Missouri) Senior High School, is making a semi-circle around the comely young teacher/director, Miss White. We have been practicing for a performance of "Escape from Time," a 1930's comedy about a hobo/hero who poses as a visiting therapist at an old folks home. Miss White is not impressed with her Thespians at this moment, and she has stopped the rehearsal to give us a pep talk.

As Linda Roper takes a step back to create a space around Miss White, her arm swings at her side in a casual arc like the pendulum in a grandfather clock. At the same moment that she retreats and her arm comes down, Martin Pruitt steps forward. He is making room for students beside him to move toward the center of the semi-circle.

Linda's hand is half-closed, almost making a fist; and it collides directly with the flap of blue jeans material covering Martin's zipper. The blow is solid enough to make a sound—thump! The boys who see it wince.

"Boys and Girls," Miss White is saying in her sweet, first-year-teacher's voice. In the general shuffle she is ignoring or did not notice the collision between Linda and Martin. Evidence of a silent gasp, however, is visible on some of the girls' faces. "Listen to me, listen to me, puh-lease."

Miss White stands erect with her arms folded around a large, annotated version of the script pressed to her breast. In "Escape from Time," the handsome Mr. Entwilder is saddened by what he sees in the nursing home; and he decides to wake up the numbed residents to the joy of life. He also falls in love with a beautiful young nurse, the only one on the staff who already knows how much everyone needs revitalization.

As Miss White speaks, Martin, who cannot stop the instinctive recoil of his pelvis away from Linda's fist, but who is somehow able to keep from crying out, silently doubles over. To anyone in the dramatic frame of mind, like Miss White, he might seem to be taking a bow.

"We must get more feeling into our lines," Miss White pleads, looking around at each of us. "Some of you are just going through the motions."

Martin's head is down, though the pain, it will turn out, is not so severe as those who see it at first assume. Or perhaps we witnesses, surprised, have exaggerated the sound of contact.

Some in the circle of students gathered around the director had first tittered, then as quickly fallen silent, when Linda hit Martin. In those days, attention was never directed toward genitals, male or female. So we saw, we responded in a kind of shock, and then we denied according to convention.

I was standing, by the way, down the line from Martin in the semi-circle that faced Miss White. For reasons I will explain, I had been watching Linda Roper as she backed into Martin Pruitt; so I saw clearly the reactions of both parties.

Miss White pulls Mike Davidson, the male lead, out beside her into the center of the circle. "When Mr. Entwilder kisses Nurse Primer," she goes on, "He has to move as if he means it." Squaring off in front of him, she takes his two hands and places them firmly on her own shoulders.

Miss White's instructions do not matter much to me. I have only a minor part in the play, as a friend of Mr. Entwilder, a fellow tramp who urges him to leave the nursing home and his, at first cavalier, then more serious romance with Nurse Primer. In three acts I never set foot on stage but speak to characters from the other side of a high garden wall, part of the scene's backdrop.

"You are not kissing your sister in this act," Miss White chides Mike Davidson. "You are stricken with love."

Mike is ordinarily comfortable standing out in a crowd, but right now he cannot control a blush rising from his shirt collar. Mike feels awkward, as any of us boys would, because Miss White is very pretty and very young, and because his girlfriend, Marcia Hall, also in the play, is watching from a position just a few steps away from me.

Just as Marcia and Mike made up a couple, Linda Roper and Martin Pruitt were, in the language of the time, "going steady." In fact, this pair provided a model for me of what was possible in the world of teenage romance. Linda and Martin embodied not just the public image of dating—he carried her books, she wore his letter jacket, they came to all the parties together—but around them had grown the reputation of love's private beauty as well.

"Kiss me," Miss White commands. Mike Davidson stands frozen in front of her, his hands locked on her shoulders, his face pale in confusion. He is tall, much taller than the diminutive blonde woman who just last spring was a senior drama major at Southwest Missouri State College. So holding her requires his bending over, as if beginning the kiss he has been ordered to bring to her lips. But she must pull herself up to him and slip her small hands behind his neck to draw him close.

Did Linda and Martin, the perfect couple, go, as we put it in those supposedly innocent days, "all the way"? It was the question we asked about any relationship that lasted several months. Close friends claimed, betraying sworn secrecy, that Linda and Martin had separately admitted to intimacy. But, as we all know, what we say we do may not be—especially in sexual matters—what we really do.

Such questions were difficult for me to resolve, given my rather limited experience. Even though I had, with neighborhood pal Marcia Terrell, advanced to amazingly intricate stages of petting, I could not really imagine taking the final logical steps.

I now know, however, the answer to the ultimate romantic question about Linda and Martin. I figured it out only recently, as I've said, when the picture of her hand bouncing off his crotch rose magically once more in my memory. It's not new information about those two that provides the answer; it's my own expanded frame of reference from thirty years of experience in life.

In fact, now that I think about it, I realize that I also understand Mike Davidson's embarrassment far more fully than I did at the time: he was having an affair with Miss White, the young teacher/director. (I must have learned this at one of our class reunions, the fifteenth?) It was not kissing her that was a problem for Mike: it was kissing her as if this were not a regular thing for him!

The same principle applies to Linda Roper, whose action, after she hit Martin, I haven't yet spoken of. The picture of her face, not Martin's, is, in fact, what has most haunted me ever since the event. When her hand rebounds off her boyfriend's privates, she looks over her shoulder (she does not spin around) and says, almost (but not quite) nonchalantly and with a little smile, "Whoops."

The look on her face—not of alarm or shame or surprise—and the way the little "Whoops" slips out of her mouth now tell me something I could never have known at the tender age of sixteen: Linda knew from experience what she had struck; she understood from past contact precisely how hard she had bumped her lover; and she could predict fairly accurately how much discomfort a blow of that magnitude would cause Martin. Nothing else but the knowledge gained from experience can account for the easy way in which she turns back to Miss White, listening to her instructions, as Martin straightens up and finds himself not so badly hurt as he had thought.

I suppose I ought to feel pretty stupid that Linda Roper at sixteen knew more things about sexual exchange than I would learn in another decade and that it would take twenty more years before chance (the sudden appearance of this image one more time in memory) encouraged my expanded knowledge to reinterpret this event from the past. But I have decided to take a positive approach to this discovery, to be grateful that, if for many years bewildered, I understand at last. I'm glad that some things which happened long ago now make sense to me, that the road I've traveled has clearer landmarks when I look behind me than when I was moving forward.

Perhaps this is why I think the life of my generation is so neatly embodied in the current fad of retracing the old path of Route 66, that famous highway in American history. Steinbeck's "Mother Road," in fact, passed just a few blocks from Fairfield Senior High School; and the story of this town's youth would be reflected in changes to that highway.

Ah, children of America's heartland near the end of the twentieth century, where are we today? Although our journey from innocence to experience is in many senses completed, there are important stages in that process we are only now ready to understand. I would love, for instance, to linger over the story of Linda Roper and Martin Pruitt, and not just their parts in the junior play. The mythic pattern of their romance, I have only recently begun to suspect, shaped their classmates' future far more than anyone could have predicted at the time.

Our lives are, really, open books, stories which, though written, can be read and reread with profit. To determine the future we must visit, and revisit, the past. In some cases—like middle America's 1950s—the past at least seems a pleasant and fortifying place. I propose, then, keeping a seat at that table for a time before looking down the road which we will soon have to travel.

Mark Landon

St. Louis, Missouri

Volume One: The Body

Part One: Breaking Out of the Circle

Chapter I

When I saw Archie Baker curl the index finger and thumb of his left hand around to make a circle, then poke the middle finger of his right hand through that ring and pump it in and out several times, I had no idea what he was showing me.

"It's how you make babies," he said, with a wicked grin and a chuckle of pleasure.

It sounded to me, of course, ridiculous.

I must admit, however, that I did not at that time know where babies came from. One of the most remarkable things about the American middle class of the 1950s was its ability to maintain ignorance about fundamental aspects of human behavior. Despite all the space sex took up in the world, some remarkable adult sleight-of-hand managed to keep it out of the sight of children.

This was first time that enormous force in human behavior was being shown me, and I was dumbfounded. But the seed, so to speak, had been planted. And the rest of the beast would be born into my adolescent mind in the days that followed this first hint of the procreative principle.

The Great Expedition into the woods west of town facilitated my complete awakening, and that was inspired by Roger Peterson, not Archie Baker. Our neighborhood leader claimed to have heard not only of breathtaking vistas past the lost mine but of an old Indian chief living in an abandoned shack at the foot of an open meadow. We all wanted to go, whether we believed him or not.

"Go on!" scoffed Billy Rhodes, my best friend at the time, a fleshy boy with dark hair worn in a genuinely flat flat-top. We were standing in the shade of the elm tree in the Bakers' front yard, waiting for Cathy, the last of our party, to join us on the expedition's staging ground. "There're no Indians living around here."

"Wanna bet?" challenged Roger and then added. "I heard it from a hobo." The concept of the friendly hobo had a wide circulation among kids in these days. The dropout from hard work and formal education, living on his wits and nature's bounty, represented a logical extension of our childhood selves. Roger's bold claim to association with such a figure tended to dwarf even the assertion that "Indians" were hiding in our woods.

"A hobo?" asked Marcia, her round mouth falling open in the middle of her round face. She and Dennis were the youngest of our group. "My Mom said not to talk to any hoboes."

"Ummm," said Roger, squinting off into the distance, his brows furrowed beneath a tumble of long brown hair. "Perhaps she should talk to some." Marcia's mouth, already open as she contemplated the land Roger traveled outside the Circle, opened even wider.

We called our neighborhood the "Circle," by the way, because its three principal streets formed a loop along the side of Piney Ridge on the western edge of town.

Limestone Drive ran west along the bottom of the ridge, rose gradually after a flat stretch, and then, three houses past mine, curved sharply to the left, south. No more than a hundred yards after that turn, traffic, both automobile and pedestrian, generally abandoned Limestone for Oak Street going east because Limestone continued south up the ridge only as a gravel road past a few, widely separated houses. Oak Street, after reaching a tenth of a mile back east, merged with Hill Road. Hill was another gravel road coming down from the top of Piney Ridge, a site from which you could see the entire town of Fairfield spread out over several square miles of gently rolling Ozark hills. The combined routes of Hill, Oak, and Limestone, then, came together at one spot at the bottom of our neighborhood, completing, or so we thought, a perfect circle.

Had we been able to climb even higher than Piney Ridge, however, and look down from, say, one of the small planes, which, to our great excitement, occasionally dropped leaflets advertising upcoming auctions or going-out-of-business sales, we would have seen that the network of streets below was more a stretched out oval than a perfect circle, the shape, perhaps, of someone's kidney, bowed out on the south (the Oak Street) side.

On the other hand, of course, such a bird's-eye view would have disguised the many ups and downs that shaped our lives within the familiar, elongated loop. Up there, we would have lost the ability to follow the rises and falls of our little world, unless we had something like one of those instruments geographers use to detect elevation changes in photographs of terrain to be mapped. Without such special, three-dimensional glasses we would have flattened the rise from the Browns' house to the Bakers', the dip in the middle of Oak, the long descent of Hill Road.

Whatever our perspective on it now, the Circle was known at this time to be rich in climbing trees, free-running dogs, and a blissful ignorance of almost everything outside its magic limits. In other words, the material for the adventure of growing up literally surrounded the children of the neighborhood. Simple numbers guaranteed excitement, as on the streets that constituted the Circle were exactly fifty houses, each containing at least one family of two. (There were no asymmetrical, single residents in those orderly days of America's post-war prosperity.)

For the children of varying ages in each house (future babyboomers) the neighborhood provided playmates of approximately the same grade and sex within a few minutes' walking distance, and that across no streets but the Circle's own self-contained and connecting circuit. With Billy Rhodes, Archie and (his younger brother) Dennis Baker, Marcia Terrell, Roger Peterson, Cathy Williams, and a score of others, I lived in a world as full of possibility as a young boy in the state that gave birth to Huck Finn and Tom Sawyer could want.

Like any limit natural or imposed, of course, the Circle had come to represent a boundary, a line which, we knew, it would be necessary one day to cross. This unseasonably warm October day marks, in fact, our first real effort to break out of the Circle. While we had all skirted the Springer house and explored the banks of Springers' Pond, no one we knew had really tested the country beyond, an area reported to contain a forgotten mine, a farmhouse with bad dogs, and a lookout point from which you could see, on a clear day, all the way to the Gasconade River.

There are many ways to categorize the seven members of that intrepid band setting out on a new adventure—by age, grade in school, sex, size, hair color, church affiliation, favorite hobbies. But the grouping that stands out in my memory, from a vantage point some thirty years later, is along a scale of gullibility. We represented the full range of suckers, from the utterly unquestioning to the rarely caught skeptic.

I would like to pretend that I was among the most wise in the party of seven, already rendered a bit jaded and cynical by experience, that difficult master. But the truth was that I was still quite near the top of the graph, among the most willing to believe what anyone, especially anyone older or in authority, chose to tell me.

Oh, I was not so innocent, surely, as Denny Baker, who had been told by his older brother Archie than the gas he habitually passed was blue, visible to the rest of us even though he never saw it himself. Archie was always alert to his brother's "barrooms" (our word, derived from that old joke about the difference between a saloon and an elephant breaking wind: one is just a barroom, but the other's a BARROOM!). Accused of a "barroom," Dennis always denied the act and refused to look at the blue cloud Archie claimed to see floating behind him. But we could all read the deep flush on his face as evidence that he believed the deed to have become visible.

On the other hand, I was hardly so deep into the world's secrets as Roger Petersen, who had found a book on the top shelf of his parents' closet that contained "actual drawings" of male and female genitalia and who had connected those drawings, although not absolutely correctly in all the details, to the furious noises he sometimes heard from the master bedroom late at night when he should have been asleep. His enigmatic pronouncements on the nature of life, delivered with a squinting look into the distance, mystified and sometimes scared the rest of us.

We were, as I said, at the top of Limestone's gradual rise west. Smiling at the arrival of our last member, Cathy, I saw something that confused my picture of a future characterized by farmhouse dogs, forest Indians, and traveling hoboes.

I saw, just to the side of Cathy's shoulder, the tall figure of Mrs. Van Meer watering with a garden hose a small plot of chrysanthemums in her front yard. I'm certain that at the time I had no idea of what gives me such pause now in remembering this scene. I saw that she stood there in a bright red swimming suit, her long, white legs outlined by the green hedge behind her. Water from the hose knifed in a long arc through the warm air of Indian summer.

I suspect that, at the time, if this image registered in any familiar context at all for me, it was that I saw Mrs. Van Meer as a version of Wonder Woman, lariat in hand. As I recall the image now, however—more than thirty years after the event—this woman's face under a broad-brimmed, white sunhat might seem to turn slowly toward me. One eyebrow lifts, the faintest hint of curiosity. Her lips are slightly parted. In a question? A smile? A farewell? A welcome?

In other words, I know now this journey was not just across space but through development: I was another step nearer the very moment of my discovery of sex.

II

Mrs. Van Meer was a unique character for the Circle. Unlike almost all other couples in the neighborhood, she and her husband, a coach at the state college in Fairfield, had no children. Perhaps that's why she had time to do such things as plant flowers and plan a wardrobe. Most of the Circle's parents were so busy with work and raising children in that heady post-war time that their dress was functional more than aesthetic, their yards little brightened by ornamental shrubs or flowering plants.

We kids would often notice this tall, attractive woman, poised on the lawn in swimsuit and sunhat or stepping to the car in a long evening gown; but we lacked an adequate frame of reference to interpret her. I saw her for a second on that day of the Great Expedition, but how her figure might have provided an oblique commentary on my journey was at best the vaguest of suspicions.

With Cathy now included, then, the seven Circle children start off in an irregular formation down the white gravel lane to the Springers' house. As our group makes its way, let me say some more things about the individuals in this party and what they will encounter on this watershed day.

Marcia Terrell lived directly behind my house on the opposite side of the Circle, our backyards mirroring each other over a low, wire fence. A tomboy who loved to build everything from sandboxes to tree houses, Marcia could run as fast, jump as high, and throw as far as most of the boys her age in the neighborhood. Her hair was what we called then "dirty blond"; and her long, bony arms and legs were always scraped and bruised from an active life.

Marcia was, however, sometimes bothered by her family. She struggled with a father who loved to tease and a mother who seemed to fear the world outside her own house. Mr. Terrell told Marcia, for instance, that the upstairs bedroom built into the attic of their house was detachable, a separate unit hinged at the roof line. In the case of high winds or tornadoes, he claimed, they might have to let the top floor go. He showed his daughter a huge red switch marked "danger" in the hall linen closet (actually a cut-off switch for the furnace) and said all he had to do was throw it for Marcia to fly off like Toto to Kansas. Marcia knew that this was a joke; but if, at night, a blustery storm from the north tore over the house, she had trouble sleeping.

Her mother worried less about the house coming apart than about anyone or anything coming inside her home. She almost never went out, even getting her groceries delivered from Tucker's over on state highway 00.

Whenever Marcia started chewing on her lower lip, I knew some recent event in the Terrell family was troubling her. If I had known what would cause her to gnaw her lip at the end of this particular day, I guess I would have called off the Great Expedition before it ever got started. But we never do know such things ahead of time, do we?

The Baker brothers, now filling their pockets with stones from the lane as they walk, have already been introduced. Archie in particular, whose potential includes the role of bully, will throw these stones at rabbits and squirrels we jump along our way. In contrast, Roger carries a small, homemade slingshot. His targets are always inanimate, puddles and rocks, at the ends of safe lines of fire.

Billy Rhodes, walking beside me, is saying that he's heard you can smoke grapevines, do I want to try? It sounds ridiculous, just the kind of thing Billy would find out about, but I say "OK" because that's what boys do. Billy is our crazy one. We say he will do anything, and he usually does.

That leaves only Cathy, as old and nearly as wise as Roger, even more confident of a prominent role in the world's future. She sees herself through stirring films of America's triumph in the Second World War. (Though we heard in our young lives reports of fighting in Korea, the battles that shape our notions of heroic behavior are movie versions of the landing at Normandy or the retaking of islands in the Pacific.) Cathy imagines herself not as the wife who stayed at home to worry but as the double agent living on a knife's edge behind the lines. She has flaming red hair, which requires vigorous shakes to show her profile or to frame a strong gaze into the future. She is beautiful. The only sign of self-doubt in Cathy is a slow blink, during which the world she sees is replaced by a better one she has imagined.

One might wonder why such a promising young creature is joining us lesser mortals on this Saturday adventure. But in those days there are no malls for her to hang out in, with ten movies at a single cinema. And cruising the downtown did not become a regular activity of young people until they were old enough to drive. Not everyone had television sets.

I think, too, that staying inside with other girls her age, playing at dolls or reading teen magazines, would have restricted the free range of Cathy's imagination. Any ordinary structure would have failed to provide the background against which her life should be played out: her cover blown after a lover blurts out his passion to his captors, the heroine has to find her way across the mountains to the border with a small band of resistance soldiers.

No one was really the absolute leader of this little group, I should note. That was one of the beauties of the Circle, that its many young citizens formed, dissolved, and remade groups; established, dismantled, and recreated pecking orders. There were so many of us that anyone getting neglected in one bunch could find another set of companions to roam the neighborhood with. Even within the seven who set out on the Great Expedition, individuals would pair up in one order on an outward trek, regroup in different patterns for the return.

The Circle was, then, because of its numbers, a fairly open and democratic society. And the carefree kids with their eyes wide open to the world tripping down Springers' Lane had little apprehension of the divisions and exclusions they would face even before this day was done.

About seventy-five yards from the Springers' (where the group now arrives) the lane crossed a dry branch, turned south, and rose to a parking space in back of the house. We slipped off the lane at the branch and skirted the north edge of the pond. Most of the run-off that filled this round, man-made body of water came down the southern slope, joining a little creek, which trailed off the pond like the tail of a tadpole.

The house, above and to the left of us as we walked, was only a couple of years old, for Colonel Springer had recently retired to Fairfield after thirty years in the Army. One of his favorite late tours had been at Ft. Leonard Wood, forty miles away and greatly expanded during World War Two. Colonel Springer and his wife had planned since that time to buy property near the base (relatively inexpensive in those times) and build their dream house overlooking the rolling Missouri countryside. And their long front porch, with an equally long patio beneath it, did enjoy a spacious western view over the pond.

In another few moments most of us gained a similar, though lesser view from the tops of two rock hills next to the north shore of the pond. These flinty mounds had been created by the rock and dirt scooped from the ground to make the pond. Marcia, Dennis, and I were on the first man-made hill, Cathy and Roger on the second. Archie and Billy, still at the bottom, were skimming rocks across the pond, seeing who could get the most hops from a single throw. Above, we had a preview of what we hoped to find at the end of our trek, the grand vista reaching to the Gasconade.

"Look there," I said to Marcia and Dennis. "I bet the open place we're looking for is just on the other side of those hills."

A small creek issued from the base of the earthen dam that was the pond's western shore. The dam reached from a continuation of Piney Ridge on the south across to the Missouri Pacific railroad tracks running along an embankment on the north.

"That's pretty far," noted Dennis.

"We can make it," I claimed. "I don't see any sign of a farmhouse or mine, though."

These railroad tracks, by the way, ran through town and were a major freight and passenger route from St. Louis, that crossroads for Midwest traffic, through Oklahoma and Texas and on to the far West. Route 66 ran right alongside the tracks.

From the other hill, Roger said. "They're down there. First the mine, on the right, then the farm." Cathy did not say anything, but pursing her lips and shading her eyes with one hand, she readied herself, I suppose, for the possible loss of some resistance soldiers in the effort to slip past enemy outposts.

I noticed then that Marcia was looking not out over the creek but back toward the lane, her lower lip sucked in on one side. "You ready?" I said to her.

"Sure," she said, turning around quickly. "We're not going to see any Indians, though, Mark." A pause: "Or hoboes." As she started down the side of the hill, she pulled her jacket around her as if it were cold.

III

Just past the pond two paths went west: one followed the creek that issued from the bottom of the earthen dam, the pond's western shore; the other path crossed that creek and ran along the east-west hill, which was a continuation of Piney Ridge. The division of our party along these two paths was not so final as Frost suggests ("Two paths diverged in a wood . . ."), but it led to a significant "difference" in what each of us learned on that memorable day.

Billy, Marcia, Dennis, and I took the creekside route, later to become known, in the lore of the Circle, as the "Low Trail." Billy wanted to look for smokable grapevines, and the tall sycamores along the creek were covered with the climbing plant. In the woods east of the Springers' house we had already found the traditional use for grapevines—not harvesting grapes, of course, but swinging from one side of a dry creek to the other on vines which reached forty feet up into tree branches.

Roger, Cathy, and Archie took the "High Trail" because they were acting as scouts or lookouts for the whole operation. From the side of the ridge they figured they would spot the mine and be able to plot a course around it. At the head of this party walked Roger, chewing on a dry stalk of grass and squinting wizard-like into the distance. Archie, who would have liked to challenge Roger as the first on the trail, took up a long piece of whitened hickory for a walking stick. And Cathy came last, her hands swinging free. The slight smile playing on her face suggested that she was letting these boys go first only to make them feel important, that she anticipated a time when she would have to step forward and direct us all to safety.

Of course, this division into smaller groups increased the chances for confusion about the status of our overall mission. We were still within easy hailing distance of each other, but the oaks, which hold their leaves late in fall, and the evergreens, which were abundant on the rocky creek side soil, caused us to lose sight of each other frequently as we marched westward.

Each group also found new things to examine and evaluate along their separate ways. While we relayed the most important observations across the creek, lesser items and small reactions were kept back. From their vantage point, the High Trail group caught a glimpse of a column of smoke on the horizon. Was the smoke from a house or the mine? They called out that they saw the mine. Did the space between those small hills represent the path to the open space? They thought so, and told us they could see where we should go.

Down below, the thicker growth along the creek bottom directed our attention to mossy rocks and moist fern clumps low to the ground. Billy stopped where a number of grape vines hung from a pair of tall trees; but he found they were green, too hard to break off. Eventually, he sawed away at a small vine with his pocketknife, looking back down the trail toward the pond.

Billy whispered to Dennis and me that the two rock hills looked like a woman's breasts, didn't they? I didn't think so, but I pretended to agree. I tried to suggest that a portion of the ridge was the rest of a woman's body. She could be lying on her back if the two hills were her breasts. Marcia, pretending not to hear, scuffed her feet in the damp earth. We called up to the others that we couldn't see much along our way.

A question occurs to me now as I remember both these trails, which I would walk many times in the next few years. It's a question this story will answer only in part.

Each path was well worn, the upper one winding around rock outcrops and between clumps of bush, the lower paralleling the creek. Flattened dirt, dry on the High Trail and moist on the Low, made easy walking; and no vegetation grew in the path's one- to two-foot wide centers. I wonder now who made these trails, and who was using them at this time? Were they as old as the Native Americans who first lived in these woods? Or did early pioneers coming overland out of Virginia and Tennessee plot the logical routes from town to village, water crossing to camp, outpost to lookout?

Just as puzzling, who or what was using them now to prevent their being overgrown? Did animals pad down these ways on their daily hunts or scavenges? Since only small creatures—rabbits, squirrels, possums—inhabited those woods, I wouldn't think they could have accounted for the wear. There were few homes out this way, as I would eventually learn; so it is unlikely local residents traveled routinely along the High or Low Trail.

Both paths were fairly near the railroad tracks and went in the same general direction. Was this a route for an army of continent-crossing hoboes moving east and west along a major thoroughfare? Or were there other neighborhood children playing all around us whom we never noticed or ran into?

I cannot, in the end, identify all the creatures besides us who had covered this same ground, though one person in particular must appear here before I end my account of this particular adventure. I do believe that these routes we followed in childhood were determined in large part by the landscape, taking the easy walking ways around high rocks and across shallow waters. Paths, lanes, highways, railroad tracks were shaped and directed by the land itself. Human patterns of transportation were molded onto a framework of rock and soil so large we seldom glimpsed it or measured its power over our lives.

The country past Springers' Pond is all changed now, of course, from the days when it was untended woods. A high-class subdivision extends over much of the area, developed from a new road put in off the state highway running south from Fairfield.

Even if I went walking within the same geographic coordinates today, the lay of the land would be altered. Some hills have been leveled to make building sites, depressions filled in to improve drainage. The creek itself is, I think, underground, part of the town's storm sewer system. All this territory is within city limits, countryside become residence. The Circle's High and Low Trails run only in memory now, their sources and purposes hidden in the past. Piney Ridge is still there, of course, and Springers' Pond is the same. But to determine all the little shapes that once directed us from day to day requires both a powerful memory and some imagination.

In that lost landscape, the two paths converged about a quarter of a mile past the pond at the end of a ridge. The Low Trail group came up from the creek bottom to see Roger and Archie sitting together on a large boulder, Cathy standing higher up the hillside and looking west. Their pose stands out clearly in my memory because it includes a second clue (after Mrs. Van Meer) to what this day's exploration is really about.

The Low Trail group had been delayed while we waited for Billy to burn up an entire book of matches trying to light a grapevine. He could light the stick, and it did smolder cigarette-like for a minute or so; but it was too green to draw or stay lit. (We would eventually find, by the way, through trial-and-error, that you can smoke grapevines. It just takes a section dry and porous enough that you can suck air through it. They taste terrible.)

One other event slowed us on the Low Trail. Marcia was lagging behind, kicking at sticks and small rocks in the path. I went back to bring her up with the others.

"You know when your dad goes off to work?" she asked me, looking up. Ahead on the trail, Denny was trying to push past Billy to be first in our group to meet up with the others.

"Sure," I answered. All our fathers left their houses on the Circle at almost precisely the same time every morning for work, 8:00. A few mothers, teachers and nurses, worked too, but they were a tiny minority.

"What does your mom do all day?"

"Um, cleans up, I guess. Cooks." I'm not sure I had ever really thought about it much. She did what all mothers do.

"Wash clothes, vacuum?" inquired Marcia.

"Sure. Must be. Listen to the radio. Call on the phone."

"Yeah."

"Do you want to stay home?" I asked, to keep us moving.

"I came home early from school once." She pushed a branch reaching across the path out of her way.

"Were you sick?"

"No. I just left after recess." Most kids walked home from school, less than a mile from the Circle. If it was cold, we could get picked up by a mother in our car pool. There were no second cars in these families yet, so each wife generally kept the car home one day a week to car pool and to do errands.

"Didn't your teacher notice you'd left?"

"Not for a while. Later she called my mom."

"Were you home then?"

"Sure, I just hung around the neighborhood until it was time to be home. When the phone rang, I was in my room and I listened from the hall."

"Your mother didn't know you'd skipped out?"

"No, she got mad at Mrs. Casey. Told her I came home with the other kids, just like every day. Why did she do that?"

"I don't know."

I didn't know at all what Marcia was asking about here. This conversation seemed pointless, but at least I had kept her moving, catching up with the others. I could hear Billy and Dennis calling out now to the High Trail group.

"Do you think there really are hoboes around here?" Marcia asked, chewing her lower lip. She looked over toward the tracks on the high embankment beside us.

"Sure," I responded. I had seen men walking along the railroad in town. Some were simply taking a convenient route across Fairfield; but others were vagrants on their way to other places. "They walk along the tracks. You've seen them."

"Do they ever come in the Circle?"

"Naw. What would they do there? They're on their way to California mostly," I claimed.

We had caught up with Billy and Dennis now, as they had gotten into a shoving match to be first. Dennis slipped and got one foot into the creek. He screamed, but it was in mock terror. We all laughed. Billy and I reached down to pull him up as Marcia grinned from the bank. Then we all started to run toward a clearing up ahead. We burst into the open together and found that we'd connected with our other group, Archie and Roger sitting on a boulder, Cathy surveying the future.

That moment and that scene have remained fixed in my memory, one of those visions that represent a discovery along the road of life. I was at a point when a new frame of reference was becoming apparent all around me that would forever modify how I live and think, though I only saw it then and did not fully understand it.

What I saw was the two boys leaning their heads together, whispering conspiratorially. I saw Archie look back over his shoulder at Cathy, grin, nudge Roger with his elbow. Then he made a gesture with his fingers, and I knew what he was talking about. This was his loony theory about how babies are made.

IV

Before I describe again the gesture Archie was making, Roger's response to that gesture, and my own reaction to Roger, I must explain how weak I was at this age in metaphor, in symbolic representation of any kind. Perhaps this was a unique or at least rare quality among my friends; but I would like to think I was not outrageously distinctive in this regard. I do know that I have been, from my earliest years, consistently literal minded. I like one-to-one correspondences: name to object, description to action, response to stimulus. This down-to-earth approach is not at all uncommon among Midwesterners, I think.

Such preferences are advantageous in many spheres of activity, leading to precise communication, the speedy satisfaction of desire, a knowledge of where everyone stands. However, there are other situations that require a more flexible system. The discussion of sex Archie was having with Roger, and indirectly, of course, with Cathy, was such a situation.

Let me give you an example of my tendency to cling to concrete expression and unequivocal statement.

I was no more than five years old when my father bought me a first kite, the standard diamond-shaped, paper affair with two sticks providing the crisscross frame, We had bought it together downtown at Ben Franklin's, the five-and-ten-cent store. I picked out the color, white. The kite came rolled up, two sticks side-by-side inside the paper.

Excited, I watched Dad peel the paper from around the sticks and lay the pieces out on the livingroom rug of our house on Limestone Drive. He placed the two sticks across each other making a "t" shape, laid them on the opened kite paper, and looped a string that ran through a seam on the outer edge of the paper into slots at the ends of each stick. With the paper now tied to the wood structure, a piece of string was stretched from one end of the horizontal stick to the other, bowing the kite so it would not bend or rip in the wind. Presto—from kit to kite!

To do all this, my father had been kneeling on the rug in his brown corduroy pants and a plaid flannel shirt. Now he rocked back on his heels, chuckled to himself. Looking not at me or at my bemused mother watching over her knitting from the green easy chair, he began a lengthy explanation of how, as a kid, he had rigged his kites, of how kites, in fact, should always be rigged.

"Never follow the instructions included with the kite," he said, shaking his head. "They don't make any sense, and you need to learn on your own anyway."

Those official instructions featured a short anchor string running from a spot on the vertical stick two inches below the top to another spot on the same stick two inches above the bottom. This string was supposed to go on the down side of a flying kite, through holes poked in the paper. The string you hold in your hand to fly the kite was then tied in the middle of this short anchor piece, allowing the kite to oscillate back and forth in the breeze, since that anchor piece would not be restricted horizontally.

My dad, however, insisted that a kite should fly in a fixed, steady position at the end of its string. "No waving or waffling," he stipulated. "That kite should sit up there like a star." He also thought it stupid to put holes in a kite's paper.

To prepare my kite for flight, then, he ran strings from each of the diamond shape's four corners to a single knot in the middle, at which the flying string was then attached. And a rag tail, which the instructions referred to vaguely as optional, was mandatory in my father's scheme. It held the kite steady in rapidly shifting currents and sudden gusts of wind.

Whatever the strength of his reasoning, my father's kites flew, this one on the first try in front of our house.

There was little room for take-off, with the wind out of the north-northeast providing a flight path over our neighbor's house (the Franklins'), across the top section of the Circle toward Limestone as a gravel road. But there seemed no worry on my father's face as he took the kite in one hand, dangled it on its string a minute, looked back across the street toward Cathy Williams's house for leaves to move in the trees (the sign of a good wind coming). Then he raised the kite with his right arm, released the string, backed up across our front yard and street.

The kite rose in little jumps over the garage, cleared power and telephone lines, pulled its tail softly over trees at the corner of Marcia Terrell's yard. It was up.

He did this so well, my father, that it never occurred to me to want to do it myself, to remember that this was, after all, my kite, not his. But he thought even of that, of a need I hadn't expressed to be more involved in the action.

"Watch the ball of string," he said, dropping it on the street between us. The kite was rising so steadily now that, as the string unwound and went through his fingers, the ball bounced and hopped on the pavement at my feet. "Tell me when I'm about to run out of string, so I can stop."

The string was wound around a cardboard cylinder; but my father, again from his own great experience, knew the end of the string would not be tied, or not tied carefully, to that core. He had already selected and set aside a stick on which he would tie and then rewind the string. He would let me fly the kite holding on to that stick with both hands. Later he would catch the string on notches at the ends of this stick and, twisting his wrist back and forth, bring the kite in as speedily as if he were using a fishing reel.

He would do this with my second kite, not my first; tomorrow, not today.

You see, I had been so carried away with this experience that when, almost immediately after he told me to watch the string, I saw only a cardboard cylinder spinning away from me downhill, no string attached, I just stood there dazzled. How thoroughly and accurately my Dad had foreseen events! The string would run out, he would have to catch it, I would have to sing out.

Well before I could get over that wonder, turn and tell him that now was the time, the string slipped through his fingers and raced off on its own, over the Franklins' into trees on the other side of the Circle and beyond.

"Whoa!" said my father, taking a few rapid steps into our yard after the string.

"Whoa!" I called, as much in echo as in the spirit of my charge to inform him that the string was now at an end.

My father, who had, of course, lost many kites in his day, laughed and looked at me. "That one got away from us, didn't it?"

I agreed, not really feeling guilty or sad at this turn of events, since things had gone, overall, quite well: the kite had been put together; it flew.

My dad looked toward where the string trailed through treetops and across backyards of houses on Oak Street. "I bet you can find it," he said. "Go on up the hill and look."

Thrilled at this new mission, I took off immediately. I would like to say I went swiftly, but five-year-old legs do not cover ground quickly. It took me several minutes, running all the way, to make the turn at the top of the hill and then cover the level stretch to where Limestone ended as a paved road. But just twenty or thirty yards past that point I saw my kite, lying face down in the middle of the road. I had found it!

However, I also found myself at an unexpected impasse: what was I supposed to do now? My father's instructions had been very specific and featured the key words "go," "look," and "find." I had carried out all three tasks; but I felt there might be something more I should do.

Still, my father had not said to do anything else. And I, like most kids, didn't want to do something I wasn't supposed to do. He specifically did not say I should do anything to the kite other than find it. I had, after all, hardly touched the kite during its rigging and flight.

Yet, it occurred to me that my kite was in a vulnerable position there in the road. Looking around at woods, back to houses on the Circle, I decided to move the kite over to the side of the road, just as a precaution. In setting it down again, I noticed that a little breeze threatened to carry it off into the bushes, so I placed a few small stones on the kite's edges to hold it down. Then I ran back to tell my father of my success so far and to get more instructions.

Again, he was not upset at this development, but he asked why I had not brought the kite back with me. Bring it back, I realized! Of course, that's what I should have done.

"Well, no loss," he said. "Let's go together and get it." And off we went.

Alas, that delay proved costly. Despite its being less in the way of traffic, my first kite had been run over by a passing vehicle, leaving several black smudge marks, one gaping tear, and a crushed horizontal stick.

We got another the next day, I'm happy to say, but the larger problem of my literal mindedness was not so quickly resolved. My refusal to get beyond the most direct content of speech or gesture was still causing problems years later when I confronted Archie's crude representation of sexual activity on the Great Expedition.

What I saw Archie doing on the rock at the end of Piney Ridge was the same thing he had showed me a few days earlier in my own backyard: he looped the first finger and thumb of his left hand together to make a circle; then he stuck the middle finger of his right hand through that ring and pulled it in and out. He grinned widely and nodded his head.

"That's what you do," he said.

Crazy, I had thought: you can't make babies with your fingers, rubbing them together as you can two sticks to make fire.

But now he's telling Roger the same thing. Either he's sure about this, or he's trying to show up Roger, prove he knows more. But then Roger's reaction to Archie confirmed my own notions.

V

I must explain once again that I did not then have the slightest idea where babies came from. So I took in this graphic representation a second time and recorded it in my mind. He seemed awfully confident about this, strange as it sounded to me.

Although I saw Archie, Roger, and Cathy in this tableau for only a second, I continued to puzzle over what their exchanges might mean as I followed the Low Trail group out into the open. Billy, a blackened grapevine clamped between his teeth, outraced Dennis to the rock where the two older boys sat. Climbing past them to where Cathy stood, Marcia took up a similar lookout position. I kicked a round rock, worn smooth from being washed in the creek, up the hillside.

"This way," called out Cathy, starting down the hill to the west. She was angling a bit to our left, across the end of a slim valley which reached back behind Piney Ridge.

Roger rose from his rock and pointed ahead and to the right, where the top of a gray cement building rose over the treetops. "The mine," he said simply, as if the discovery of this mythical landmark were nothing, only the first in a series of breakthroughs he had planned for us.

At the same time, I became aware of the sound of machinery, trucks, a low rumbling, perhaps coming from underground, out of sight. I had probably not noticed it earlier because we were down low at creek level. Marcia, Billy, Archie, Dennis, and I fell in, in that order, behind Roger and Cathy.

I am reasonably sure I knew then that storks did not bring babies. It had something to do with doctors. Mothers, wives, women were involved, getting bigger and bigger around the middle until, after visiting the hospital, they came home with infants. Perhaps I understood that babies developed inside the mothers, though I am sure I never asked how it all got started.

At the bottom of the hill we came to another creek, dry except for a few stagnant pools here and there. Archie used his walking stick to vault across it, though that was hardly necessary. Billy checked out the grapevines swinging from a tall sycamore but saw nothing to exchange for his current smoke. He said this water came all the way from Arkansas.

I was at this time aware of the anatomical differences between men and women, thanks to one succinct father-and-son session conducted when I was about five years old. The follow-up lecture, however, was still only in the planning stages, and its delivery came some months after it would have done me the most good.

We must have been coming even with the mine now, which lay to our north along the tracks. When we had turned somewhat south, the Missouri Pacific had curved northward; and we were probably several hundred yards away from the main portion of the mine. We all talked in low voices, looking off toward where that gray building would be. Would we be in trouble if we crossed onto the mining company's property? What did they mine there anyway?

"What do they mine there anyway?" asked Marcia up ahead.

"Gold, I hope," claimed Billy.

"Sure," said Archie with a sneer.

"I bet its bauxite," offered Roger. There was a pause, probably because no one else had ever heard of bauxite. I thought his answer was "boxed ice" and concluded that the operation would be interesting but not very profitable.

"I think it's diamonds," offered Marcia. "Precious jewels."

"There is gold around here," I said. Dennis waved a piece of rock, pulled from his pocket. Pyrite, I knew without looking, "fool's gold." There was a lot of it in these Ozark foothills, and everyone in the Circle, at one time or another, had to go through the ritual of being shown some, being told it was real, learning the truth.

"Let me see your rock, Dennis," said Cathy, stopping for a moment in a little clearing. "The one that's gold." He handed it to her, smiling. He knew she knew.

"See those shiny spots," he said, carrying on the old joke anyway. "If you can melt down the rock, the gold sinks to the bottom."

"That piece's worth, oh, probably fifty bucks," added Archie.

"Yeah," I chimed in, wondering why we were carrying on this charade so long with Cathy. She was not only our senior but a creature of another order. She had her eyes on a world beyond the Circle, beyond Fairfield, out there in places like New York City and Hollywood.

We had all gathered together in a little clump now, watching Cathy examine the rock. Pushing a rich wave of red hair back behind one ear, she turned Dennis's find over in her hand, weighed it, scraped a section with her thumbnail. "Gold," she said, a statement not a question. She blinked once, and her eyes glittered in the shade of the creekside trees. She handed it back to Dennis. "We must look for more."

She turned and began to follow the creek again, her eyes scanning the ground. I saw puzzled looks on the other faces, except for Roger who squinted up at the sky, as if he was judging, by the height of the sun, the hour of the day and our distance from the North Pole.

Look for more, I wondered? How dumb can she be? We all know it's just a rock, no more valuable than the flint and limestone that are everywhere around here. Still, I began looking at the ground too. Maybe it was gold?

What was actually mined in the operation north of us, by the way, was nothing. Well, they did produce gravel, crushed rock, but not intentionally. This was a demonstration mine run by the college in Fairfield, South Central Missouri State. The school had a strong metallurgy program and used the mine to demonstrate technique and to experiment with new equipment.

There were two main tunnels dug back into a limestone hill, and little trains on small tracks bumped down into the dark. Digging it deeper, the operators would haul rock out, which would be piled into small hills on the edge of the property. There were also several square excavations into the surface outside the mine's opening, some kind of model strip-mining. We would all take the tour in high school a few years later, not much impressed by this small-scale operation.

I wondered about the lost mine (now found) and its purpose as I walked behind Cathy on the Great Expedition, but I also kept replaying in my mind the vision I'd had where the two trails came together. As I had kicked my smooth stone uphill, a vague suspicion came over me that this matter of babies, this realm of human activity by which the species keeps itself on the planet from one generation to the next, was bigger than I had imagined. There was something out there very important whose shadow I had just glimpsed. The full body was going to come into view, I felt, very soon.

I remembered none of the words Archie had used earlier to explain sex to me, except perhaps "man" and "woman," "his" and "hers." There was something too about juices, and pleasure. But I had dismissed this theory as absurd. For a time I wondered why we needed an explanation of this natural event, anyway. There had always been babies; there were babies now; there would be more babies. Did it matter where they came from?

All of a sudden our party came to a halt, the bunch of us in back bumping up against Cathy and Roger at a turn in the trail. A high wire fence stretched across the way. Hearing the low grind of engines and the muffled clanking of machinery nearby, we looked at this fence and at, every ten feet or so along the fence, conspicuous "No Trespassing" signs.

These were not the familiar hand-lettered paper or cardboard posters designed to keep hunters away, but institutional, machine-made, metal signs aimed at all passersby, especially, we assumed, at children. We would not try to cross this fence as we had climbed over the rusted barbed wire ones we occasionally came to in other parts of the woods. Even Roger would not challenge this limit.

At first, I had thought Roger's response to Archie's hand rubbing was an immediate endorsement of my own judgment: he had laughed, throwing his head back and hoo-hooing to the sky. Yes, I had thought, exactly. This was the stupidest thing I'd ever heard, babies from fingers. I couldn't imagine anyone's being naive enough to believe it!

But then a second thought raced after the first, caught up with it, left it in the dust. Perhaps Archie did have this baby making business all wrong, but what Roger knew about it might be far more unbelievable, wilder still than Archie had ever imagined. And if that were true, how far was I from understanding what actually was involved? Perhaps not fingers and thumbs, palms and knuckles, were used but, what? feet? elbows? backsides? Was it just a man and a woman (marriage), or did it take groups?

Roger looked down to the left of the high wire fence marking the borders of the mine property. Although there were a lot of bushes, he thought he could see where it turned back west. "Come on," he said in a quiet, slightly strained voice, waving us after him.

We had to climb the side of a steep hill, using low-hanging limbs and small bushes to pull ourselves up. Behind us, the sounds from the mine seemed to be rising from a low rumble toward a deeper call, a throaty moaning. In addition to the underlying roar we also heard now a thumping, like a huge hammer striking the ground or two giants bumping into each other. Nervous, we all wanted to get through this section of the woods.

The moment after Roger laughed at Archie's explanation of baby making on the end of the High Trail, I saw him look back over his shoulder at Cathy, and wink. To Roger's wink, Cathy returned a small smile. She knew? Girls knew? What was this? Something was going on here that I'd missed. Who else knew? Billy, Dennis? Surely not Marcia! Was I the only one who didn't know?

Halfway up the hill the fence did turn back to the west, and we could see a clear way beside it. The roar of the mine was louder still, and Roger started running at half-speed along the fence. We were still in thick brush, scrub oak that had grown up after land had been cleared, and could not see far in any direction. But the fence continued west only another twenty-five yards or so, then turned sharply north; and the ground gave way before us toward an open meadow.

The sounds of the mine fell behind us as we continued to run.

Part Two: Coming Full Circle

Chapter VI

And so we ran on, away from the mine and its subterranean noises, away from our nervousness at being somewhere we shouldn't be, ran along the side of a low ridge headed west, seeing beside the trail, through gaps in the scrub oak, a small farmhouse at the end of a brown meadow (a farmhouse with a small yard in which two small dogs seeing or hearing or smelling us began a shrill chorus of barking), ran down the end of the ridge though high grass and occasional evergreens, down across another dry creek, leaping from a big rock on one side over to a soft muddy bank on the other, ran up toward the southwest to avoid a drop-off above the creek, itself running far from its source of Springers' Pond, ran over finally a rounded and tree-covered hilltop to burst into the open and see before us all at once what we had sought from the beginning, the goal of our expedition, the open space from which you could see, it seemed to us, forever.

We could not see, of course, forever. But certainly for miles we looked out over rolling green countryside lying now in the bright sun of midday. The Gasconade River was even out there somewhere, though we couldn't pinpoint it. Below the hazy blue horizon of cloudless sky and brown land it had to be winding its way toward the Osage, the Missouri, the Mississippi, the Gulf of Mexico, the world's oceans.

We would learn in later years exactly where to look for the river by coming very early in the morning, when mists would rise from the water, visible to us at this distance as a thin gray ribbon on edge. But for now we simply looked at miles and miles of land and were satisfied, elated even, at the prospect laid out before us.

We saw also to our right the railroad tracks heading west, down a long incline toward that distant river. And running more or less parallel to the train tracks, a thin white strip appearing and disappearing on hillsides and across valleys was Route 66, the major east-west highway from Chicago to Los Angeles, coming through Fairfield out of St. Louis on the way to Tulsa, Oklahoma.

We didn't know it yet as Steinbeck's "Mother Road" because none of us would read that great work before high school. And even then, we didn't automatically connect that road across a fictional landscape with the reality before us.

While some of us were thinking of what it would be like one day to travel down the open road we could see plainly, we had no idea what was coming toward us along that same path. For me the result would be an awareness of new possibilities, but Marcia's meeting would send her into an enforced isolation.

To the south we could see great reaches of wooded countryside, dotted with occasional fields and marked here and there by high hills. From this point to the heart of the Ozark Mountains along the Missouri-Arkansas border lay only small towns little changed or changing in this or the last century. So tiny were most of them that we would not even learn their names until high school, when our football, basketball, and track teams went on the road to compete.

The foothills would gradually flatten in the other direction as in another fifty miles they reached the Missouri River, the line which divides the state across its middle into generally open prairie land (north) and hilly forests (south).

For perhaps half an hour we stood looking, hands shaded against the sun, and talked about places we would one day go, things we would surely accomplish in our futures.

"As soon as I get out of school, I'm going west," said Cathy, unpacking a sandwich she had been carrying in her jacket pocket. "To California."

"I'm going farther than that," countered Roger. "To Hawaii. Or Japan. I'm going to join the navy."

"It's Minnesota for me," said Dennis, pointing due west. His understanding of geography was not strong.

"I'd like to build a road out there," I said. "I wonder how they put bridges across rivers."

"They build the whole thing back at the factory," explained Billy. "Then just push it across on tractor tire floats." Billy never hesitated to answer questions, whether he knew anything about the subject or not. This was a habit that would make school increasingly difficult for him in later years.

We had been walking around among a number of large sandstone rocks in this newly discovered field, rocks which jutted out of the ground as obvious observation points for our party. Most of us gravitated now toward the largest slab near the center of the field. At its side grew a small tree providing partial shade. Marcia and I sat down on the shade end and took out the sandwiches we had packed for lunch. Cathy and Roger (who was already eating an apple) stood in the center. Billy and Dennis walked out in front of the slab to examine some of the low, thick clumps of brown grass that dotted what we, having arrived, were now officially calling the Open Space.

Archie stood on a smaller rock about twenty yards behind us, leaning on his hickory staff. "I'm calling this 'Archie's Rock,'" he announced from his spot, with a tone of command, even challenge.

No one responded, perhaps because, although we were familiar with the neighborhood practice of claiming territory, we seemed to sense that this was for now a community place, a find for the group rather than individuals. Even when we asserted special rights to places, it was usually less an effort to exclude others than an attempt to define oneself, to find a comfortable place within the group. We did this, for instance, with the Vacant Lot Tree.

The "Vacant Lot Tree" grew, of course, on the "Vacant Lot." One address on the fifty-house Circle had no building at its site because the property had been set aside in the original planning for the neighborhood. It had been reserved for a proposed street, a second exit from the loop of Limestone, Oak, and Hill. This potential road, never actually built, was to have crossed over the railroad tracks and linked up with Route 66 on its way into town. (Later, of course, this highway became Business 66, as a bypass was built around Fairfield.)

About two houses down and across the street from my house, the Vacant Lot was considered community property, often a playground or small park for kids on the Limestone side of the Circle. The curb turned into the lot at the edges of the neighboring properties, making it possible also to pull cars onto the unoccupied land. When more families began to buy second cars in the 1960s, this spot became an unofficial parking lot for the immediate area. In one of the cars parked in that lot my own sexual initiation, begun on the Great Expedition, took another delightful step forward.

Behind where these cars would be parked was a site of more innocent play, a massive pear tree. The Vacant Lot Tree was a great climbing tree, one of a number of big-limbed, expansive pear trees scattered throughout the Circle. Before it was developed, this land had been a farm with an orchard of cooking pears. Dr. Masters' House (corner of Hill and Oak) was the old farm residence, a stately two-story house with columns and a separate garage, significantly grander than all the one-story, two-bedroom houses other families lived in. (I'll have more to say about that house later on.)

The Vacant Lot Tree had been divided up by our gang of seven, each person having a limb or fork specifically designated as his or her own. Dennis had the lower section of a long branch reaching south, and I was out at the end. Roger had the highest fork on the main trunk; Cathy her own limb reaching east, Marcia one going west. Archie claimed a secondary upright trunk below and to the north of Roger, and Billy the fork from which these two trunks began. Many summer afternoons and evenings of my youth were spent lying or hanging or sitting in this tree, seven or fewer of us, talking about events in the neighborhood, stories we had heard on the radio, things we wanted to do.

At about this same time there was at least one other set of kids who had parceled out the Vacant Lot Tree. My brother Charles, heavy Joe Martin, the Bell sisters, and two boys from Hill Street did a lot of things together. And on days when we younger kids were roaming the woods or headed for town, this second, older gang might be occupying our places.

I remember no battles for exclusive rights to the Tree, the different groups somehow alternating occupation as if there had been an early treaty or some time-sharing agreement about the property. There were also Circle kids temporarily unattached to any specific group who might climb the Tree and sit alone in one of our spots, or join others already there when there was room for one more. We felt no need to contest a newcomer's right to a place, and there always seemed to be enough space in this tree for everyone.

It came as a shock to learn one day that my brother's friends divided the Vacant Lot Tree into parts different from ours. No one sat in Roger's fork, but each of the two boys from Hill Street took one of its two main branches. The limb Dennis and I claimed belonged to just Charles; and the Bell sisters shared Cathy's west-reaching branch.

This alternative division of space should have taught me something, but it didn't—at least not at the time. I was staggered by this denial of what I saw as the natural order, asking my brother again and again how he thought this branch contained places for two, this other space for only one, why that fork didn't require a person sitting in it. Two years older and wiser by more, he only laughed at me. Eventually, I gave up trying to understand their system, pretending it didn't exist and that our way of organizing The Vacant Lot was the only way it could be done.

Archie's appropriation, out in the Open Space on the day of the Great Expedition, of a sandstone rock big enough to park a car on, then, was complicating a fairly innocent day of discovery. So rather than turning to claim other spots on the field or to challenge his place, we went on eating, watching the view.

"I wish we could stay here all night," said Cathy. "Watching the stars come out."

"Yeah," added Roger. "Make a camp."

"Better look out for the Boogey Man," advised Billy. "He'll be coming to get you!" Dennis, who was often threatened with the Boogey Man by his brother, Archie, looked up nervously.

"Yeah," said Roger ironically. "He comes out here in the middle of the wilderness every midnight, figuring there'll always a bunch of kids looking at the stars."

"Maybe we ought to be starting back," offered Dennis, glancing off into the woods.

In a whisper not everyone heard, Marcia said, "I'm not going home." I was still sitting beside her.

"Ah, I know what you mean," I said softly, leaning toward her and nodding my head at the horizon. "What a beautiful place."

"No. I mean I'm not going home, ever," said Marcia. And when the tone of her voice made me turn to look, I saw that she was chewing her lower lip furiously and that a single tear stood in the corner of one eye.

VII

I would love to be able to report that, as soon as I spotted a tear in Marcia's eye, sensitive young person that I was, sensitive but also wise in the ways of the world, I performed some delicate and appropriate act to relieve her distress.

For instance, *I put one arm around her shoulder and gave her a reassuring squeeze.* Or, *Laying a hand upon her arm, my younger self kept it there with just the right pressure and for just the appropriate length of time to show a concern that would not fade over the years stretching out before them.* Perhaps, *Mark then found words that revealed a great understanding of the young woman's sorrow, words that did not embarrass or burden her, but words that one would have thought beyond the reach of a boy so young.* Or even: *Sighing himself, the future scientist-poet-religious leader Mark Landon found a tear rising to his own eye, for he was overcome with a sense of loss and sorrow greater and more lasting than anything Marcia could imagine; and that recognition, coming as suddenly and powerfully as a stroke of lightning, overshadowed her tiny grief.*

I did not, however, do or say such things. My literal-mindedness often required that I already have specific instruction or previous experience with a situation in order to know how to act. And a girl's weeping from unknown causes in the middle of the day on a forest excursion went beyond any circumstances with which I was familiar.

Sure, my younger sister Beth cried often enough, but I generally knew (or was) the cause of her unhappiness. And my mother could well up at sad stories passed around our family or the neighborhood. But here in the Open Space with a person about my own age, a person whose experience pretty much matched my own, I was confronted with something new, a condition for which I possessed no immediate resources.

I was saved from the embarrassment of revealing that I had nothing to say to Marcia by the fact, announced in a sudden chorus of cries from the entire group, that Billy was setting the woods on fire.

Billy had concluded that the solid tufts of dried grass all around the hilltop, each perhaps a foot in diameter at the base and as much as two-and-a-half feet high, were natural, ground-based torches. Surrounded as each was by dry dirt and flinty rock, they could burn, Billy thought, without setting fire to neighboring clumps or nearby bushes and small trees. And he imagined this clean burn of a single bundle as a grand sight, a fitting celebration of our accomplishment in reaching this goal.

Billy also decided it would be good for this commemoration of achievement to come to the rest of us as a surprise, so he gave no warning before putting a match to a potential beacon fifty feet in front of our observation rock. Within a matter of seconds an area the size of a one-car garage was blazing.

(Although he used one more of the matches by which he had been lighting his grapevine to ignite this little bonfire, it is characteristic of Billy that he already had in his young life obtained his own cigarette lighter, trading a dozen comic books to Heavy Joe Martin for a battered silver Zippo. He had not found an easy way to get lighter fluid for it, as grocery store and drug store clerks in small towns had a way of knowing your parents in those days, and word of your purchases could sometimes beat you home. Still, the empty Zippo rode in Billy's front jeans pocket every day, and we would occasionally see its sharp rectangular outline against his thigh. Roger was always teasing Billy about a habit of fingering the lighter as he walked, and I would laugh along with everyone else, though I was not always sure what the point was. "Got something in there?" Roger would ask, and Billy would blush. "Play with it, and you'll break it," he might caution. "Don't set yourself on fire now.")

Billy was not on fire yet, but the way he screamed for help suggested he might soon be. He had his jacket off and was beating at the edge of the burning area. The others ran down to join him, hollering too.

Chaos quickly established dominion over us. We knew something had to be done, but we weren't sure what. Billy, Marcia, and I began stamping at the fire on one edge, where the wind was slowing its spread; but on the opposite side the flames were too high for any of us to try stepping in. Roger and Cathy composed themselves enough to study the wind and conclude that the fire was moving toward a line of evergreens on one side of the field, and they began to scrape a fireline in the dirt ahead of the flames. Picking up sticks and a sharp rock, they hurried to dig a shallow trench across the fire's path.

Meanwhile, whenever the fire jumped to a new big clump of grass, there was a frightening burst of light and heat. The burning grass and small brush made crackling and hissing sounds as a gray smoke grew thick and caustic, throwing some of us into coughing fits. We continued to shout at each other and at the flames themselves.

Despite these efforts, however, the fire spread with relentless appetite, soon the size of half of a basketball court. Working on opposite sides of the burned area, the seven of us were being moved farther and father apart as the fire grew.

I saw, through smoke and dust and the shimmer of heat across a distance, several dark forms swinging coats to beat at flames and stepping high to stomp out smoldering ashes. On another part of the circle of fire I saw a lone figure bent over making a second fireline, digging with a sharp stick. Busy myself at similar tasks, I felt inside the steadily growing realization that from this one spot might begin a forest fire that would devastate not just our woods but the town of Fairfield, the entire county, even more.

The screaming of questions and instructions, the sounds of stamping and slapping, the roar of air feeding the fire and a hiss of combustion inspired a panic far greater than had the mine's ominous rumbling earlier, which had sent us running along the site's fence line.

In the confusion of the scene, several specific images stand out even after all the years since this event. At one terrible moment I rose up from a crouched position, from trying to roll a large rock up against another to block one line of the fire's approach, and saw a small evergreen, just about the size of a good Christmas tree, burst into flames. It was almost an explosion, the fire catching several dead branches and shooting up the trunk into the sky. I felt at that moment that all was lost, that we would not be able to stop this fire, that it would chase us back past the farmhouse (gone in flame), past the mine (would that explode?), around Springers' Pond (too small to stop this devastation), and on to the Circle at least, back to shame and punishment beyond imagining.

But even at that instant, through the towering tree of flame, I saw on the other side of the fire, or thought I saw, more figures than belonged to our little group struggling to turn back the inferno. Several individuals even seemed bigger than we were, not giant forms, perhaps, but larger than young teenagers, working at ground and brush to help put out the fire. I didn't have or take time to examine closely these figures, ghostly outlines across the smoky haze, and I didn't actually count bodies to determine whether they were extras to our party or if I was seeing the same persons twice. I went back to my task of trying to put a barrier across the northern side of the fire, so it was a momentary vision that I wondered about later.

A third sharp image from the heart of the conflagration remains in my memory. Across one section of smoking ground, through the haze, I see Cathy Williams in a kind of silhouette. She is standing facing me with her legs slightly apart. Holding her jacket by the collar in both hands over her head, she leans forward and swats at a burning clump of grass by her feet. And as she bends down and to the side in this swinging gesture, her torso turns sideways to me. She has, I see, I realize, breasts!

She has been wearing beneath her jacket a thin white blouse, now one button undone at the top and the bottom pulled loose. So through the fabric of her blouse, light behind her, the sharp outline of breasts is visible. I realize that I never knew girls I knew would one day have breasts. (She will have great breasts, by the way, well into middle age, high, firm, and large for her slim figure.)

There is something about her legs, too, that will take even longer for me to figure out. Her feet spread a shoulder's width apart. she delivers a blow to the fire and raises her jacket over her head again. And I see her legs in her jeans, long legs thin at the ankles but rising through strong tight calves and full muscular thighs to her body. And her waist, sharply drawn against the dark background of evergreens and washed by waves of thick, gray smoke, is thin at the belt line, making her hips round and prominent. The picture (another Wonder Woman?) stays with me, though I do not understand exactly why.

Did we put out the fire? Not really. The wind shifted or died down, and natural barriers brought an end to our mini-forest fire. We did not realize exactly when we had gained the upper hand, but at some point I found I was making remarkable progress in stamping out one section of edge. And then I looked around, and others were stepping back, catching their breath, pointing at how what we saw now was primarily blackened ground, smoking embers.

There were shouts of encouragement, renewed efforts to make sure the fire would not spring to life again, and then a general recognition that we just about had it under control. A final phase of scurrying from place to place, some triumphant stamping and swatting, several marches around the perimeter and we knew the crisis was over.

In all of this, of course, I completely forgot the tear in the corner of Marcia's eye.

VIII

After our experience with crisis, the little party from the Circle was stunned, struck with the enormity of what had almost happened. We stood around and looked at the blackened ground. I did not remember for some time Marcia's near crying earlier, or her fierce declaration that she was never going home again, because even she seemed to have forgotten the cause of her distress, to have been completely absorbed by the fire.

As was so often the case on that day, of course, I was misreading the signs right in front of me. For Marcia, the fire was the little event of our expedition. Her personal confrontation was yet to come.

Meanwhile, Roger, sitting on the observation rock, began a series of nervous jokes: "Did you see a bear in a highway patrolman's hat when we first came up here? I think I saw him drop a cigarette."

"No," I said. "I was too busy looking at some boy scouts rubbing sticks together to pay any attention to bears."

Then Dennis: "Me, I was ducking the lightning in that terrible storm."

Without anyone's taking the lead, we found ourselves standing up, brushing off our pants and jackets, preparing to start back toward the Circle. Although there were a number of jokes at Billy's expense as we began to wander down the way we had come, no one seemed to want to make him out to be any different from the rest of us. We all got in trouble; this was just one of his times. Even Archie, still looking for some way to take center stage among us, knew that what Billy had done, any of us probably would have, had we been the ones with the matches that day.

"Which way did we come?" asked Cathy before we had gone very far at all. The trail, if we had really followed any route that definite on the last stages of our journey to the Open Space, seemed on the reverse course less distinct, its edges blurred by clear patches of ground, openings between trees or through brush. We were also confused by the similarity of hills climbed and dry creeks crossed.

We knew the general direction we wanted to go, east; but a number of theories on how to proceed now contended for our allegiance. Roger claimed it would be easiest to go somewhat south and east along the bottom of a ridge, keeping that between us and the mine. Marcia advocated heading more northward, directly toward the rumble of machinery in order to get home more quickly. Probably just to be different, Archie insisted on following a path up the valley toward the south. Billy decided to join him, perhaps hoping to recover his self-confidence by separating himself from most of the group for a while.

"We'll all meet where the two paths came together after Springers' Pond," Archie told us; and he and Billy moved off quickly. No one seemed to want to go with Marcia close to the mine; so, in the end, she came with the rest of us.

We hiked quietly now, each lost in thought. Dennis was particularly self-absorbed, shaking his head from time to time and muttering. I was just ahead of him, so I could hear his little, explosive exclamations: "Whew!" "Humpgh!" "Aghrrf!" "Kphfph!"

Marcia walked in front of me, looking, I noticed, apprehensively around her. There was a cool afternoon breeze rustling through the woods, and I saw, looking behind me, clouds gathering in the west. Was she thinking about her father's teasing, saying the attic bedroom would be jettisoned in a storm? Had whatever inspired those few tears returned to trouble her as she walked? Or was it still the effects of the fire, a letdown after the crisis?

Ahead I saw Roger and Cathy walking side by side whenever the trail allowed; but they did not seem to be talking much. They too were subdued now, keeping a steady pace on the road home.

Looking at them, my mind turned back to Archie's story of what men and women did together when they were married. Kisses, I thought to myself; what's involved there? Do kisses have something to do with this baby business?

Approaching a creek that ran from the ridge down into the little valley to our right, Roger and Cathy stopped to examine some unusual rocks. She may still have been looking for fool's gold, he perhaps for small rounded stones to use as slingshot ammunition.

I had lately been thinking a lot about kisses. In the romantic movies I'd seen, remarkable interest was shown in this activity. When hero's arms wrapped around heroine's shoulders and waist, when heroine disappeared in this embrace, cameras zoomed in on smooth profiles. Heads twisted neatly to the right angle. Lips met lips. (I didn't realize until much later that such neat camera work also obscured the bodies beneath those kissing heads. Again it would take Martin Pruitt and Linda Roper to teach me what was off-screen in our movie world.)

All this seemed no more exciting than kissing my own wrist; yet Hollywood was insisting that there was more, much more, to this lip stuff than I had understood.

Marcia and I stepped across the dry creek bed. Then she stopped a minute to listen for the sound of the mine, actually a bit less loud here in the shelter of the ridge. We also waited for Cathy and Roger, who were still considering the rock formations made by water rushing down the ridge during storms.

The event of kissing seemed bland enough to me, judging from own lips' experience of plump maternal cheeks, my face's contact with a grandmother's or aunt's simple dry smooch. In the movies, though, there were differences. Those lips were sometimes wet, for one thing. Glistening on the silver screen, their moist quality was not the pasty smudge of lipstick but some strange tonic to the parties involved, a subtle catalyst to love linked with the music of orchestras and breathless meltings.

We were all on the way again, Dennis growling and woofing behind me. What was his problem, I wondered, not realizing he was trying to disguise his "barrooms." The wind from the west was stronger now, and in the far distance, did I hear thunder?

What could the secret of a kiss be? What else besides lips played a part? Well, tongues, I supposed. In one movie I remembered the woman's lips had parted as the man's face neared; and in that dark space between her lips her tongue moved in a way I could not interpret—out? up? around?—and toward a purpose simply unfathomable.

We moved into a circular field where large rock outcrops created a logical route toward a gap in the ridge. We would cross there and probably be able to see the mine ahead and to our left.

Teeth? No sensation there. Only scraping or grinding possible in that contact; and I imagined heads drawn sharply back, grimaces in anticipation of visits to the dentist, if kissers crashed together.

We passed through the little field of boulders. Although there were no large trees in front of us, the ridge rising on both sides of us blocked the side views. A path of sorts disappeared ahead into a clump of cedars, over which I thought I saw the cement block of mine building. The thumping of machinery was louder here.

The little thing that hung down at the back of the throat? It was visible when Goofy, falling down into some bottomless canyon on the *Wide World of Disney*, threw open his mouth in a desperate scream. The "uvula" (I didn't learn its name until ninth grade biology) served no purpose that I knew. Was it a miniature, second tongue, mimicking that larger body in chewing or speaking, turning food over beneath teeth or framing tiny faint words lost in ordinary speech? Maybe that was how Dennis was making his irritating little sounds behind me.

The ground softened beneath our feet as we traveled on a bed of fallen cedar needles. I lost sight of Cathy and Roger where they wound through the trees no more than twenty feet ahead of me. Either Dennis was falling behind or I couldn't hear him now.

I didn't seem to have any control over the little thing in the back of my throat, though when I examined my uvula in the bathroom mirror, stretching my jaws and turning my head into the light, it jumped around in there. Could some people move it when they wanted to? My father could wiggle his ears, using muscles along the cheek and neck; but try as I might, I could produce only furrows in my brow and, after too many minutes of grimacing, a dull headache.

I was being hypnotized by Marcia's walking form ahead of me, legs swishing in her blue jeans, hair swinging back and forth, heels rising and falling above the soft ground. The sun went behind the clouds; and a soft wind blew over the treetops, smelling faintly but sweetly of rain.

Was there some method I hadn't glimpsed to the uvula's involuntary quivering, a secret process it was involved in I'd never been told about? Could it recede and extend on command? Was it stronger than it looked, its soft dangling shape misleading? Were men's uvulas the same as women's? What would happen if you lost one in an accident? Did uvulas make babies?

"I SEE DENNIS'S BARROOM!" somebody yelled suddenly in a tremendous voice. I jumped straight up, then whirled around to see Dennis, ten yards behind me, blushing so furiously his faced glowed a fiery red.

"Who is that?" screamed Marcia directly in my ear, almost hysterical. I looked where she was pointing, to our right, and saw a huge Indian standing in the shadow of a tall pine tree. Although his form was shaded, there was no mistaking the giant headdress of war feathers; the erect posture, one arm raised; the wooden and stern face fixed on us.

"WHAT ARE YOU KIDS DOING IN MY WOODS?"

"Who is that? Who is that?," hissed Marcia, pulling at me arm.

"You can't see farts! You can't see farts!" shouted Dennis, furious.

"YOU KIDS ARE IN TROOUUBBBLLEE!" the Indian moaned, threatening.

Marcia leaned her head on my shoulder, crying softly now. "No, no, no."

Instinctively, I circled her shoulder with one arm.

"I'M GOING TO SCALP YOU!" the Indian cried.

Dennis picked up a rock and threw it directly at the Indian. To my horror, I saw it bounce neatly off his forehead.

"AIEYEEE!" the Indian called. Then he began to fall forward, away from the tree's trunk, directly at us.

"YOU KIDS ARE . . . " Thump! He hit the dirt with a soft sound.

Cathy and Roger were laughing. From behind the pine tree stepped Billie and Archie.

IX

The Indian was wooden, an old storefront character.

Archie and Billy had found it on the crumbling porch of an ancient log building farther up the valley. Apparently, the structure had once been a small country store. Years ago, a north-south road ran up this little valley, an alternate to the main road east (now Route 66) on the other side of the railroad tracks.

This was a long time ago, maybe even before Fairfield was incorporated. The little road circled around the back of Piney Ridge into what was or would become the town, and the main road made the long climb where the Missouri Pacific line now lay. In places of this now remote part of the woods we would in succeeding years discover sections of the old roadbed, and we could imagine forgotten traffic winding along the sides of hills and curving over the tops of ridges.

On the site of a small spring along that road, facing west and the setting sun, stood (according to a hand-lettered sign found inside) "Store," which originally may have served the logging operation that cleared whole forests in the last century. After the timber business closed down, hill people perhaps came there to shop without having to walk or ride all the way into Fairfield. Or maybe early settlers bought supplies here while trying to farm the rocky countryside left by the clearing of trees. And perhaps trappers and pioneers made this a last stop on their way to the western territories.

With the extension of the railroad, however, this route was used less and less, until eventually it was abandoned altogether, left to grow wild again in scrub oak and cedar. Now Store was almost invisible, set back against the ridge and surrounded by brush.

The wooden Indian, presumably Store's token, was actually pretty beaten up, his facial features unrecognizable after decades of exposure to weather and insects, the original colors faded to a dull brown. But from the distance at which Marcia, Dennis, and I saw him, leaning against the huge pine tree, his form was recognizable, even striking.

Billy later told us that he and Archie had jumped when they came upon the old building and saw "Chief-Who-Lost-His-Face" looking out a broken window. When he didn't move, though, they investigated; and Archie had the idea almost immediately of setting an ambush for us. The Indian was light enough that the two boys could, with some effort, carry him. He'd been hollowed out in part by termites. While we were looking at rocks in the little creek, then, they were hauling the storefront character into position along our route.

Although the ambush succeeded in terms of Billy's aim, distracting our attention from the fire he had started, it failed in its primary goal for Archie. He had wanted to scare Roger or to make him appear afraid in front of Cathy.

Roger immediately claimed that this was the very Indian he'd told us about, who lived in the woods, his little joke. And we could never tell whether he had known about a wooden Indian all along or just made it up on the spot. He gave us that wizard look of his, a sly grin; and Cathy's smiling silence on the subject tended to be interpreted as confirmation.

The scare worked far better on the rest of us, more on Marcia than we understood for some time: it was the next-to-the-last scare she would face on the Great Expedition. She was so angry at the trick that she announced she was walking directly north to the tracks and would follow them back to the Circle.

"I'm going with you," said Dennis. He wanted no more barroom jokes.

"This way'd be shorter," said Archie, pointing southeast. "Go over one more hill, and you come down on the other side of Springers' Pond." He meant on the south side of the house, not near the driveway we'd originally followed.

"Is that right?" Marcia asked the rest of us, hesitating. I tried to think it through myself, remembering where we'd walked today and the earlier trips we'd taken as far as the pond from the other side. I couldn't decide, but not only because I needed an aerial perspective, the proverbial bird's-eye view, to calculate distance. I got to thinking also about how frustrating it was that people like Archie could never be counted on to give a straight answer.

Perhaps Archie did believe the distance was shorter along the route he proposed, though I'm pretty sure he was barely suppressing a grin. He might have been hoping to pull another surprise on us, the wooden Indian trap having at last brought him into prominence within the group. There could be some interesting landmark or feature along the route Marcia was proposing that he didn't want her to find out about. Or he might simply have wanted to be in control here, the one who knew the territory and guided the others.

I was troubled then, and have been troubled in later life, by what I consider a distressing human failing, the willingness to misrepresent things because it serves a personal desire unrelated to the situation at hand and to the concerns of others. It might be that I was a slow learner in this regard, hopelessly taking in what I heard or saw at face value far longer than I should have. And I am still a sucker for deceit, for irony, despite the many times I've encountered it, the repeated experience of being mistaken in others. It seldom occurs to me that falsehood can serve such remote ends.

Whatever my own shortcomings in perception, however, Archie was lying: we could have gotten back to the Circle much more quickly following the tracks. Ironically, however, things would have been much easier for Marcia and Dennis if they'd taken his deliberately false advice and come with the rest of us. Going their own way along the tracks, they ended up in the wrong place at the wrong time. The rest of our return trip, on the other hand, though longer and less direct, was simple and uneventful.

This matter of being in the wrong or the right place, at the wrong or the right time, is another troublesome thing to me. The decision to go back one way determined other, unrelated events. Chance was responsible. And chance did not distribute pain and happiness fairly. Yet this occurs all the time. Some people live entire lives blissfully sidestepping calamity, while others seem to have an unerring, unconscious attraction to disaster.

This principle was most forcefully brought home to me a decade and a half later in Vietnam, where too many people I knew ended up in the wrong place at the wrong time. I thought then that this was a product of the special theater of war. Now I know the same frame fixes events in peacetime as well in conflict.

What did Marcia and Dennis find on their walk home? It was death, I am sorry to say. They found a dead man lying in the ditch along the side of the tracks.

He would turn out to be "John Doe," some hobo, the Fairfield police assumed, on his way west. The empty pint bottle lying near his feet, traced to a liquor store in town, provided a clue to the circumstances of the event, though the immediate cause of death was drowning. He lay face down in three inches of water.

Average height and weight, without distinguishing physical characteristics, middle-aged, no driver's license or social security card, the dead man was anonymous. He was never identified, never linked to any of the many accounts of missing persons emanating from distressed families and friends throughout the land. Not even traced to a specific region of the country, the dead man had slipped off all the social maps of his time, disappeared from the coordinates that were guiding the rest of us into the future.

He was so neatly prone, parallel to the tracks and centered in the ditch, that Marcia and Dennis almost walked past him without noticing. According to Dennis, who later told Archie, who passed the story on to the rest of us (perhaps accurately), Marcia literally fell down when she saw the corpse. We understood only weeks later why the event struck her so hard.

The dead man was dressed in dark slacks, a brown sports jacket turned up at the collar. He wore no hat, and his dark hair was surprisingly neat. How Marcia could have thought she recognized him from the back is not clear, though we all knew eventually that she thought for a moment he was a man who had been secretly seeing her mother.

My own mother told me about it afterwards, that some Circle residents had seen what they thought at first was a salesman calling on Mrs. Terrell more often than was customary. Marcia must have seen him once or twice herself when her father wasn't home (perhaps that time she came home early from school), and she came to her own conclusions.

So it was not only the encounter with death that so overwhelmed her near the end of that autumn day; it was also a personal panic that the tight world of her family had been invaded, her parents' lives corrupted by outside forces, perhaps also from within. And now, she thought, one party lay dead along the railroad tracks.

Of course, it was not anyone she or her parents knew, a fact Marcia probably accepted even before she and Dennis, racing their own panic, reached their homes on the Circle. She had, Marcia admitted to herself, been seeing her mother's visitor everywhere today. (If, by the way, there really had been anything going on between her mother and some man, nothing came of it. The salesman, whoever he was, stopped calling.)

So Marcia escaped direct knowledge of betrayal, though she did have to deal with death after she told her mother what had happened. She led the police to the spot, told about finding the body.

She apparently handled this well, better than Dennis, who had told no one at his house and who would have denied everything had not Marcia come with the police to have her account corroborated. Still, the event and her memory of that event, to be buried from her conscious mind for many years, lay down a certain path for her future. For her, betrayal had become connected with death.

I, of course, was in other places at the moments of her crisis, unaware that terror and disillusionment could threaten our little lives. I was lucky, I guess, able to hold off for a few more years a direct encounter with finality. Even though I gradually learned all the details, Marcia's experience remained for me a story, something that could be controlled and kept at a distance, like a radio show or movie. In fact, what I bumped into myself at the end of the Great Expedition was more exhilarating than depressing, a moment of exciting discovery.

X

As we walked, Billy and I got to thinking about the abandoned country store, "Store," about how it would be fun to have a store of our own in the Circle. It would be a kids' store, we said, run by and for kids. It would have things we wanted—toys, candy, comics—at prices we could afford. And there would be a place for us all to get together, talk and play games.

After we had passed the area of the mine, we began to feel the temperature falling. It was not only getting late in the afternoon, but the heavier clouds gathering over the Gasconade probably meant an evening thunderstorm. At the top of the last hill by Springers' Pond, Cathy looked back over her shoulder, red hair flashing in a ray of sun filtered through distant clouds. "Come on," she said. "We want to get back before this breaks."

What appealed to Billy about the idea of a store was its operation, the stocking, display, and movement of goods. He foresaw trips downtown to get odd things (spools of thread, from which we could make little rubberband-driven cars) at going-out-of-business sales; trips to make bulk purchases of standard items (string, balloons, safety pins); and trips to do research on pricing, merchandising, advertising. The more we talked, the more complicated and expansive the operation became in his view. The business's only boundaries at this point were our imaginations.

Ahead of me Cathy picked up a rock, another piece of fool's gold, bigger than any I'd seen. She squeezed it in one fist as she walked, a smile playing over her face.

For me the appeal of a store lay not in the operation but in the planning and construction. Where in the Circle would it be built: in the Vacant Lot, at the base of the neighborhood where Hill and Limestone came together, at the intersections of several backyards near the very heart of the Circle's fifty houses?

62

It had to be central, accessible, but private too, so that customers would come regularly but where we could keep an eye on the building. Too, we didn't want it conspicuous enough that parents would ask questions, interfere, or try to take over.

What shape should the building be? A simple square, one room with a counter and shelves, customers moving up and down orderly aisles to check out the merchandise? Or would we want to be more innovative, creating, perhaps, a round building, stock grouped in pie sections of the outer wall, with a booth at the center to carry out transactions?

We came out now on the south side of Springers' Pond, following a narrow path running along the edge. Across the still water we could see the two rock hills, resembling, in Billy's eyes, the breasts of a woman. Behind those mounds the railroad tracks rose on the high embankment, but we did not see Marcia and Dennis, presumably ahead of or behind us in their parallel journey.

A store might be more than just a place to buy and sell goods, Roger said to Billy; it could be a place to hide out, a place to get away from the ordinary world of school and family.

"Yeah, a clubhouse," Archie added, getting excited about his own version of the idea. "We could have meetings. Only members. With a president." I could see his eyes go hazy at the prospect of running this club, of dominion.

"We'll have to build it first," I pointed out.

"It needs to be at a hidden location," put in Cathy. "Where no one but us knows." She was thinking again in her other contexts: Allied forces had set up a base camp to which she returned after operations within enemy territory. The night before, face blackened for the night mission, a pack of explosives slung over her shoulder, she had said goodbye to the wounded officer whose assignment she had to take over. When she came back, pulling off a wool cap, bright hair springing out, she learned that the soldier, her lover, had not lived to hear of her success.

"Why not use the tree house?" offered Roger. He and his father had built a great tree house in his backyard, with roof, walls, even a window. You climbed up on little boards nailed to the tree trunk, and entered through a hole in the bottom. He had stocked it with comics and several books he would not let anyone else see.

"It will have to be bigger than that," said Billy. The scheme in his mind's eye already required a main room and a storeroom.

We came out now on Limestone as a gravel road, the top of the Circle, near the spot, in fact, where my first kite had met its untimely end. The breeze was stronger, heavy with coming rain. Billy began to worry that he was going to get in trouble for being late and for getting rained on, so he proposed going down Oak, then cutting through to the other side of the Circle at the Kings' house. (We all knew about the place where the fence was bent down behind the Kings' and we could hop over from Oak Street's backyards to Limestone's.) I decided to go with him, but Cathy, Roger, and Archie went the other way.

When Archie stopped at his house, Marcia had not yet brought the police to interview Dennis; and Dennis was playing with toy soldiers, not letting on that anything unusual had happened on his way home.

Roger and Cathy took their time, I later figured out, coming down the hill. Her house was nearly opposite mine, next to the Vacant Lot; and Roger lived further down the hill. Had he continued without stopping at Cathy's, we would have met each other somewhere on Limestone after I left Billy's.

Billy and I ran down Oak, jumped the fence, and came out at his house, in the middle of the north side of the Circle. I stayed for a minute to finish talking about our store. Behind us on Oak Street the police car summoned by Mrs. Terrell must have arrived by this time to hear Marcia's story.

"Let's scout around tomorrow," I proposed. "Look for a good place to set up shop."

"I'll start getting some things together tonight. I already have enough smokes to sell." He pulled a dozen sections of grapevine out of pants and jacket pockets. He had gathered them all along the way of the Great Expedition. There were also three books of matches.

"Umm, we'd better be careful with those." I advised.

"Oh, yeah. Sure. OK."

"Anyway. See you tomorrow."

"Right."

The last exchange was not really necessary, of course: we knew we'd meet the next day because our lives unrolled together in the Circle. All of us either met at the neighborhood school bus stops in the morning, or on other days just piled out into the neighborhood to join up with whoever else was there and looking for something to do.

Unaware that a police car, with Marcia inside, had pulled around to the top of the Circle, I started up the hill toward my house. Just as I left Billy's, I spotted, under a bush in the front corner of his yard, an old rubber ball. Once bright red and perfectly round, it was weathered and chewed, probably by Billy's dog, Stumpy. I toed it out from under the bush and began kicking it up the street.

Kicking something along the street, by the way—a rock, a ball, a tin can—was a regular activity for me and my friends as we moved through our neighborhood or to and from school. As far as I know, kids have always done this.

I did not, however, kick the ball with the authority and skill of a developing soccer player; for that sport was unknown then in this part of the country. I had no concept of the goals and defenders, teammates and passes, zones and sides I would one day understand in great detail through my own children's involvement with the game.

On this particular late afternoon, then, as the dark came on and the first drops of an evening shower began to fall, I nudged and skimmed this lopsided, soft portion of an old ball up Limestone. Thinking about the things that had happened in the woods today and what might happen with a store tomorrow, I did not respond at first when I saw out of the corner of my eye Cathy and Roger on the front porch of her house.

There were no lights on at the front of the Williams' house, her parents probably in the kitchen at the back. A street lamp opposite the Vacant Lot threw only a little light to her porch. And, because of several intervening branches blowing and bowing in the wind, Roger and Cathy were to me shadows among other shadows dancing against the house. And their two selves made, at the moment I did actually see them, one form, a single silhouette to my suddenly attentive eye.

There were kissing, I realized, wrapped up in each other's arms, mouth to mouth. Kissing, I thought; there it is! I'm looking at it. Lips on lips.

"What good is it?" I thought, still puzzled by the operation at the same time I was startled to find kids I knew, kids not that much older than I was, engaged in this fabled activity, this movie event.

I stopped under the single elm tree in my own front yard, looking across the street at the motionless pair. The old ball I had been kicking lay at my feet. As the rain started to come more heavily, I saw the shadow split, one half sliding down the steps away from the other. The shape on the porch raised a hand to wave. The other shape just glided away, into the trees, through the rain, down the hill.

Then lights came on in the living room of the Williams'
house, to Cathy's right as she stood with her back to the
front door. She did not move from the porch for another
minute, though, as I could tell now by the indirect light.

I could not read the expression on her face, but I could
make out the eyes and mouth. Perhaps I only imagined
the slow spreading smile there. But I could see what she
did next; and then lights went on in my own mind.

When the shadow that had been Roger was gone into
the night, and the light that had come on was not
followed by the appearance of her father or mother,
Cathy took one hand, the hand that had waved perhaps,
and lowered it below her belt, between her long, lean
legs. Holding her hand there, she leaned back against the
door and her mouth fell open in a sigh that, I still believe,
I could hear within the storm breeze.

And in that instant I understood: it was not fingers that
did it; or lips and tongues. That was it; those were they;
this to that.

"Oh, ho!" I thought. "Ah, ha!"

Volume Two: Landscape

Part Three: Setting Up Shop

Chapter I

We did not build and stock our neighborhood store that year of our youth, though I do want now to tell you of how we finally did reach that goal after some minor setbacks and with a final bizarre reversal of fortune. Our store building was delayed in part because Marcia and Dennis's walk home changed for a time the attitude of our parents toward life in the Circle.

Suddenly convinced that vagrants and shiftless characters were roaming the outskirts of their children's world, mothers and fathers grew more cautious about letting us stay out after dark or allowing us to walk to and from town alone. They required frequent reports of what we were doing, where we went and with whom, if we had talked to or seen anyone they might consider suspicious.

Their concern was at first reassuring, for we too were unsettled by the image of a fallen man at the side of the railroad tracks. But then we began to find such attention to the details of our lives irritating and distracting. It was difficult to play freely and openly the way we once had when we anticipated long question-and-answer sessions at the end of the day. Nor could we organize easily for any cooperative purpose, such as establishing a neighborhood kids' store, when all stages of the operation would have to be explained to anxious mothers and fathers.

It was during this period of worry that the great system of calling in children was established on the Circle. Billy's dad inspired it, as I recall, since he had such skill at whistling. Joining a thumb and first finger of one hand, he put them in his mouth and produced a note that could, we felt, penetrate forests and cross the prairie.

Mr. Rhodes had always used this whistle when he wanted Billy; and now other parents felt that they needed similar methods of reaching out to their children, summoning them home or at least generating reassurance that they were close by. Most, however, could not master this famous whistle and had to develop alternatives. Even the few who were able to imitate Mr. Rhodes' shriek did not want to use it because it was Billy's call. Each family desired a specific signal by which children knew to check in with parents, confirming the security of home and neighborhood.

A version of the police whistle, usually red and white plastic, became the standard instrument for calling children, though there were several interesting variations; and patterns of sound identified the individual audience. The Bell sisters from the Oak side of the Circle responded to a single long pull on a whistle; Archie and Dennis's parents used a long and two short blasts; the Landons (Charles, myself, and Beth) were alert to one long and three short. Patrick Froemer responded to the ringing of an old farm bell, once used daily on the three hundred acres his great grandparents had owned in Ohio. Karen King went home to something like retreat, sounded on an ancient trumpet, improbably, by her mother. And Heavy Joe Martin, whose father had served throughout World War Two on a Navy destroyer, was burdened with a sound that could not be ignored, a booming fog horn.

In all, it was quite an operation, the Circle knitting itself together with a variety of means in a common purpose.

While the system was born of crisis, it proved so useful that it was maintained long after the great fear of strangers diminished among our families. Even when we all grew too old to need such attention, parents who could not immediately locate their high school or even college age children around the house resorted to the familiar call, whatever it was. When I hear a whistle today, in fact, I cannot help but wait, after the first long sound, to see if it will be followed by three short. And if I did one day hear such a call, I doubt that I could resist answering (”Yo!“) and trying to report in.

A few kids did escape this network. Roger, for instance, simply ignored all signals. Cathy's mother either had absolute confidence in her or, some suspected, lacked sufficient interest and never called. Poor Marcia, though she did eventually get to leave her house, did not often go far enough or stay long enough to need summoning.

So throughout the Circle's summer months in particular, when we stayed out until dark and sometimes beyond, the order of daily life, especially its closing down for the night, was punctuated by whistles and responses. That long pull right now, for instance, announces that it is time for Tricia Bell to leave Cathy Williams' house, where they have been playing canasta with two friends from across town.

”I'm coming!“ she calls; and more shouts relay the message (”She's cooommmming!“) across our connected streets and adjacent yards to Oak Street.

The fact that it's near dinner time at the Landons' this fine late afternoon in July is also conveyed (one long, three short) from the top of Limestone down past Roger's house to the bottom of the Circle, and then back up the hill to the Vacant Lot, where Billy and I, more than a year after first conceiving of the possibility, are resurrecting the idea of a community store.

Billy and I are sitting in his father's beautiful 1946 De Soto, parked just off the street in the Vacant Lot. This is one of the places we sometimes use to avoid the web pulling children in for dinner or demanding our presence when dark approaches. We claim we cannot hear our whistles inside the car, though it's warm enough to have the windows down. It's a ruse familiar to us and our parents, good for delay but not escape.

This is the Rhodes's second car, by the way, which they have taken to parking here rather than in their driveway, where their new 1955 Chevrolet sits. Since the town owns the Vacant Lot, no one objects; but when others become two-car families, rights to such extra public space will be debated.

The Rhodes don't drive the De Soto much any more, keeping it, I suspect, for sentimental reasons; but they have approved our sitting in it, listening to the radio, so long as we don't dirty the upholstery or leave trash behind. And it becomes one of the key places where we pretend to be beyond the reach of grownups and their ideas, able to discuss the present and plan a future on our own terms.

"We could run the store right here, out of the trunk," offers Billy, waving a hand over the backseat, though without much conviction. As we talk Harry Caray and Joe Garagiola are calling the Cardinals-Giants game on the radio. It's tied in the bottom of the eighth.

"There really isn't enough room here," I note. "And the Vacant Lot is too busy." I wasn't even mentioning that parents, in particular, could watch what happened here.

"How about the field behind Dr. Masters'?" This wasn't much of a field, just an extra lot owned by the doctor. He kept it mowed, but a stand of trees in the back corner did make a good private spot.

Billy punches a button on the radio, changing stations. Now we have the St. Louis station that plays popular music, in the midst of that major change from Big Band and Swing to Rock 'n' Roll. A soft Elvis is on, "Love Me Tender"?

Fairfield is, by the way, in a funny place for radio reception, if you discount, as we generally do, the local station (too much bad country music and farm prices). We can get some St. Louis stations on certain days; but weather or sun spots or who-knows-what often generates a lot of static. Jefferson City to our north comes in on many days; but we haven't found more than one music station there we like. Springfield is no farther west that St. Louis is east, but we can't get anything that way. And south is the heart of the Ozarks, a realm, for all we can learn, without radio.

"Masters' field is too much at the bottom of the Circle. We need to be more central," I point out.

"Roger's tree house, then?" It's centrally located, but we both know it's too small, no way for kids to come by, for traffic to move past merchandise.

I spin the dial on the radio, searching for something different, something new. At night or as the evening comes on, we can usually pick up far-away, more exotic signals. New Orleans sometimes, where Dixieland jazz bands pound out song after song. Occasionally, the East comes roaring into Billy's dad's De Soto. Cincinnati, Indianapolis, even that important city of radio, Pittsburgh, link us up with the larger nation, seats of power. They seem to have more news than anything else. Or the West calls to us, Kansas City, Omaha, Denver filling up the car's interior with other voices, odd accents. We think we're cowboys.

"Old Man Simpson's garage?" asks Billy, with more hope than accompanied his other suggestions. This is a possibility. Mr. Simpson owns a double lot in the middle of Limestone's rise up the hill, several houses down from me. At the back of the empty lot is a garage he doesn't use. But would he let us have it?

I pretend I don't hear the second Landon whistle. Too much longer, however, and my mom will get angry.

Billy tunes the radio again, passing up news, sports (the Giants have picked up a run in the top of the ninth), music. What else is there?

Sometimes, of course, reception is terrible all around. Signals from every direction, from far away and local, crisscross the Circle and cancel or jam each other. At times what we seem to get is a cacophonous jumble, a windy howl.

"Now, if we could drive," speculates Billy, sitting up straight behind the wheel and sighting ahead with a knowing grin. "We could take the old De Soto around, that would work. Have several locations for our store. No, a moving store, that's it! Mobile shopping."

We both know it will be years before we can drive, but the idea has genuine appeal. I sit up straighter too, my arm out the window, holding the roof as if we're cruising.

The Cardinals are threatening in their half of the ninth. My mom's third whistle sounds. I'll have to go.

"I know," says Billy, starting to open the door on his side. "The Bells' bomb shelter. That's the place for us."

I reach up to cut off the radio as Stan the Man Musial tags one, Harry Caray makes his famous call. "Holy cow, it might be outta here..... it might be..... it could be..... it is! A hoomme ruunn!"

I like and don't like the idea of the Bells' bomb shelter. It calls to mind a horrendous threat to everything I love; but it also hints at something unbelievably interesting, which the Bell sisters represent at this impressionable stage of my life—that is, what comes after lips meet lips in acts of love.

II

The Bells did not have the only bomb shelter in the neighborhood. There was, after all, in the 1950s a nationwide scare about the possibility of nuclear attack. And most people at least studied the lay of their land for places to go in an emergency. In an area where tornadoes were sighted almost every year, a corner of everyone's basement or a storage cellar had already been designated as a safe spot.

While most families, like the Landons, contented themselves with such knowledge of potential shelter, others were driven to more tangible measures. The Bells had enlarged an old root cellar in their sideyard, originally part of the farm on which these houses had been built, digging it deeper into Piney Ridge. This cave or underground house had battery electricity, bottled water, and a system to circulate air through a variety of filtering devices.

Marcia's mother had demanded that the small finished room in their basement be surrounded by a second wall of cement blocks and topped by a sandbag roof. This, of course, also added a new layer of irony to Mr. Terrell's joke about the detachable second floor, where Marcia slept. Storms could now be seen as a minor worry.

The Johnsons, at the edge of Limestone as a gravel road, reportedly had also reinforced the wine cellar beneath their kitchen with steel and concrete. And Billy's father had begun bricking off one corner of their basement, but the wall got up only as far as his waist before he lost energy and interest. In the space that would have been a shelter he had stacked a dozen one-gallon cans of water and five boxes of surplus C-rations, obtained somehow from Fort Leonard Wood.

These actual structures and other planned, proposed, or imagined shelters suggested interesting scenarios for the future of the Circle, stories radically divergent from what might be predicted by the general principles controlling our day-to-day life.

Sitting in the Vacant Lot Tree or out in the Open Space, we speculated about what it would be like to hole up in our basements for weeks, months, years rather than go to school every day. Much of the material in our environment then became irrelevant, as streets, stores, offices no longer shaped the actions we would take or guided the movement necessary for survival. Inside tiny cubicles, our lives would be directed by the allocation of food and water (little variety there), by the use of three games included for recreation (Monopoly, Scrabble, checkers), and by the one exercise tool (a jump rope).

Even more scary was the action forecast by the shotguns and boxes of shells stashed in the beams of many basement safe spots. Would we be going out in hunting parties to scavenge for supplies, taking back alleys and crosscountry routes to break in and steal, to ambush and retreat? Or would the rifle be used to hold off desperate individuals or bands of the sick and dying who had failed to find cover during the first blast of nuclear war? Would we turn away neighbors and friends whose shelters had proven inadequate? What if one family member had failed to get inside in time? When we were out of food and the world outside a waste land, would we turn weapons on ourselves?

These fantasies also inspired a new vision of the Circle: what an approaching Russian bombardier might see from his high-flying airplane. His special assignment was to knock out this Midwestern center of technology and commerce.

We talked about this character, Ivan, frequently, whether he had children, parents, a home, if he knew about baseball, television, hamburgers. We imagined Ivan sighting through his instruments, visualizing us, his targets. He did not seek out the biggest and most expensive homes as his first targets, but those with the best bomb shelters. They were the families he had to hit, preventing an eventual American victory. So new lines of importance sliced through our terrain, highlighting vigilance and foresight rather than wealth and local political power. The Terrells, Johnsons, and, most important, the Bells, marked the line of the country's inland defense.

At this time the Bell family figured in other frames of reference as well, particularly in the dreams of adolescent boys. When Billy suggested the Bells' bomb shelter as the site of our proposed kids' store, then, he was mixing contexts for me at least.

This was a good business location, near the middle of the Circle but not where everyone would be watching. It was also a good structure. There was a spacious front room, which served as living and sleeping quarters, and then a separate storage area in the back with a chemical toilet. But the space was also inhabited in my mind by fantasies of what had or could go on in a bomb shelter with the alluring, fascinating Bell sisters.

There were, as I said, two daughters in this family, Tricia, who was nearly the same age as my brother Charles (he is three years older than I), and Susan, two years younger. They were both pretty, like their mother, blond, bouncy, happy girls, almost young women. And unlike Cathy Williams, whose mythic stature completely removed her from my sexual imaginings, they were so friendly, so enthusiastic, so much fun to be with, that, although older, they figured prominently in my hopes for experience in the line of love.

This was, remember, more than a year after my breakthrough about the meaning of kisses and lips, about where babies come from. I was not, of course, interested yet in the latter: but I understood now the symbolic nature of the former, the fact that kisses meant more than lips and lips.

Not all points of confusion about such matters were erased, however, and new questions arose continually. Why the acts I contemplated went under the general term of "necking," for instance, hardly made sense to me, especially after it had taken me such a long time to find out what body parts were involved in which phases of the operation. New terms as well, whose literal and metaphoric meanings could present difficulty, were always surfacing: "back porch," "wheels," "hung," "circus," "chest goodies."

Still, I certainly wanted to, perhaps was desperate to, find out myself how this whole business worked, whether some sort of fire would run through my entire body when I made contact of this sort. But. while my dreams and my daydreams were full of improbable, exciting encounters, I had found no real life situation over the past fifteen months in which to pursue this desire.

As I trotted across the street from the Vacant Lot, then, calling to Billy that I would talk to him tomorrow, a puzzling combination of associations tumbled through my mind. Were we going into a partnership with the Bell sisters in order to organize our world apart from the rule of parents? Could the material of our concerns—licorice sticks, balloons, water pistols—displace the stuff of grownups—canned food and water, emergency signals, a shortwave radio?

Or were we going to approach the Bell sisters in order to enter a world of sexual experience, off limits for us before now? Would we soon be transformed from short, skinny high-voiced boys who pestered everyone into husky, tall, rough talking men in whose arms beautiful women melted?

I remember this confusion most in the shape of a recurring dream I had in these months. Perhaps there were several dreams, which have now become mixed in my memory, dreams of great intensity but each of a different kind. I recall these dreams or this dream as made up of bomb shelters and blond bombshells.

The first dream was inspired, I presume, by the presence of safe spots in my neighborhood and by graphic images from World War II movies and news clips. All those pictures of the D-Day invasion and of air raids over Europe gave this first dream its basic black-and-white elements: dark, cloudy sky; squadron after squadron of bombers in precise formations; strings of bombs falling, tumbling toward their targets; a landscape exploding in puffs of gray smoke and flying debris.

In this dream I am standing in front of my house on the Circle, looking north over Cathy Williams' house, Missouri Pacific train tracks behind that, the great highway, Route 66, behind them.

Above the house and trees appear the planes, hundreds of them, black crosses wing to wing, engines droning. I see them, and I know my world will end in a very few moments. There will not even be time for farewell. Although my family and friends had to be somewhere nearby, in my house, in the other houses, no one is in sight; and I seem to face this destruction alone.

The dream never goes much further than this, the sky filling with planes, my ears with the sound of their approach. I awake in a sweat, glad, after a few moments, to realize that none of this is actually happening.

The other half of my dream, or the other dream, is scary, but less ominous. Susan Bell and I are alone in some dark space, inside a darkened room, perhaps her bedroom. (Are we hiding from the bombs?) And, in one of the things I most like about this dream now, there is music playing, strings, an orchestra. (This is the background for the few romantic movies I have seen at the Uptowne Theatre, neatly transferred by me to my dream life.) As that music swells, I put my arms around Susan and draw her close. Her eyes shut, and she leans her head to one side, ready for my kiss. I start to kiss her, gently, sweetly.

This part of my dream is not scary. It follows the pattern I have absorbed from the culture around me. What worries me is that there is no feeling in my lips or arms as this is going on. I do not experience Susan as a physical being.

This makes sense in an adult frame of reference, of course, for she is only a figment of my imagination. But after this dream I wonder if it means there is something wrong with me, if I am not going to be ready when the occasion for love finally does arrive.

I am excited, almost breathless when I awake, by the prospect of the dream; but I am also uneasy, troubled by the fact that what occurs is so empty, so without fire. I want something to happen to me, but I do not know yet how to imagine it.

Soon, of course, something will happen. But not as I imagined it.

III

My worries and hopes about what might occur in the Bells' bomb shelter diminished considerably the next day, however, when Billy told me that Old Man Simpson had said we could use his abandoned garage for a kids' store.

"He did?" I asked Billy. I couldn't believe it was going to be this easy.

"Sure. Come on." Billy had knocked on my door in the middle of the morning; and we were now walking down Limestone to inspect the building, make our first survey of the space available. This was good, I thought. Not only do we get this prime location, but I can keep my scenario of business success separate from my dreams of romantic entanglement.

"What do we have to do for Old Man Simpson?" I asked Billy, unwilling to think there wasn't some price to pay.

"Well, the place is pretty dirty," admitted Billy. "We'll need to clean it out, put some things up over the rafters." Apparently, the garage was being used for storage.

We passed Mr. Simpson's house and started up the two concrete strips that constituted a driveway. He never used the driveway, parking his car on the street, as did many in the Circle. The building itself was a neat one-car structure, with double doors that swung open from the middle and a small side door near the back—public and private entrances, according to Billy. He already had keys to the padlocks on each.

Opening the side door, Billy pulled me into the dark. (It would be weeks before I learned how much I was in the dark about my best friend's schemes.)

"There's no electricity, of course, so we'll have to be a daytime store," he offered. "But look at all this."

He pushed open one of the wide front doors to let in light, waved a hand at several stacks of long, unpainted boards in the middle of the concrete floor and a broad workbench running across the back. "We can make shelves along the walls and store extra items back here under this bench."

"Hey," I offered. "We could pull the bench out, make it our counter. We'll be behind it."

"Of course! And over here," Billy added, pointing to a wooden cabinet attached to the side wall over the bench. "We'll keep our books, the receipts and the money."

"What do we do with that stuff?" I asked, nodding toward several large piles of metal pipe and even more stacks of roof shingles. "Does it have to go up there?" I pointed to the space under the roof, over the rafters.

"Well, yes. But that won't take us long. Then, we clean up, and it's ours."

It wasn't going to be that simple, I thought, as the metal pipe would be heavy and difficult to handle. The floor also had an oily look, as if a leaky car had once been kept in here; and dirt was mixed in with the grease. But I couldn't get over our luck in having permission to use this place.

True, Billy was good at talking people into things. He was a charmer with his crazy schemes; and we kids usually fell for his enthusiasm, taking up his causes as if they had always been our own. Still, Mr. Simpson didn't seem to me the kind of man we could even approach about such a project.

We called him "Old Man Simpson" because he walked with a cane, slightly stooped, slowly and deliberately. Although thin and angular, he never seemed to me frail or old like his wife. Although the cane was always with him, he used it almost as another limb, pushing things out of the way, tapping something to draw attention to it. His hair was dark and thick, standing up on his head like the bristles on a brush. He also had sharp, shrewd eyes.

We did not have to speak loudly to him, as we did to other older people on the Circle, to Billy's grandmother, for instance, who spent six months of the year in Fairfield and the other six months back in Chicago with her other daughter's family. Old Man Simpson heard what was said and spoke with authority. We generally stayed out of his yard.

Still, I began to get excited about the prospect before us. I could build shelves along the wall, and also display cases and bins to fill with loose items, bulk sales. There would be a wonderful variety in my shelves, I thought, some deep and tall, others short and spaced closely together—room for all manner of products. And there would be pleasure in the arrangement of goods, food items in one area, toys in another, clothes and decorative items hanging conspicuously.

We would also pay attention to the movement of customers, what they saw when they came through the double front doors, how the counter and bins should direct traffic by the best buys but lure people on to things that would yield us the biggest profit. And we could build special features into our position behind the counter, a drawer for the cash, a bulletin board that would hold reminders, tall stools to serve as perches from which we could keep our eyes on everything. It was going to be great.

It was going to be great, but right now it was a dirty garage filled with junk. Several days would be needed to store Old Man Simpson's stuff and more to organize the space into a functioning store. But it was, after all, summer; and neither Billy nor I was old enough to get a regular job while school was out. We each had a number of yards around the Circle to mow once a week; and various tasks were assigned regularly by our parents. But, by and large, the days and evenings were free, available for just such a project as starting our own business.

That summer, now that I think about it, was the last before we faced adult responsibilities like employment. In the next year I would have my paper route, delivering the daily local paper to approximately fifty downtown businesses and nearby residences. That took about an hour and a half, with more time one day each week to collect. Billy began that next year working in a nursery for fifteen hours a week, sticking seedlings into peat pots and setting up trays of bedding plants.

Since we had already seen what happened to older kids in the Circle, like my brother Charles who now had a fulltime job at a small printing company downtown, we recognized that our days of freedom were numbered. The store was perhaps a last major project of innocent play. At the same time, it could be a preliminary step toward the world of work, a world with rewards that had been beyond our reach so far.

There was one specific object associated with the jobs and the lives of older kids in the Circle that got caught up with my hopes for the store, for setting up shop on our own, for running a business of sorts. I wanted that bigger and stronger body that was required in the next phase of adolescence, a body capable of bagging groceries at the A & P, carrying the rod for a local survey crew, bringing in hay and loading it in the high lofts of barns through the heat of August.

Such bodies began to appear on boys in the late junior high school years. For the girls, of course, it all happened earlier. The Bell sisters had been towering over us for several years, and even Marcia Terrell was suddenly taller than I was. But the boys my age on the Circle had watched Charles, Heavy Joe Martin, and that crew bulk up, rival their fathers' heights, drop their voices down into wells. And we wanted that stature, that power.

Seeking signs of our future size and influence, we began to look at ourselves in new ways, from altered angles. It was in most cases too early for facial hair to be conspicuous; but in other regions of our bodies changes could occur swiftly, dramatically. We looked down in the mirror now, not straight on, and hoped for big things.

We learned of possibilities, of course, in the showers after gym class at school, those difficult times of discovery. Twelve months' development can make a big difference at this age, and the few older students in these classes were abundantly men among boys.

One individual each year, as I remember, gained the reputation of being the biggest in school. The boys hanging around Miller's Drive-in would call the new title holder "L.D." as if those were his initials; but we all knew they were shorthand for a certain prominence. Those of us whose manhood had not yet blossomed secretly hoped that one day we would become our group's "L.D."

With a brother three years my senior, I was confronted by what I was *not* at home as well as at school. Charles and I shared a bedroom downstairs, a finished portion of the basement (perhaps the place where a bomb shelter might have been); so I could see daily what I hoped was my future. So far, I had known only disappointment in my body. Charles, on the other hand, was large boned and huskier overall. He would, in fact, end up several inches taller. So to all the usual sibling rivalries I added one more, a desire for greater gifts.

Under these trying circumstances, I took to somewhat strange habits of dressing and undressing, my back to the center of the room, my gestures sudden and jerky. I was both hiding myself and trying to avoid additional evidence of what I was supposed to be accomplishing. Only in the bathroom, with the door locked, could I examine myself closely, try to decide if I was at last making progress or still stuck at some plateau.

Sometimes I could believe, with the light at the right angle, the perspective carefully controlled, that those thin wisps of blond hair were the beginnings of a more manly, dark bush, that, compared to what I was a month ago, surely there was growth, change, bulk.

Of coarse, it was terribly difficult to tell about these matters. Was I changing or not? Was I just hoping, pretending? Should I accept an inevitable, punishing smallness now and go on with my life?

How could one be objective about this, anyway? Should I take measurements? How about photographs, before and after? Was there anyone I could ask for advice, for help? Billy was easy to talk to and loved just this sort of question. And here we were together in the privacy of our new store. We could even make comparisons.

But you know how it was in those days: there were some things just too hard to talk about, even with your best friend. And Billy was already glassy-eyed anyway, telling me about a deal he had set up for ten thousand pop sickle sticks, our first purchase. At this moment I just didn't see any way to ask him, or anyone else, for that matter, if I was ever going to be a man.

IV

My concern with one area of the body inspired a new vision of the human community. I organized a vision of my peers focused at only one point in each individual.

Of course, I couldn't literally look at this point; but I found myself speculating, guessing, making calculations based on a personal and no doubt faulty logic of proportion, correspondence, extrapolation. I typed and classified according to size, or to rumors of size, or to hypotheses of size. It made me see my world as a collection of parts: small, average, large, extra-large. Everyone was placed in a group, determined by shared characteristics. My main worry was that I didn't like the set within which I had to fix myself.

A similar ranking of girls went on regularly, of course, within the Circle's population of boys. The size and quality of breasts were much discussed, though at this time more within my brother Charles' set than my own. Too many of us were preoccupied with our own insecurities to be confident judges of others.

Still, we knew the definitions of terms (a "herman" was one cubic mouthful of boob, for instance), though such understanding was certainly abstract rather than experienced. We could fall right in with confident assessments ("Tricia Bell, definitely four hermans"), echoing the head-shaking exclamations of praise and the hearty guffaws of dismissal.

But I was, after all, in my dealings with the opposite sex, still trying to get up to the level of lips and kisses. These other body parts had been for me more mythical than real, out of reach literally and figuratively. However, I was soon to have one more lesson in my sexual education.

These body ranking sessions occurred at particular times, as I recall, times when we were by ourselves, away from parents, often in dark or secluded places. One situation where the links and limits of personal and social identity were mapped out on the Circle was during games of Kick the Can. This was for us a favorite pastime of summer. While those days of July were being filled by Billy's and my labor transforming Old Man Simpson's garage into a functioning kids' store, for example, the same evenings were being shaped by marathon sessions of Kick the Can. And in the close, humid dark of neighborhood hiding places, two or three or more boys whispered and wondered at the magic of nature.

I had assumed at various points in my adult life that everyone growing up in the 50s played Kick the Can and thus spent nights of youth much like my own, but I have learned that this isn't true. The game obviously figured for certain groups and subgroups within the nation but not for others. I'm not sure whether it was primarily or exclusively a Midwestern event, a middle class activity, or just small town entertainment; but I know that in Fairfield we whiled away many a summer evening playing Kick the Can. And in the process we were always sorting and arranging in our own minds the elements of life and love.

Here's how we played this more complex version of Hide 'n' Seek. Games were best begun at dusk, for the close texture of night contributed, as I said, to the game's special flavor. Any number could play, but the larger the group the better.

Someone was "it," and his or her goal was to find and capture everyone else. "Base" was an old tin can set on the curb. If Roger and others who lived near the bottom of the Circle got up a game, we established the base in front of his house. With Archie and Dennis Baker at the top of the neighborhood, the can generally sat on the curb near the lane to the Springers' house and pond. And sometimes I played with kids on the Oak Street side of the Circle, and base then was at the house of the Bell sisters, sometimes, in fact, near their root cellar/bomb shelter.

From this center for any given night, those who were not "it" spread out in all directions and hid to start the game. The one who was "it," after counting to a suitable number, perhaps 25, then moved cautiously away from the can, trying to spot any of the others.

If he or she did see one of those hiding, a race was on, the two trying to get to the can first. "It" had to put a foot on top of the can and count "1-2-3 on whoever" for that person to be caught. To avoid being caught, the hider had to beat "it" to the can and kick the can from its spot on the curb. If "it" caught all the hiders, then he or she was no longer "it." The first one caught became the new "it" for the next round of the game. And off we all went again.

Unlike regular Hide 'n' Seek, however, this game included a way for people who had been caught to be free again. Hiders who had been captured were made to stand in a place selected by "it," perhaps under a tree near the base, until the game was over, that is, until "it" had caught everyone else. If, however, another hider could run in and kick the can from its perch before "it" counted him or her out, then all prisoners were free; and they scattered to hide again. "It" then had the whole search and capture to repeat.

I remember many times, when some others had been caught and I was still hidden in some secure location, enjoying the quiet sense of my own secrecy or the soft pleasure of whispering, gossiping, dreaming together with Billy or Marcia or Dennis. I would hear a mad race suddenly begin, runners pounding across someone's lawn or down the middle of the street, breath pushing from lungs and returning. Then a mighty clanging would sound through the night as the can shot off a runner's foot and bounced across the pavement. "It's" scream of exasperation was jarring in the summer night, but that cry was usually lost in the shouts and laughter of the hiders.

Why all our adult neighbors were so tolerant both of this noise and of the essential trespassing in this game I don't really understand. We hiders moved through the neighborhood as if it were a field laid out for the game of Kick the Can, not a section of town with individual lots whose owners paid property taxes and kept up appearances. We climbed trees, leapt over porches, ducked behind bushes, and raced up driveways as if they had been put there to provide us hiding places and lanes of escape or attack. In any official description of the land there might be streets and fences, property lines and boundaries, domiciles and lesser structures, water pipes and telephone poles, storm sewer routes and plains of drainage. Yet at night in the summer the Circle was organized along our lines: at the center of the universe was this can we kicked; and arterial spokes ran outward to select places of hiding and along paths of searching.

Perhaps this wide open travel was allowed because so many of the people living on the Circle had kids of their own, whether they were playing this particular game or not. Some parents had children old enough to be interested in different activities, and others might have had infants or small children already in bed. But so many of these post-war citizens were on the same cycle of family development that we almost shared a single, communal life. And that larger framework allowed children free-running games, neighborhood access.

My own kids have not grown up in a similar world, I am sorry to say, for property owners today, it seems to me, draw surer lines around their territory and block off private space. It might be that I remember this incorrectly, exaggerating my parents' neighbors' tolerance, but I think larger social changes are also involved.

In any case, on the night of the day Billy and I had spent many hours trying to remove a sticky mix of oil and dirt from the cement floor of Mr. Simpson's garage, we found ourselves crouched behind a bush in the Peterson backyard, near the base of the large oak that held Roger's tree house. In front of us a streetlight illuminated the corner of the house and the side yard. Susan Bell stood in the middle of Limestone, looking in our direction but glancing back over her shoulder as well. She was "it," and we were hoping she had not spotted us.

"Keep down!" I whispered to Billy. He was looking over the top of the bush; I lay flat to look underneath. He dropped down beside me.

"Did I tell you what I bought for the store?" he asked me.

"Quiet!" Susan had turned sideways so she could look back at the base and forward to where we were. She was doing a little sidestepping dance into the Peterson side yard. Something must have told her we were back here.

"I bought six hundred sponges."

"Shhhh. You what?"

I punched Billy on the arm. Didn't he see her coming? Susan was advancing now at a slight run, still looking back at every third or fourth step. Good grief, I didn't want to get caught. I would be first; that might mean I would BE "it" for the next game!

"Sponges, all colors. A dozen boxes of fifty each."

I began to gather myself for a run to the base, hoping I could beat Susan. Hmmm, that was sure a lot of sponges.

Susan, by the way, was a great "it." She didn't seem to get frustrated when someone kicked the can, freeing all her captives. She would throw up her arms and laugh in good-hearted acceptance of her fate. I, on the other hand, was generally a bad "it," feeling resentful if I had to spend the whole night looking and finding. I grew especially frustrated when one last person beat me back and kicked the can to start another round of the game.

Now Susan made a dash right at our bush, and Billy yelled out, "Run for it!"

He and I leaped from our hiding place and raced after Susan. She was leading us both, though, and already counting, laughing, "I got you! Ha-ha! One-two-three-eeee!"

In the middle of the Peterson's front yard, Susan stopped dead in her tracks, for the can was suddenly sailing down the street in front of her, banging and bumping. Roger had come from above Billy's house. He had kicked the can, and there weren't even any prisoners yet.

Although Susan stopped abruptly, I didn't, running right into her. We went down together on the soft lawn. Neither of us was hurt and would ordinarily have been giggling at the accident. But we were both blushing furiously.

In trying not to land on top of her, I had held on as we hit the ground. When we rolled to a stop, my left hand ended up on her right arm near the shoulder; but my other hand rested for an embarrassingly long moment directly on her budding left breast.

V

Oh, the difficulties of youth! There was probably nothing I wanted more at this moment in life than just such physical contact with the opposite sex as this accidental falling of my hand on a young girl's breast. And I don't know, by the way, that Susan didn't share a similar desire. Did her hand explore some part of me in our tumble to the ground?

For my part, hours of daydreaming had been devoted to scenarios in which such events transpired: an unintentional bumping into each other as we walked along the street; an unexpected turning around the corner of a building into one another's arms; a coincidental crossing of paths at which sensitive extremities innocently met. So intense at this age were the sensations inspired by the mere idea of body-to-body contact that my fantasies actually went no further than the moment of encounter. Even my imagination did not know what came next.

And then when it actually did happen, my right hand on Susan Bell's left breast, I felt only panic. I leaped up, red in the face, though, in the dim light of the street lamp, who could tell I was blushing? There was, I think—though again in the dark it was hard to know—a corresponding, excited embarrassment in Susan's face.

Thank goodness Billy had kept running when he saw Roger kick the can, crossing the street and making off for a new hiding place. Roger too just waved in Susan's direction and, characteristically, melted into the night. So she and I scrambled up, stumbling over some sorts of apologies, checking that the other wasn't hurt in any way. You OK? Sure, you? Fine. Fine.

She trotted over to get the can and return it to the curb. I waited for her to close her eyes and start counting. Then I turned to find another hiding place, glad to get away one minute, mad in the next to go back to that touch.

It was not always Susan, of course, about whom I entertained fantasies, but she was one of my favorite subjects. Already she had the height of her sister, though her figure had not filled out to the perfection granted Tricia's. The Bell girls resembled each other quite a bit, in fact, both slim and athletic, bright and enthusiastic. When Susan wore her hair pulled back in a ponytail, as she did this evening, she looked still like a girl, long-legged in Bermuda shorts and a bit awkward, sometimes shy. With her hair down at shoulder length and wearing a dress, however, she could at a distance easily be mistaken for the poised, womanly Tricia.

Susan stood on the edge of achieving a new identity, ready for the experiences appropriate to that context. My feelings about her were similarly balanced between the almost asexual friendship of childhood and the burning curiosity of a young male. When I fell on top of her in the Peterson's side lawn that warm summer evening, I was certainly in search of a new version of myself and my place in the world.

Running away from the first accidental glimmers of that new person, and from a maturing Susan, I hid this time by myself, behind Old Man Simpson's garage. I probably was drawn to this spot by the nagging knowledge that much work still needed to be done before Billy and I could begin our neighborhood business.

We did have all the pipe and roofing materials put away, although, in the end, that required installing a floor over the rafters to make a more distinct attic in the back half of the building. Mr. Simpson had come out one day to check on us and, pointing with his cane, told us we could use the four-by-eight-foot sheets of plywood in his basement. I felt we didn't really need them, but Billy convinced me this would keep us on good terms with our new landlord. While adding about a day and a half to our work schedule, we learned some useful techniques for getting large material up to that height and anticipated some benefits in the ultimate arrangement of the store.

Crouched now behind the building, watching and listening for Susan, who was again on the lookout, I heard the sound of a train in the distance. Trains played a regular role in Kick the Can because of the noise they generated.

Passing between the houses on the north side of Limestone and Route 66, these trains were less than a hundred yards from where most of us were hiding. We could not, however, see engines or cars because they were actually below the level of our street when they passed the neighborhood. In order to keep the tracks from rising too steeply, a deep cut had been dug through the base of Piney Ridge just behind the backyards of my neighbors across the street. We called it, of course, "the Cut."

Every day quite a number of freight and several passenger trains passed through the Cut on their way in or out of town. We could hear (and feel) them, though we were so used to that traffic that they often roared past unnoticed. I seem to remember (but perhaps I'm mixing in images from movies again here) clouds rising from the Cut, as if there were still steam locomotives in those days. Most, if not all, of the trains were diesel powered.

"One-two-three on Roger," sang out Susan in the distance. Wow, she had our senior player! Someone would have to come through to free him now. I decided to sneak up to a tree in Old Man Simpson's front yard, try to see if anyone else had been caught.

Both "it" and the hiders rewrote the basic tenets of their strategy at train time. There were two kinds of train noise familiar to Circle residents, and knowing the difference made you a better player of Kick the Can.

When trains came from the west, making the long pull up to town from the Gasconade River valley, we would first become aware of them as a low rumble far in the distance, punctuated only rarely by a muffled, off-pitch whistle. Especially with the big freight trains, more than a hundred cars, that rumble grew louder and louder, minute by minute, little by little, as the train struggled up the twenty-five mile incline to the plateau on which Fairfield rested.

Trains coming through town from the east, on the other hand, kept up a fairly steady speed of twenty-five to thirty-five miles per hour, blowing their warning whistles frequently. At the Circle they were already picking up downhill speed and were past us in a few minutes.

Long east-bound trains, giving plenty of warning as they approached, then, usually kept "it" close to the can. Hiders often used the more sudden, explosive sounds of westbound engines to cover a rush to kick the can. The sounds I heard tonight were getting loud fast, a westbound train. This was just what I needed to kick the can and free Roger.

I peered around the trunk of the large oak in the corner of Simpson's yard. There, gathered on Roger's porch were two, three, no five people! I really must have been daydreaming behind our store while the game was going on. Susan had everyone but me and who else? Ah, Billy. He was still out too.

From where I was, I could not see Susan. She must be out searching; I had better be careful. Back behind this bush to make a plan. Let's see: do I want to make my run from below or above the can? From this side of the street or the other? Slowly by way of various cover or in a mad dash out in the open? I don't have too much time to think, as the train is whistling often, going across the streets in town.

In a pause between whistles I think I hear a race, the slap of sneakers on pavement. Then I do hear Susan, "One-two-three on Billy!" Uh-oh, all caught but me.

I decide on the back way, by Old Man's Simpson's garage, the place at the Kings' where the fence is bent down and you can cross over to Oak Street backyards. My plan is to go past the can and the streetlight, come out two houses farther down, trust everything to surprise and speed. My timing should be just right, for the train has stopped whistling so frequently. It must be leaving downtown and heading out to our neighborhood, the edge of town.

I slip between houses, in a crouch go down a driveway beside a parked car. I can look through the car's windows, check if there is any sign of "it." She would not be able to see me through the glass, more a mirror on the streetlight side where she is. The train is roaring, very close now.

Up the hill I see long-legged Susan walking away from me on the other side of the streetlight. Ah-ha, "it" is looking in the wrong direction! I step out into the street, quietly so she won't hear me, though there's not much worry about that now with the train noise.

I don't have to run fast, as she doesn't turn around, just moves on up the street, pigtail swinging. She's not even looking back to check the base. I wave casually to the crowd of captives on Roger's porch. They spot me. I can see their excited gestures, pointing toward the can I am to kick. They make preparations for getting freed and hiding again.

The train's engines must be just behind Roger's house now. I can't hear anything, though I can even see Billy's mouth wide open as he screams at me. He's cheering me on, like everyone else.

Susan has never turned around. Boy, how dumb can you be! She's gone much too far from the base, especially considering the fact that there's a train on and she had everyone but me caught. She is usually a much better "it"; but now she'll have to start all over again.

I take a final glance at the porch where everyone is pointing toward the can and cheering. I start my acceleration toward base, toward, I think to myself, the greatest can kick every recorded in Circle lore, a kick so devastating the can may never be found, a kick to punctuate the arrival of a new, bigger, more powerful me.

The game may, I think, have to be suspended until replacement equipment can be found, newer players at my higher level. And stories, surely, will be told about this famous emancipation of prisoners.

There at the base, however, inexplicably stands Susan, smiling. She points at me. I am caught? As I look, bewildered, up the street, I realize in a flash that the person walking up the hill is Tricia, Susan's sister.

Part Four: Open for Business

Chapter VI

Of course, I took quite a bit of ribbing after that game for my goofy run at the can. Billy regularly reenacted my coming out into the light, waving to the captives on Roger's porch, going into a wind-up to put toe to can and inaugurate another round of hiding. He laced his recreation of events with commentary, pointing out how everyone on the porch had yelled at me that Susan was right across the street, but that I couldn't hear because of the train.

I tried once to explain that I had seen Tricia walking up to Cathy Williams's house and had mistaken her for Susan, but this admission only heightened my reputation for confusion. And finally in Billy's rendition of the action came the look on my face when I spotted Susan standing with one foot on base, smiling. For a good while, no game of Kick the Can could begin without an account of my performance, or at least several winking references. I was, in a way I hadn't sought, famous.

Part of me didn't mind this notoriety. The linking of myself and Susan in some bond, even of mistress and her fool, appealed to me, gave me a feeling that this incident was part of a process tying us together, leading to more, and more interesting, contact. I couldn't quite find a way to integrate this sequence of events with my sexual fantasies, though I did sometimes daydream about the two of us being "it" together.

Standing in some shadows near the base, we watched everyone else making preparations to run in and kick the can. We had a plan (though I didn't work out the details) whereby each one of the hiders would be caught, everyone taken completely by surprise. And as we stood side-by-side, perhaps hand-in-hand, in the darkness, we shared this knowledge, this power. She whispered to me; I whispered to her. We were a team. We worked together.

Something like this did, in fact, happen. But it was even more erotically charged than I could have predicted.

Billy was my regular companion during the next few days, however, not Susan by nights. He and I had finally gotten to the point in the establishment of our store that we were looking for merchandise and thinking about how it could be displayed.

I had already put in some of the shelves. And I had made drawings of the whole scheme in my room at night: tall, deep shelves between the upright beams on the wall by the small back door; shallow, close shelves on the opposite side. There were also to be cabinets behind the counter in the back and four large bins spaced symmetrically in the area between our counter and the front double doors.

My drawings were ridiculously elaborate, probably owing to the frustration of spending so much time cleaning and storing Old Man Simpson's stuff rather than building our own structures. I included front views, top views, side views. I labeled sections and indicated the order of their assembly; number and type of screws and nails had been meticulously calculated. Everything was cleverly interlocking too, as I remember, shelves with tabs that fit into frames with slots. I wasn't at all sure I had the carpentry skills to accomplish this beautiful construction, but the whole concept took my breath away.

When it came down to installation, in fact, both my own competence and the nature of partnership affected the layout of our store.

The tools I had and knew how to use, all hand-me-downs from my brother Charles, consisted of a basic but somewhat rusty handsaw, a hammer with one claw missing, and a wooden-handled, standard screwdriver. I couldn't bevel joints or countersink screws, insure right angles or level planes, design or make trim. Too many of my measurements turned out to be inexact; some boards were warped or marred by flaws; many nails bent and screws insisted on following odd angels. Wood that was supposed to be smooth and finished was rough and coarse; pieces that should have been exactly the same size varied remarkably; most joints had gaps and spaces. Despite these shortcomings, there were shelves of sorts along both walls, reasonable bins stood in the middle of the floor, and a cabinet could have been built on the back wall.

These shortcomings of construction were overlooked by Billy, though he occasionally offered what I took to be inappropriate suggestions about design. "You know," he said one afternoon. "We'll want some place to display our comic books. Could some of these shelves be slanted?" He was pointing to where I intended to put my closely set shelves.

"I was thinking that we'd put small items over here: yo-yos, marbles, miniature cars and trucks."

"I know, I know. But by putting the shelves in at an angle, and then a little strip on the bottom, you would have a great place for comics."

He had a point; and his scheme did represent a challenge. All my shelves were level, everything in my design a right angle. "I'll see what I can do," I conceded.

Billy had other suggestions too as we worked (he wanted some baskets suspended from the rafters, for instance), though most of his time was being spent finding stock. He had an amazing ability to come into odds and ends that nobody else wanted, leftovers or rejects for which he apparently paid nothing or next to nothing. And he had reasons why kids would buy these goods.

His latest acquisition was a dozen pairs of metal runners for standard, one-person snow sleds. Without the sled body there in front of me, I thought the red strips were awning supports or porch railings of some sort. Billy explained that kids in the neighborhood, when they knew what they had, would build wooden frames or attach the runners to other things like packing crates to make their own sleds. And since our investment was so small, he said, what was the risk?

In this particular scheme Billy was, I must admit, prescient. I hope you'll indulge me in a moment of digression to explain.

Later that summer the town would pave Hill Street, formerly only a gravel road south of Oak Street without gutters or storm sewers. Since Hill went to the top of Piney Ridge at a very steep angle, a new, great sledding hill was born. Up to this time we had done all our sliding from west to east on Limestone, which was fine but not really fast, not nearly the breakneck ride Hill would prove to be. Sledding for all the kids on the Circle after this summer was done south to north.

Not only was the ride from the top of Piney Ridge to the bottom of the Circle fast, but the new, paved Hill Street run had several fine options built in: a hump that was easily transformed by some added snow into a jump; and a difficult hairpin turn from Hill onto Oak.

The hump in the pavement was just above the intersection where Oak "T"-ed into Hill. Here sled speed reached its peak, as the rest of the run was steep enough to maintain momentum but not to add to acceleration. So, if we built up the hump with several dozen shovels full of snow, packed it down and slicked it over with a bit of quickly-freezing water, we created a daredevil leap scary even for veteran sliders.

The other challenge of the run was to sweep right, around the hump, and make the sharp left up Oak Street, which, at the speeds we reached, was not an easy maneuver. Many times we piled or rolled into Dr. Masters' side yard, unable to steer the sled through that sharp angle. The turn could be made easily by dragging your left foot; but that was considered a flagrant failure of nerve.

I remember this Hill Street run most vividly as a nighttime experience, a winter version or inversion of our summer Kick the Can games. In this activity we were all together, going basically the same direction (up and down Hill Street) rather than radiating outward from the center or base, the can; but it was a communal event that organized and related all the participants.

The landscape was, of course, transformed from its ordinary state, with trees, bushes, and buildings wearing extra coats of ice. Wind-driven snow often distorted the shapes of familiar objects, fattening telephone wires, adding height to mail boxes, and obliterating the borders along yards and even between street and ground. There were many fewer cars than usual, and those moved slowly, grinding with chains or slipping on snow tires. Muffled pedestrians also moved in the tracks left by large vehicles or down snow-shovelled walks rather than following paths across yards.

As we picked up our sleds, several of which were, in fact, home-made versions using Billy's surplus runners, and started our runs at the top of the hill, our relationship to this altered landscape was also affected by changed senses.

Ear muffs or hats with flaps dampened the sounds of children calling and talking, placing objects at one remove from ordinary perception. Street and porch lights created strange shadows and bright spots ahead of us down the run, shaping and marking elements of the whole. When it wasn't still snowing and the sky clear, there would be stars out in front of and almost below us, since we looked over the Circle, over Route 66 and the town to the distant horizon. Each sledder, especially during the ride, entered into a private engagement with this special world.

We wore galoshes in those days, too large rubber boots with snapping metal clasps in which our feet, still within their regular shoes, tended to knock around. Every step expelled air from the tops with an explosive "foofff!" And the take-off came at the end of twenty-five or thirty whooshing steps building to a run.

We flung ourselves down onto our sleds and entered another state of existence, the gliding, racing, bumping ride over ice. Freezing air on our faces made us squint and took the breath out of our mouths. The sounds of those at the bottom of the hill, those climbing up for a ride, and those gathering at the top for their run were in totally different frames of reference. Those at the bottom belonged in the future, those at the top to the past of our present. It was, as I remember it, almost like flight itself.

This was, of course, not at all the future Billy and I were forecasting, individually or jointly, as we labored that July to create a kids' store for the Circle. As he roamed the neighborhood and the town for good buys on standard and exotic items, and as I drew and calculated, shaped and built shelves and bins, we were imagining futures that never quite came to be. But the material we gathered and the skills we developed did combine to make a very exciting world and to generate wonderful experiences like sledding on wintry nights down the glassy slickness of Hill Street on Piney Ridge in the Midwestern version of 1950s America.

VII

Even as I neared the end of my shelf- and bin-building, and as Billy stacked his sled runners and other odds and ends in the corners of Old Man Simpson's garage, I felt new purposes for all this work growing within me. The effort involved in establishing the enterprise and the visible outcome, the store itself, were impressive. And I hoped to impress Susan with what I had done. If, moved by the beauty of what I had accomplished, she were inspired to reward me in some tangible and tantalizing way, that was, I decided, only appropriate.

I saw Susan and myself alone in the newly arranged store as an advanced form of a game younger kids on the Circle played called "Under the Umbrella." This game, despite its name, actually involved a parachute rather than an umbrella.

Archie and Dennis Baker's father, who had served as a bomber pilot in the Pacific, had come away from his war days with several white silk parachutes. On summer evenings or in the fall, we would sometimes get out one of these relics and spread it across their or another front yard. The cords from which a crew member hung beneath the chute had been removed, so what we had was basically a large, soft tent without poles. We all got under the smooth cool material and created another one of those special kids' worlds where old games are played again and new ones invented.

The silk cloth was so limp and flexible that it fell around the individual to the ground, closing each off from the others. And the whole parachute was so big that a dozen small children could crawl around under it for some time without touching each other. To make a bubble or small room holding more than one of us, we would have to stand and hold out our arms, sometimes throwing up a section of material to give us a sense of space. Or we could sit three or four in a circle, and our heads would hold up the portion of parachute around us in a mini-canopy.

What was so much fun in Under the Umbrella, as I remember, were the endless possibilities for arrangement: everyone in his or her own private spot; four or five little cells of two or three together; several large places of half a dozen kids; one huge room holding everyone. In this protected little world we could play with cards, cars, dolls or toy soldiers, marbles, comics, and much more. Anything you could do outside the umbrella became somehow another game under the umbrella, thus doubling the range of activities available to us.

You could even play Under the Umbrella at night, with flashlights; but this sometimes turned scary, especially for the youngest. In the day, you could always see through the thin, light material, making out shapes and forms, shadows and outlines; but at night you could get cut off from everyone in your own swirls of silk. You would not be sure which way to turn to get hooked up with the group or your special buddy again. And during the day we usually had a mother reassuringly close by, checking out the window, for instance, from time to time to be sure that no one was suffocating beneath these folds of material.

From outside the parachute, a position I generally took now that I was somewhat older, all one saw were bumps, little ones and big ones, some moving, some still. There was plenty of talking and laughing as kids moved around and found each other or began playing some specific game in a particular spot.

Few sessions of Under the Umbrella went without some tickling—one child sending another jumping and then racing away beneath the silk on hands and knees. It was this tickling that appealed to me now, I guess, as I thought of myself and Susan under the roof of a new kids store.

On the day before we were to open our store I invited her to stop by the garage on her way to the evening's game of Kick the Can. Of course, I had to tell Billy what I was up to. We had agreed to keep the project secret as long as possible, letting surprise be a first step in our promotional campaign for the store. Billy even had some elaborate ideas about a grand opening, but the time and energy we had spent cleaning, stocking, and building caused them to fade in the last phases of preparation. Still, he was not happy with me for leaking word of our enterprise.

"Aww, she'll tell everyone," he complained. "Some surprise!"

"No, she won't. I'll explain it all to her."

"Sure, sure. She'll tell her sister, who'll tell Cathy Williams, who'll come by to see. I know how word gets around with those girls." How true this was I'd learn before long!

Billy was arranging two dozen, one-gallon wastepaper cans on the shelves by the back door. He had bought the last of a shipment Ben Franklin's had been unable to move downtown. Each one had the map of a different state painted on the outside, though none was Missouri. None, in fact, was even a Midwestern state.

"Not only that, but they'll get it all wrong. They'll think it's going to be a beauty parlor, or an ice cream shop. Or some sort of dress store, with clothes and fashion stuff."

"Susan's not going to tell," I insisted.

As we talked, I was trying to insert a sliding panel into a groove in front of two of my large shelves in the back of the garage. Billy thought we should have some places where more valuable things could be kept out of the sight of browsers. Customers in the know could ask for them. What special merchandise was to fit in these secret places he never said, but I liked the challenge of constructing them.

"They'll come in here and demand that we put lace curtains on the windows, leave out bars of lilac-scented soap to make the store smell good. They'll want colored candles and lamps hanging by chains and paintings. It's not that kind of store!"

I thought Billy was being completely unreasonable here, so I just let him ramble on. These were not real threats to our enterprise. And I certainly wasn't asking Susan in to consult on the shape of our business, but to see it and wonder, wonder at the drive and spunk of the guys who had come this far. And then . . . then, well, whatever would happen, would happen.

Some of the things I was forecasting did come true. Susan met me at the garage early that evening, for instance, before most of the other kids had finished dinner and come out for Kick the Can. And she was impressed, both with the idea and the reality of our store.

"You know," she said. "You could put a card table out front, near the street, with some sale items. People would stop to look at them, then come on in the store."

I had to admit this was a pretty good idea, although I wasn't concentrating too well on salesmanship right then. I was noticing that Susan's hair, pulled up in a ponytail, bounced when she talked. My, what a cute, lively ponytail!

"What I like is ten-cent sales. When you buy one thing, and the second costs only a dime?" She looked at me enthusiastically, raising her eyebrows with the question.

I knew what she was talking about of course; and, again, she seemed to be making sense. However, as she turned back around, my eye happened to land on the point at which her left arm and shoulder disappeared into her pullover top. That short sleeve was rather loose, and I wondered if she knew what I almost caught a glimpse of there.

"And, another thing. Make a poster, with the store's name on it—it does have a name, doesn't it?—and then hang the poster on the inside of one of your double doors, in front?" She was pointing, a beautiful, long finger at the end of a long, beautiful arm.

"Yes."

"Then, when you're ready for business, you swing the door wide—presto! Your sign is in place, and everyone knows you're open."

This was all great advice, but it didn't seem to be leading the conversation in the direction I had hoped. Susan was rubbing her chin thoughtfully. It was a very pretty chin, rounded not pointed, a perfect foundation for her very attractive lips.

Since I'd made my breakthrough about lips, by the way, I had begun to realize the variety and character of lips in Fairfield. I had been astounded to discover the range of possibilities, the suggestiveness of individual types. Big lips, little lips; thick and thin; wide or narrow—these differences were meaningful. Often they revealed, I thought, character and behavior.

Billy had a wide, open mouth, and this seemed appropriate to his appetite for adventure, experimentation, investment in crazy schemes. Marcia Terrell had thin lips, and, when she chewed the lower one, she reflected troubles in her family. Roger's steady look into the future was sometimes accentuated by a soft whistle he let slip through perfect lips.

But Susan's lips were distinctive in their smile. The corners were always dancing up in the beginnings of a grin, and it gave to her whole appearance the sense of enthusiasm, interest, fun. As she looked around Old Man Simpson's garage that evening, in fact, a smile played all around her face.

We were now at the counter in the back of the store, where Billy and I proposed to stand and pass out goods, rake in cash. At this moment, though, Susan stood behind the counter, as if she, not I, were the proprietor. And I wobbled around in front of her, wondering what to do next, struggling to continue or begin conversation, sporting a goofy grin as disguise for my growing panic. She had her hands flat on the counter, fingers spread, and was smiling out over the prospect.

I hoped that Susan's joy was not inspired simply by the transformation of Old Man Simpson's garage into a kids' store but also by the chance to share this vision with one of the operation's founding officers. She seemed genuinely caught up in the idea and the very near reality: a store was being born here, to coin a phrase. She looked at me happily; I certainly looked at her happily.

At this moment, however, I disparately needed some way to tie all these real and potential things under the roof (or umbrella) of my kids store together: fingers, smiles, lips; sharing, grinning, tickling. I had done wonderfully to envision and then compel an arrangement of all the things I wanted. They were within touching distance in one place, and everyone seemed willing. But now I was stuck. I simply did not know what to do next.

How did one, I asked myself, get to the next stage in this kind of operation?

VIII

Outside Old Man Simpson's garage, which tomorrow would become the Circle's first kids' store, the humid heat of a July day descended to the warmth of a tolerable summer evening. No breeze stirred, but insects and birds kept up a melodic hum. Down near Billy Rhodes' house children's shouts announced that a regular session of Kick the Can was about to begin.

The sounds of nearby traffic suggested families on their way to Dairy Queen and ice cream deserts, while the pull of automobile and truck engines in the farther distance hinted at summer vacationers resuming their journeys to other towns, drivers with cargo headed for different states.

In the quiet semi-darkness of the moment, Susan Bell leaned across what would become a store counter and kissed Mark Landon on the lips.

I must have gone numb all over, and I remember only a kind of buzzing in my ears that went on for perhaps a minute. Susan slipped out the side door and was gone before I was fully restored to consciousness. I remained frozen at the moment of wondering how I could get Susan Bell to let me kiss her just once. Then I started from the spot, hurried through the side door.

I turned the corner of the garage in time to see Susan running easily down Limestone, ponytail bobbing. In one hand she carried a tin can, probably taken from Mr. Simpson's trash, to serve as base for Kick the Can. I went after her.

It had been one of those moments: once passed, you wonder if it really happened. Your experience was so dreamlike that you begin to think perhaps you only thought it happened.

This fear haunted me especially on this night because no turn of strategy or accident in that game of Kick the Can led to Susan's and my being alone together. There was no chance for a squeeze of the hand as confirmation, an embarrassed look into each other's eyes.

The game went on—first Billy was "it," then, for a long time, Archie Baker—in the same pattern that shaped most of our nights. I hid, I ran, I was caught, I was freed, I hid again. Susan did the same, but always in another circuit, with other hiders. The only connection we had was the can she had taken with her, which our feet alternately kicked. And the one moment that occupied my thoughts, that tumbled around and around in my dizzy head, stood out there in the past, or in my imagination, inaccessible, unverifiable.

There was also another difficult question: if something had indeed happened and not been dreamed, did I feel anything at the moment of my lips' first real contact with significant other lips? Was it, I worried later, like my recurring dream, which went up to the moment of kissing but then ended in a kind of deadness, the absence of sensation?

Or, was I so struck with sensation, so full of feeling, that I was stunned, my nerves' circuits burned up with feeling and no record of the event, as memory, left behind? Had I been kissed, or was it all a dream? Did I experience real lips on lips; or had I blacked out during the action and thus missed everything that occurred?

To make all this even more unsettling, chance did not throw me together with the object of my desire for a number of days after our encounter in the store, that game of Kick the Can. Part of the reason, of course, was Billy's and my opening for business.

Although for much of our days the store stood empty of customers, just the two of us dusting stock and spinning scenarios of success, we were almost always there. In the evenings, before Kick the Can, kids did come by, many interested in both buying and selling. They picked over our assortment of stuff and offered us what they claimed were good buys on their own cast-off toys and miscellaneous mementos.

We spent, in fact, much more time haggling over prices and making deals, as sellers and as buyers, than we did actually completing transactions. Also, our store was from the start as much a center for social gathering and gossip as a place of business. All these activities took up hours; but Susan, this week, was not involved in any of them.

The time-consuming nature of our store also derived from the kinds of merchandise Billy managed to collect for sale. I have already mentioned the two dozen sled runners, the mountains of pop sickle sticks, the piles of sponges, the alien wastepaper cans. Billy's idea of what was a good buy for us and what would sell to others led him to the filling of bins and shelves with: two hundred backs of stand-up 8"x1O" picture frames with their fold-out, triangle supports; fifty boxes of garden hose washers; perhaps a thousand of the little bars that hold bands on wristwatches; several stacks of tiny lamp shades; a huge sack of replacement cane chair bottoms; uncountable mason jar lids.

I never understood what people, especially children, were supposed to do with all these parts of things. Billy always had an argument about how they could be used, but experience proved that few or no kids were going to invest in the possibility of such circumstances arising where a garden hose washer would save the day.

Our food and candy line was similarly eccentric, owing in large part, I learned in time, to our limited capital and the clever salesmanship of downtown merchants. Billy was a sucker for the results of confused packing at a far away plant, misdirected loads of material that could not be returned, loose shipments of bulk items that no one wanted in the first place.

So in our store were cartons of ice cream cones (we had no ice cream); thousands of tiny little jars of boysenberry and other exotic jellies, the kind that restaurants serve with toast or rolls; a bin full of canned asparagus, each can slightly damaged in transit; packs of baseball cards in which the cards were blank, the gum an unpopular apricot flavor; baskets full of defective cake decorating kits, the cones through which icing was to be squirted sealed shut.

Only the comic book section of the store was an immediate success in terms of activity, though whether this was making any money or not was another of my concerns.

Billy had convinced me to add my collection to his own as a base from which to begin a buy-sell-and-trade operation. He managed this part of the business, and comics came and went with dizzying speed. Two-for-one deals, returns, credit purchases, loans, partial issues, stack sales were but a few of the ways he kept things hopping. All I could tell was that my favorite comics were gone within the first few days, though occasionally thereafter I might catch one recirculating through the system; several I purchased as soon as I saw them again.

Despite the amateur and ad hoc nature of our efforts, the business was a heady affair; and I was whirled along for a time in the excitement and novelty of events. All the while, of course, I was still keeping my eye out for Susan, hopeful that a follow-up opportunity to our encounter in the dark would somehow develop. I saw her only once within the next week, however, in one of the few times not taken up with running or getting ready to run the store. And that sighting brought on the ultimate sexual encounter of my summer.

Billy and I were playing a game of marbles. There were two primary versions of marbles in our childhood, Little Circle and Big Circle. In Little Circle, a game I have since found to be pretty much universal, each player drops an identical number of marbles onto a spot in the dirt, creating, it is assumed, a random pattern. Then, with the toe of a shoe, someone draws a circle around the marbles. The diameter of the circle varies depending on how the marbles fall and on whom you play with (the older the players, the larger, generally, the circle); but it usually ends up being about three feet.

Then players take turns shooting from outside the circle at the marbles with heavy "shooter" marbles: each marble driven out by a "shooter" is kept by that player. Every time you knock out one marble, you earn another shot; and if your "shooter" stays in the circle after a play, you shoot from that spot rather than outside. Thus, good marble players make their shooters stick in the circle, often cleaning out the pack from that close range in one turn.

If this form of marbles was widespread in America among my and earlier generations, Big Circle was probably a unique variation of another regular game. I've also heard this game called "Chase."

Chase involves one player shooting out ahead of another toward some distant finish line, the edge of a yard or someone's driveway. The second player shoots in pursuit. If one player hits another's marble, he or she gets a free shot further along the way toward the goal. So you want to stay well away from your opponent unless you have an almost sure chance to hit him. The first player to reach the end, obviously, is the winner.

Our local version involved shooting marbles all the way around the Circle, the entire neighborhood. It was, at least in theory, an all-morning or all-afternoon affair. But we didn't always get that far, and any game whose range went beyond three houses was called "Big Circle," though it technically covered only an arc of that large circuit.

Billy and I were playing Big Circle near the end of that week of the neighborhood's first store and my first kiss. I had initiated the game in part to get Billy and myself out of Old Man Simpson's garage, where I was beginning to feel I spent all of my time. I also hoped in this different setting to elicit from Billy a more direct account of how the business was doing than I had been able to gain thus far.

We had made it all the away round the top of the Circle and onto Oak Street, only three or four houses from Susan's and Tricia's. As Billy's marble landed two feet from mine (an easy hit and an extra shot coming for me), I saw Susan Bell standing beside her family bomb shelter, looking in my direction. We were far enough apart that I could not see her eyes or read the expression on her face; but surely her whole posture gestured to me.

Didn't her hands turned palm out by her hips in a kind of entreaty ask me to make arrangements to be with her again? Didn't the slight tilt of her head toward the secret space of the bomb shelter indicate that this was to be the place for our next rendezvous? Didn't the smile I knew to be dancing at the corners of her mouth say to me, here are joy and wisdom, love and desire, truth and fulfillment? Didn't she say, come to me?

IX

I could not go to Susan right then, of course, as my actions were governed by a game of marbles. And when Billy and I and our marbles reached the Bell house (he enjoyed a lead of about ten feet), she had disappeared, leaving me again with the fear that something I thought had happened (Susan beckoning to me) might only have been a dream, an imagining.

As I was getting ready for bed that night, I had a second confusing experience, another feeling that reality and fantasy were in danger of getting mixed up for me. Charles was sitting at his desk, trying to clean the printer's ink and grime from beneath his fingernails after a day's work. Rather offhandedly, he said that he heard girls were getting interested in me.

"Me?" I was surprised. I tried to disguise a combination of shock and pleasure, however, by sitting down on my bed and turning to pull my pajamas from beneath the pillow.

"That's what I hear," he insisted. He cut on the lamp at his desk to see better.

"Girls—hunnh!" Until I had more information, I thought it best to keep to the standard pre-pubescent line that girls could not interest me less. I took off my shoes and stuck them under the edge of the bed.

"You may not like girls, but it could also be the family curse—good looks." He looked at me and grinned.

"Ha!" I tried not to let him catch me eying myself in the mirror on the closet door as I pulled my shirt up over my head. Charles was already almost six feet tall, and I had heard he could date anyone in his class. But I didn't think I was following in his footsteps.

"No, I'm serious. That's what I hear, You're being talked about."

"Oh, yeah, by who?" I put on my pajama top.

"I don't know, neighborhood girls, kids on the Circle."

Maybe there was something here. Maybe Susan had said something to Tricia or to Cathy Williams. And word had gotten back to Charles through the circuit of older kids' gossip. How could I find out more, though?

"Well, I told Tricia Bell you were getting to be quite a little lover," Charles added, getting up and heading through the door to the unfinished portion of the basement, where we had a half-bath.

"Oh, I bet!" I called after him. This sounded like a joke; he was probably just putting me on. Still, he might have told Tricia? Hmm, this could be good: she would pass it on to Susan.

"Of course, Tricia's got the hots for me, you know," said Charles with a wink. That was quite possibly true, but I was more interested in who wanted me. I wondered if Susan and I had been seen going into the store? Were we already the subject of rumor?

I got no more about my reputation for romantic activity from Charles on this night, however. After he came back from the bathroom, he started telling me a story about what had happened at work that day, a co-worker's getting in trouble with the boss. This was a friend of Charles, and my brother was afraid he might get fired.

I soon lost interest in what happened, though a number of the details stayed in my mind later, as I was drifting off to sleep. Some things about Charles' friend's actions and explanations of his actions reminded me of Billy, my business partner. The more I thought about our kids' store in the last few days, the less convinced I was that things were going well. The details that had been emerging from my casual conversations with Billy suggested an operation spinning out of control more than a smoothly functioning system.

By the end of the second week of the company's existence, I decided to try to pin Billy down about some details. I wanted to determine actual sales and profits, see how we stood. His descriptions were remarkably vague, however.

"Let me see the books," I demanded finally. Whatever records we had were in the cupboard on the wall. Billy opened it and pulled out a cardboard shoe box.

"That's most of the receipts," Billy offered, though he was also digging little slips of paper out of his pocket.

I had built a cash drawer under the counter. Both of us were authorized to receive money and make refunds, if necessary. At the end of each day, Billy had added up the transactions and transferred the money to the cupboard, which had a small padlock. When he went on shopping expeditions, usually in the mornings, he took cash from that supply. So inside the shoe box were his I.O.U.'s to the company, a log of things we had sold, and receipts for what we had purchased as stock.

"How much do you think we've made?" I asked him. I was spreading things out on the counter.

"Mmm, hard to say exactly."

"Well, you know we put in some money for locks and the cash box and like that. So, we had to make something first, just to come even."

"Right." Billy, standing in the middle of the garage, was inspecting the shelves, the bins, our holdings. He held his hands behind his back, rocking on his heels, turning slowly around.

I started stacking all the slips into two basic piles, money in and money out. "What's the story on comic books?" I asked. They were displayed on the slanted shelves I had put in. The number looked about the same as when we started.

"Well, you know, we've bought and sold there. I was thinking they'd primarily bring customers into the store, who'd buy other things."

"You mean you don't think we're ahead there?"

"Can't say for sure. I'll have to check it out." He stepped over to the wall, appearing to count individual comics while he straightened the display. I had all the pieces of paper from the shoe box in two separate piles, credits and debits, basically. The debits pile was clearly larger than the credits.

"Maybe I should have kept a record of comic book transactions," offered Billy.

"You mean you didn't?" I began adding up "money out." Many of the slips reminded me of the crazy things Billy had purchased—popsicle sticks, washers, ice cream cones. The prices he'd paid were small, but most of the goods still seemed to be in the store.

"Well, I was going to, but things got kind of hectic." He stepped back from the comic shelves, eying the bin full of sponges. I didn't think we'd sold a single one of those.

"What's this—'whistles/radio'?" I asked, referring to one scrap of paper as I started adding up "money in."

"Oh, I was going to trade with an old woman at Brents' Store downtown, the radio in my Dad's De Soto for a box of police whistles. But Pop wouldn't let me take the radio out. That's nothing, nothing." He reached over and wadded up the slip, stuffing it in his pocket. I wondered what was wrong with the whistles, whether they were missing the little ball that rattles around in the inside, or pitched somehow so that only dogs or rodents could hear.

"Billy," I said tentatively. "Billy, we seem to have spent more than we've made."

"What?" He seemed genuinely surprised. He came up to the counter, and I turned the sheet of paper on which I'd been working around for him to see. It showed $11.22 more going out than coming in. "That's terrible," Billy admitted.

We had each pooled some money from our savings to start a cash drawer, so the business owed me $15.00 and

Billy $10.00. When I counted the cash available ($13.78), it confirmed our status in the red.

"We're going to have to reorganize what we're doing here," I stated firmly. I looked around the store, at the shelves and bins and baskets of things we were probably never going to be able to sell.

"Oh, I don't know," offered Billy. "We're going to have to move out anyway."

"Move out?"

"Yeah, Old Man Simpson wants his garage back."

"What? We just finished fixing it all up!" I protested. But a light already began to glimmer off in the distance. If all our stuff were cleared out, Mr. Simpson would have a nicely cleaned garage with new shelves and all his old things neatly stored.

"When did he say that?" I asked Billy.

"Oh, I can't remember exactly. A few days ago."

There was a silence before I asked. "It wasn't, by any chance, before we opened?"

"Hm? What? Oh, no, no. It was just the other day. You know, we could move most of this stuff to the De Soto, put it in the trunk, keep the business going. I know . . . "

As Billy began to lay out a scheme of where everything we had could be stored, I tried to decide how long Billy had known we wouldn't be able to stay in Old Man Simpson's garage. I didn't think—and I don't to this day—that he knew from the very beginning. I think he had gotten so excited about the idea in the first place that he was blinded to any signs or clues in Old Man Simpson's behavior that the building was on loan to us only long enough for us to fix it up. I think Billy glossed over that likelihood not to fool me, but to keep himself fooled, to keep the project alive for his own enjoyment. He was always, of course, crazy like that.

I am even more sure he was in the dark about the ultimate use of the refurbished garage. This was something we figured out months later, after we noticed an increasing number of cars parked in front of Old Man Simpson's house, after we observed that a steady flow of visitors was coming to that garage. And we realized that no women came to see our neighbor, who, his cane propped up beside him, sat in an old straight backed chair just inside the double front doors. He would open one of the doors enough to admit a single visitor to the darkened interior.

Mr. Simpson had stocked the garage, which Billy Rhodes and I had worked so hard to fix up as a store, in girlie magazines and other erotic material. His trade was small but regular, discrete but not invisible. It was all pretty tame stuff by today's standards (R-rated rather than XXX, say); but, in the years in which *Playboy* was getting established, pornographic novels, picture playing cards, and little wooden boxes you opened for surprises did not circulate through the regular businesses of Fairfield.

So, in a sense, I guess, our kids' store was taken over by a larger, adult operation, swallowed by a giant competitor. And we did not become powerful, successful leaders in our community. I am happy to report, however, that my other goal, of attracting beautiful women through the dynamics of bold entrepreneurship, was not in the end entirely disappointed.

X

The kids' store debacle was certainly not without lessons learned. Although I had had previous experience with Billy's schemes, I now understood more fully the need to keep a certain distance from my best friend's projects.

I learned that, for all his vision and drive, Billy was a person who would seldom accomplish what he set out to do. He had a habit of ignoring the fundamental forces that meant success or failure in his endeavors, though his love for action and head-over-heels commitment to an idea remained engaging qualities to his friends.

Still, the two of us had, for a time, run a business, a store conceived by kids and for kids, an operation that existed, though only briefly, on its own terms, free of adult control. The final phase of that dream came, as I have suggested, in my relations with the opposite sex, in another encounter with the alluring Miss Bell.

Once again my adventure occurred in connection with a game of Kick the Can, on a night when I felt new strength and maturity coming from my struggles. To that point, the day had been bittersweet, as Billy and I, in a series of wagon trips, hauled the last of our junk from Old Man Simpson's garage to the Rhodes' basement. Our former landlord was standing out on the sidewalk where his two concrete strips of a driveway met the street. He punctuated the stages of our eviction, as I remember, by striking his cane forcefully on the curb when each wagon load passed by.

At Billy's house three doors down and across the street we had a second distraction: on one of the hottest days of the summer, over 100 degrees, Mr. Rhodes was having his furnace cleaned. The inefficient heating systems of those days slowly caked up the insides of furnace, chimney, and ducts with thick, black goo. And every five years or so, it had to be loosened from the walls of furnace parts and sucked out by powerful machines on a large flatbed truck parked in the driveway or in the street.

So out on the front lawn that day near the end of July lay the huge canvas bag into which the soot and dirt produced in the Rhodes' furnace was being pumped by some sort of vacuum apparatus. I guess the bag that collected all that grit and grime was twenty-five feet long, over six feet in diameter, a giant, gray sausage covering most of the yard. (One of the standard ways in which older children teased younger ones, of course, was to talk of little kids who had gotten sucked into such bags, coming out, if at all, covered with soot.)

Cables, hoses, and wiring ran through a small basement window, and workmen from Gass's Chimney and Furnace Service, with their blackened faces and clothes, were regularly going in and out the downstairs door. Whenever we were coming in, it seemed, they were going out, and their equipment had to be wherever we wanted to put something of ours. Throughout the day the truck's powerful vacuum devices roared and howled out by the curb, and our efforts to communicate with the workmen or each other were frustrated by incessant noise.

Our exit from the world of retail business was made more painful, then, by the heat, by the presence of an irritating landlord, and by the circumstances of a furnace cleaning operation. When we finally got ready for Kick the Can that night, Billy and I were already bushed; and I think we looked forward to nothing more than finding a cool, quiet hiding place where, alone or together, we could lick our wounds.

The can was at Archie and Dennis's, the very top of the Circle; and Cathy Williams, surprisingly, had decided to join us on this night. She more often spent such evenings with Tricia Bell and the other older kids, but tonight she seemed to be without companions. She even volunteered to be "it," something none of us would have predicted. So we had nearly a dozen younger kids excited by the fact that our red haired, neighborhood beauty was playing with us.

As Cathy put her foot on base and started to count, Billy proposed going down Limestone toward my house, but I felt this would be too close to Old Man Simpson's for my comfort. I took off alone down Oak, making a mental note that I thought I heard a sound in the distance, probably a train. (Or was it a squad of Russian bombers come at last, crazy Ivan in the lead?)

Was I already thinking of the Bells' bomb shelter, then, as I jogged along? Perhaps, though that hiding place's primary appeal might have been its coolness, an escape from the still oppressive day's heat.

Did I hope to meet someone there that night, someone like Susan who would help me move on from my problematic business career to different contexts, new experiences? Perhaps so.

Susan was playing, and I seemed to remember her running off, as Cathy counted, in a direction that could have led back to her own house. I do know that in a few minutes I saw Susan standing under a huge elm in her side yard, a silhouette framed by a neighbor's porch light or perhaps the moon.

The gesture this young woman was making should have revealed to me that here once again was not the young Susan but her older sister, Tricia. That gesture remains one of the most enticing poses in my experience, a woman lifting her hair with both hands behind her head, letting cool air to her neck. She often will follow this act with a little shake of her head or sigh. That this event generally occurs when, because of the heat, the woman is wearing few or loose clothes only adds to its deadly attraction for me. Seeing the tall shapely form with her fair, blonde hair pulled up that night took my breath away, and I was drawn to her.

As I advanced, however, she retreated, first toward and then into the Bell family bomb shelter. A light breeze swept through the trees, shaking leaves. I heard a train distinctly now, but still pretty far away—eastbound, I concluded.

124

Before me Tricia, whom I thought to be Susan, raised a hand in the shadows of the shelter doorway, beckoning to me. I slipped across her side yard and ducked into the cave hollowed out of the hillside . . .

Now, at this point I must stop and make a confession. I am trying to tell you everything that happened in the Bells' bomb shelter that summer night, or at least everything that I remember. There are parts of that experience, however, about which I am now unsure. I can no longer tell, in fact, if they actually happened, if at the time I only imagined them happening, or if I later made them up and worked them into my memory as real events. I know that some of them are unlikely, perhaps even preposterous; yet they feel now to me as real as the other events that seemed to lead up to and follow from them. So, here goes . . .

When I stepped into the cool, damp darkness of the bomb shelter, Tricia was standing, arms at her sides, in the center of the large, main room. The only light came from outside, through the open doorway behind me; so I still thought it was Susan meeting me, responding to my inner needs and desires. She raised her hands, and I walked into her arms.

Tricia/Susan looked into my eyes and said . . . well, I'm not exactly sure what she said. I can tell you the words I thought I heard; but remember that eastbound train, a heavy freight making the laborious climb up from the river valley? It was now close enough to fill the air with a steady growl, perhaps echoing or amplified within the hollow space of the shelter.

Furthermore, as close as we were now, I suddenly recognized that I was alone with the older, more mature Tricia, not the younger, familiar Susan Bell. This person's mouth opened and closed, her lips formed syllables; but with her speaking softly and me dazed by the noise, the heat, the shock of recognition and just a hint of fear, who knows precisely what she did say.

Perhaps Tricia said, "I know you are 'L.D.'"

I might have said, "Oh?"

Perhaps she said, "I want to see."

I might have said, "Oh?"

I think I remember what happened next more clearly, more accurately. Tricia took my face in her hands (she was several inches taller than I) and leaned down to kiss me. This kiss was different from Susan's, deeper, hotter, longer. I believe at the end of it my whole body was shaking.

Also by this time the eastbound train was probably about at Springers' Pond, its several diesel engines groaning on the Fairfield plateau, though its one hundred or more cars still had to be pulled up the last of the incline. The ground in the neighborhood was beginning to shake in response to the engine's ferocious working. Did I possibly hear in that din the slight but familiar sound of a plastic police whistle?

Tricia's hands were, I think, at my belt. And I was trying to get some words, any words, to come out of my mouth. I remember, or think I remember, a number of breathy gasps, my lips bumbling against each other, my tongue flopping around the inside of my mouth. I could not move the rest of my body, which stood there in Tricia's grasp. I remember being very warm.

The train was now directly opposite the Circle, just beginning to pick up speed as it reached the level stretch through town. The sound traveling in the air drowned out any speech I might have achieved, and the vibrations running underground sent shivers from my feet to the top of my head. The lingering warmth of a scorching July day outside was matched by heat generated within this small, enclosed space. A crisis had arrived.

At this point in some versions of my memory I feel my belt loosened, my pants falling to the ground.

I don't think that's what actually happened, but I cannot be certain it didn't.

After that, perhaps, I see Tricia stepping back, looking down, to my ultimate embarrassment. And in this series of recollections, everything then goes blank. I guess I faint.

What is more likely to have happened, and what I generally recall when I think of the events immediately following the second romantic kiss of my life, is that, in a moment's pause, during which Tricia leans back and smiles playfully at me, miraculously, I find my voice. It's not, I'm sorry to say, the deep gravelly voice of manhood; but at least it's a sound, made and shaped by me. I am not tall and strong, confident and muscular; but neither have I fallen to the ground and begun to cry.

At this time, gratefully—but also a bit sadly—I hear myself say, "I think . . . I think . . . I think my mother's calling me." And I run out of the bomb shelter.

Interlude: Crossroads

Throughout the years of my growing up, my parents regularly took me, my brother, and my sister to visit our paternal grandparents in Jefferson City. It was only about an hour-and-a-half drive, and we usually went up on a Sunday to have dinner after the church hour (though we skipped church itself on that day), returning before dark.

This drive became over the years incredibly familiar, and we could identify every turn around, climb up, and dip between the Ozark foothills along the way as landmarks so many minutes away from or close to Grandma's or to home. I feel, in fact, that I could map for you that route right now, thirty years later, with an inclusion of detail that would be startling.

After enough trips to and from Jefferson City, of course, I began not to notice these landmarks: they became so familiar as to be almost invisible.

On one particular Sunday I looked for a customary feature of that landscape. On the west side of the road, behind a set of small hills, were some high cliffs in which several huge openings loomed. Something, I can't now remember what, in between the last Sunday drive and the present had reminded me of these giant caves; and I waited patiently for them to become visible through the car window, particularly as we crossed the Osage River about fifteen miles from the state capitol. I believed the bluffs were close to that river.

However, I did not spot them going up; nor did they appear on the way back. In fact, I never did see them again on the road between Jefferson City and Fairfield. Where had they gone?

It was years before I solved this little mystery, even though the answer was not complicated. Those caves I had seen were not on the road north to Jefferson City, but along the road east to St. Louis. Route 66, now Interstate 44, was the highway we took into Illinois every several years to visit my mother's family back East in New Jersey.

The exit from Missouri was notable because the old road crossed the Mississippi on the Chain of Rocks Bridge, which had a strange bend in the middle.

And it was near Pacific or Eureka, Missouri, that I had seen the cliffs. Apparently I then forgot where they were; and, associating them with riding to see grandparents, I placed them in my mind along the road to Jefferson City. A long visit in New Jersey may have put the sighting of the cliffs a considerable ways back in my brief life too, so their location in space became first fuzzy, then inexact, and finally incorrect. When I next remembered them as things I had seen somewhere, I began to look for them in the wrong place.

Of course, my attention span at this age was not always as long as was required by many tasks. Try as hard as I could to keep looking along the road to Jefferson City for those cliffs, my mind would wander, or someone in the car might say or do something that distracted me, or I could even fall asleep. So when we pulled in at my grandparents' house, I would sit up with a start, angry that I had missed those large landmarks once again. I would swear to myself to watch more carefully on the return trip. And several times during the visit it would come to me in a flash of memory that I was supposed to be ready on the drive home and this time recover these elusive natural phenomena.

Yet once more on the ride back I would fail to spot them, and I would assume I had lost concentration at various points along the way. I continued to believe that what I wanted to see was there, but that at the crucial moment I had been looking in the wrong direction.

An additional incident removed any immediate opportunity to undo this confusion. Between the trip to New Jersey on which I had first seen the caves and the family's next journey east several years later, the Missouri highway department improved Route 66, straightening and leveling its course among the hills, recharting its path nearly a half mile away from the high cliffs and caves. I did not see them on subsequent trips to New Jersey, then, because they could not be seen from the new roadway.

There's something else, too, involved in my absolute conviction that these pale bluffs were in the place I believed them to be. We did not have in those days fundamental doubts about the world around us or in the ability of our senses to perceive that reality. And I'm not talking just about children here. In post-World War II America we all felt that things had clear natures and outlines, that the tasks before us were known, the ways to proceed fixed and understood. Even in little things, like how families sat in automobiles, the world was organized.

In the Landon clan, the father always drove while the mother sat in the front passenger seat and attempted to navigate. (I say "attempted" because, of course, she never satisfied my father. Any missed or wrong turns, even unexpected complications of traffic in strange cities far from home, were somehow her fault, not the driver's. I marvel now at the patience and lack of anger that she maintained over so many miles and through so many years.)

The back seat of our family car had an order as precise and fixed as the front: I sat behind my father on the driver's side; my older brother Charles behind our mother; and the youngest, Beth, between us. Even if only some of us were riding in the car, our seats did not change, except on those limited occasions when our father was not going. Then our mother drove (she did not drive on the long trips) and of necessity sat behind the wheel.

If I was the only passenger going with my mother to the grocery store, I rode in my customary seat, the back left. It never even occurred to me until much later that I might more reasonably have joined her on the front seat. My whole view of the world for years, in fact, extended outward from that precise point in space, the rear driver's-side seat. Essential landmarks in my sense of this earth include the back of my father's head, the left profile of my kid sister Beth. If I close my eyes, I can feel them ahead and beside me right now.

You would think such consistency required that staple of car travel in the present day, seats belts; but so universal was the acceptance of rules of behavior, at least in our family, that no external restraints were needed to enforce them. We knew our places, and we kept to them.

None of my own family now, of course, accepts a system of required seats. My wife drives as often as I do and has her own car as well. My children fight about who will "ride shotgun" on every long and short journey, and I spend more time negotiating settlements and attempting to redress apparent and real inequities than I do running errands.

The world has changed, or at least the way in which we respond to and shape it has. When I think back to my childhood and its remarkable stability, I recognize the costs of maintaining so rigid a control of persons and things. But, even so, my retrospective vision inspires no little yearning for some modern version of a similar security.

If an unquestioning acceptance of fixed places contributed to my loss of the high cliffs along the roadside to Jefferson City, experience in the world eventually restored them. However, other knowledge came with that experience as well. I know now, for instance, that those limestone cliffs were dug, not by the Osage on its way to the Missouri, but by the Maramec River as it winds down to the Mississippi.

Even more unsettling, I realize that what I had originally seen as caves were really excavations made by a rock company, which was dynamiting hills into gravel for building projects in and around the growing city of St. Louis. I discovered this years later when I was in college, working summers for the Missouri Geological Survey. With a crew that was mapping a section of flat bottom land, I had come upon the scene entirely by chance. In the passenger seat of a state-owned pick-up truck, I saw the same landscape I had first encountered some dozen years earlier in the backseat of the family car—high limestone cliffs and large openings.

The loss of countryside to progress is of some interest here, but it's not my primary point: I'm more troubled by the confusion of time and space in my past. I had believed for years, for most of my whole life, that a striking physical feature of the world was in a particular place at a precise time; yet it was not there then at all. Without realizing it, I had slipped off a route taken so routinely that every detail was permanently etched in my memory and continued along a different road in another direction. What if fate had never revealed my mistake to me? I would have gone on living forever with an illusion about the fundamental shape of my universe.

Even more unsettling now, at the approximate midpoint of my life, is the question: what other switches and slips have my faulty modes of observation and remembrance accomplished? What elements of the land and my past are in the wrong place at the wrong time in my memory? Are the courses I'm plotting into the future based on inaccurate or totally wrong pictures of reality? It's a scary thought, let me tell you, particularly if you believe that you have survived life's perils long enough to gain some understanding of it.

I have, in fact, recently come to just that conclusion. I feel I know something about the Midwest, where I grew up, and about that larger entity, America. This conviction is, in fact, the justification for writing down this story of my life.

As I set out now to tell you more about my adventures and experiences, then, I can only hope to be getting most of it right, lining up landmarks I've passed on the correct paths, drawing conclusions about the nature and meaning of existence in our time based on actual obstacles encountered, genuine acts performed.

Even while I tell it as carefully and completely as I can, I worry that this story may be coming along paths that can no longer be found, through a landscape recast by the forces of time and change, down ways that may not, in fact, ever have existed. In such a perilous enterprise, a traveler can proceed only by confessing these possibilities, which I do here, and by asking for a certain generosity of spirit from readers, which I also do now.

These reservations offered, I shall continue.

Volume Three: Society

Part Five: On the Town

Chapter I

When I took a regular shortcut home after delivering papers one November evening of my first year in high school, I turned an unfocused fear of one dark neighborhood into a complete panic.

The paper had been late that day, something to do with a breaking story about a zoning commission report, so I was in a hurry to get home and not be late for dinner. And I was braving the little stretch of odd houses and dark empty lots just short of the Circle on Valley Lane.

I always had great difficulty getting through this undistinguished neighborhood, even though it was an effective short cut. Valley Lane was a thin, uncurbed blacktop crossing Black Street about one hundred yards east of the bottom of the Circle (the point where Hill went south and Limestone curved north and west to run along the side of Piney Ridge). Valley Lane going north off Black dipped down to the tracks, which were not in a cut here, and then up to Highway 66 as that now famous highway left town.

There were no street lights along Valley's entire length, and crossing the tracks after sunset was more than a little scary. I had not forgotten that time several years ago when Marcia Terrell and Dennis Baker found the body of a tramp along these same tracks, perhaps a half a mile further west. Stagnant pools formed in the ditches parallel to the railroad bed off Valley Lane, the same kind in which that poor man had drowned. And hoboes still passed through town taking this route. So, when I turned off Kingshighway onto Valley after dark, I generally found myself breaking into a little jog as I neared the tracks and then getting up to a full fledged gallop from the Knight house to Black Street and its comforting streetlight.

I picked up speed as I came down the hill toward the Missouri-Pacific railroad tracks, glancing off into the dark on both sides as I ran. Then I thought I saw a shadowy form rise up out of the ditch to my left.

Although I was already springing off the ground with each stride, I took an even more excited leap into the air at the sight of the ghostly figure rising up beside me. My legs felt as if they might kick loose from my body. They had, all of a sudden, great energy, a desire to get me out of here. I even thought I heard whoever or whatever had emerged from the darkness speak as I shot across the tracks and propelled myself up toward Black Street.

Do you know how when you walk somewhere at night, sometimes you think you hear someone behind you? But the follower's steps could be synchronized with yours, you realize, so you can't tell for sure if you're hearing yourself or another as well? That's the way it was that night: I felt that there was a second pair of feet pounding the pavement with mine; but I hoped that it was merely my own fear echoing in my mind.

And the noise behind me, "Mawf! Morden! Mahl!," surely that was just my own breath bursting from my lungs with each frightened step? No hand was about to reach me from behind, was it, land on my shoulder, turn me about? No contorted face of crazed or lunatic killer would confront me when I reached the streetlight up on Black Street, would it? Yiiii! I ran.

The hand and face of some pursuer did not catch me, however, at the intersection, for whoever was following me—and someone was after me!—cut across the front yard of the last house on Valley and intercepted my flight down Black street, his whole body appearing directly in front of me.

"Billy!" I gasped, for it was my neighborhood pal, Billy Rhodes. He had the Circle's paper route, and I could see even now under the streetlight that he carried his empty bag loosely in one hand. "What . . what are you doing?"

"Trying . . . trying to catch up . . . with you." We were both out of breath.

"I'm just on my way home. Haven't you done your papers?" I knew that he generally ended his route at his house, having devised a complicated circuit to make his own the final delivery.

"Yeah. I took a last minute detour." He had a funny grin. We were walking together now, turning off Black onto Limestone, breathing more easily.

"Back there?" I looked behind me over my shoulder. It seemed to me that, for Billy to be where I had seen him, he must have come down the tracks. "What? "

Billy stopped in the road and looked at me. "Can you get out of your house tonight, about eight o'clock?"

"I guess. Sure. Why?"

"Meet me at the Vacant Lot. I'll show you."

"I'm not going down the tracks."

"OK, OK. It's not that. You'll see."

And that's all he would tell me right then. However, I had gotten into the business of delivering papers in the first place in order to find out more about what lay beyond the Circle. And here was Billy offering me an intriguing opportunity. (What I learned in the end, however, turned out to be even more strange than I could have imagined at the beginning.)

In the summer preceding this first year of high school for me, near the end of that innocent decade for America, the 1950s, I had been mowing lawns, having developed a list of regular customers nearing two dozen. Most of these yards were on the Circle, that residential area perhaps half of a square mile on the western edge of Fairfield, Missouri. But I also had a few farther up Piney Ridge (where Limestone Street became Ridgeview Road and on Hill Street extended) and one down Black Street, which ran from the Circle out to Highway 00.

These jobs wound down after Labor Day, when school started and the weather turned cool. But I had gotten the idea that I wanted to keep working this year even after classes started. Earning just the small amounts paid to lawn mowers those days had given me a sense of independence I wanted to continue into the school year.

At that time, of course, there were not many employment opportunities for such young teenagers. We were not old enough to bag groceries at the A & P or Krogers; nor could we compete against upperclassmen at the high school for the much coveted position of soda jerk at one of the three or four downtown drug stores. My best chance would be to work for the local newspaper, the *Fairfield Daily Mirror*.

I would have liked to deliver the more prestigious and worldly *St. Louis Post-dispatch*, the afternoon paper thought by everyone I knew to be superior to the morning *Globe-democrat*. But I had missed by only a year or so being old enough to take on that task. Boys on bikes and young men on motor scooters had delivered the *Post* across Fairfield for years (country residents had to get the paper a day late by mail.) But just as I was about to reach the stature necessary for this job, they changed the system.

In those days before television news dominated the nation, the big city paper was large enough that delivery boys needed specially equipped bicycles: double saddlebags over the rear wheel, large basket in front, cloth bags over the shoulders. And even that rig could handle a maximum of perhaps sixty papers, where some routes had over one hundred customers. Pedaling this heavily loaded vehicle required the strength of emerging manhood, not the skinny legs and arms of the preadolescent. And on Sundays even veteran carriers took up to half a dozen trips back to a home base to reload their bikes.

Just as I threatened to achieve the strength and endurance necessary for a *Post* route, the man who hauled a truckload of papers more than one hundred miles from the city and then apportioned them to individual carriers realized he could do the whole job himself. He instituted a new procedure of billing and receiving payment through the mail. Then, in a battered white Chevy station wagon, with his two sons riding in the back seat and hundreds of papers in the flat space behind them, he drove around town while all three threw rolled papers out the windows. He had eliminated the middleman and taken away a means of gainful employment for the boys of my generation. (There were no papergirls then. Only Marcia Terrell had the idea of one.) Thank goodness for the locally owned and operated *Fairfield Mirror*.

When the paper was late, by the way, as it was on the day Billy came out of the shadows on Valley Lane, I didn't need to tell anyone at home that I was waiting downtown at the *Mirror* office or still delivering. Since Billy would be just as late bringing the *Mirror* to the Circle, my mom would understand why I wasn't home yet.

It was a subtle communication network, actually, these paperboys on their parallel routes. Like military units represented by pins on a war board, Fairfield's sons could be spotted on town maps taped to the backs of kitchen doors. They could be recognized by their analogous figures of the home neighborhood as in route from point A to point B or held up at intersection Y. Although she no longer whistled from the front porch for her children with a long and three short blasts, Mom, I knew, still linked up with me when she saw Billy come around the curve at the top of Limestone near the end of his route: I was on my way home.

Many mothers, in fact, knew most of the paperboys in town and where they delivered, so each had in her head a kind of situation room, where the travels of a dozen different individuals were continuously being charted. What Billy was proposing that night, however, would not have shown up on these mothers' radars. If it had, some sort of alarm would surely have sounded all across town.

II

The sixteen page *Fairfield Daily Mirror* was issued Monday through Friday. The front page generally contained national stories, taken pretty much straight from the wire services. Inside was local news, reported with great allegiance to official statements and reports by town officials.

The Sweet family, which owned the *Mirror*, was well connected politically; and grandfather William Sweet, with son Frederic and grandsons Tom, Richard, and Fred Jr., presented a consistent picture of Fairfield as an orderly and well governed community. The paper made its money, of course, from a virtual monopoly on advertising. (Its only competition was the radio station.) And prosperous businesses desired the stability represented and reinforced by the town newspaper.

Of such background, of course, paperboys remained blissfully ignorant. They handled fifty to seventy-five copies of the Fairfield *Mirror* daily but almost never read a word of what they carried. Their primary goal was the spending money they could earn each week.

Paper routes, however, were something more than a source of income to me. They were a means by which the boys of Fairfield separated themselves from identification with their families and with their neighborhoods.

In school we were easily defined by the parents who brought us the first day and who shared rides to regular PTA meetings. Those of us with older brothers and sisters also suffered from expectations, good and bad, established by our siblings. Having the responsibility of distributing the town's official record to its citizens gave one the chance to become known away from home, to take a place in the larger social structure. And, as I entered high school, I was ready, I thought, to move on to a bigger role.

Fairfield was divided into about a dozen regular paper routes of long standing, sections of town that were identified to boys my age not just by some name (Ridgeview, the Shoe Factory Addition, Fairfield Gardens) but by route number (VI, VII, and XI respectively). Roman numerals marked the outlined sections of town covered by each route on a huge wall map in the *Mirror*'s downtown office building. The same numbers were also written with indelible printer's ink on the gray canvas bags that paperboys used and on the metal plates of each route's book. Billy and I are carrying these inked bags on our way home up Limestone Drive right now.

The books used to define and keep a record of every paper route were made up of cards, about six by eight inches, one for each customer on a route. On the top third of a card would be written, in the present or some former paperboy's irregular script, the name and address of the subscriber. Sometimes additional directions were given on how to find this residence or where to leave the paper (porch, driveway, side yard, etc.). The bottom two-thirds of each card was divided by perforated lines into five rows of six one-inch squares. These squares, little tabs, were receipts for weekly payment.

The *Mirror* cost a nickel a day at the newsstand, a quarter a week with delivery. On one weekday, traditionally Thursday, paperboys all over Fairfield knocked on doors and requested payment. As a receipt, each paperboy handed to the subscriber one of these little cardboard squares, on which were printed the words, "Paid" (big letters, top line); *Fairfield Daily Mirror* (second line, medium print); and the date (small print, third line). My mother saved these tabs—I don't know why—putting them in a bowl on the sideboard that also contained rubber bands, paper clips, thumb tacks, and other odds and ends.

The cards of one route's customers were sandwiched between two metal plates (scraps from the printing process), also six by eight inches, and held together by two metal rings at the top. This collection was called, then, the "Book"; and it represented the official identity, history, and operational log of an individual paper route.

On the top plate was written, again in printer's ink, the Roman numeral for that route. The shoulder bag used to carry papers also had a pocket beneath the strap for carrying the Book. Whenever a young man decided to retire from the business, he handed over to his successor that bag and that book.

All paper routes had, of course, their individual reputations. Prime routes were downtown, where a paperboy had protection against bad weather (hot or cold) because he would be going in and out of places of business. Routes in established residential neighborhoods, the closer to your home the better, were satisfactory. (Billy Rhodes, as I said, had Ridgeview, VI, which included the Circle.) And the least desirable were those reaching out to the edges of town, where houses were far apart and often exposed the paperboy to bothersome pets and eccentric subscribers.

The downtown routes also held the advantage that their papers did not need to be folded for delivery. On neighborhood routes paperboys generally rode bikes and threw papers (so much smaller than the *Post* that someone my size could carry one hundred).

Each paper had to be folded into a shape that could be thrown to the customer's front lawn or other desired spot. Usually sixteen pages or eight sheets, the paper emerged from the presses folded in half twice, once side-to-side and once lengthwise. The traditional method called for two more folds in half side-to-side, then a triple fold top to bottom, tucking one end into the other. The result was pretty nearly a flat square, which could be grasped at one corner and sailed horizontally with considerable accuracy. Downtown delivery, however, did not require folding since the paperboy stepped inside shoe store, barbershop, or insurance agency and handed the *Mirror* directly to clerk or owner.

The eighteen or twenty boys from all the neighborhoods of town, aged perhaps twelve to sixteen, received the papers for their routes in a cinder-block room at the back of the newspaper building. We entered from the alley behind Fairfield Street (parallel to and one block over from Main), very close to where the Missouri-Pacific railroad tracks sliced across town. About fifteen feet square, the room was absolutely bare, without furniture or windows, nothing hanging on gray walls over a slick cement floor. A second door, split into a top half (hooked open) and bottom (locked shut) half, connected with the large area where the big printing press thumped and growled.

If the paper wasn't out when they arrived after school, the boys milled around in their room, sometimes watching the two press operators run the giant machine. A large man we knew only as Karl was the veteran, having been there beyond any paperboy's memory. Chester, a boy several years older than my brother Charles and who had dropped out of high school, was his assistant. When the weather was warm, some of us might wait outside, putting pennies on the railroad tracks before trains came by and picking up twenty minutes later the thin, half-dollar-sized discs pounded out by the weight of a hundred freight cars.

When the daily edition came off the press and the stacks were counted and corded together, Karl and Chester threw bundles through the open top half of the doorway to the paperboys' room. In each stack the top paper would have the route marked by a huge black Roman numeral (the paperboy could keep that extra paper for himself or sell it to a nonsubscriber). Their bundles in hand, most of the boys sat down with their backs against the wall to fold papers and pack their bags. Since Roger Peterson and I had the two downtown routes, we started out immediately for delivery.

To see myself now comfortably passing out the back door into the alley with a bag full of papers, however, would be to ignore the dangers of this first stage of the daily journey in my new profession. The enclosed space where we waited for our stacks was another of those raw arenas in which young males established relationships of power. Those not among the largest or strongest—and that included me—had to find ways to minimize head locks, punches on the arm, and other, even more debilitating acts of intimidation. Having a quick tongue and the experience of living with an older brother, I was able most of the time to talk my way out of or stay clear of harm's way.

A background for these scenes of violence was provided by the two press operators struggling in gray work clothes with the huge levers, inky rollers, and tall cylinders of paper used to put out the Fairfield *Mirror*. Looming uppermost in my consciousness were the great vertical cutting and folding blades that fell and blocked the rolls of newsprint toward its ultimate, sixteen-page newspaper shape.

Big Karl never spoke to us boys as, with huge, inky hands, he flipped switches, adjusted gears, slammed home rods. He communicated instead with the editors and owner who came from their offices on the other side of the press room, his giant head, gray haired with a black mustache, inclined deferentially. But Karl's thin assistant Chester liked to sidle over to our two-part door when the press was stopped and suggest horrors that Karl had told him about, accidents which had befallen former press operators a bit too hasty or a bit too slow. And always the story of one paperboy allowed to see the press up close losing a finger in the blink of an eye.

I had taken over Route II in the September after the Landon family's biannual visit to the maternal grandmother in New Jersey. I kept the route so long that I believe I can still tell you every stop, the name and identity of each customer; but I may be mistaken. If there were some way to go back and verify every detail, I would probably find errors in the order of delivery, confusion among the faces along the way. In any case, to recreate fully that weekday walk up and down Main Street requires more space than a single chapter.

I do, of course, intend to keep adding new chapters to this tale, folding them for sailing across yards and up to the porches of those who continue to read. I might even think about providing little tabs for receipts, markers in our continuing relationship. For now, though, let's just say that that fall I entered a new arena with enthusiasm, ready even to follow Billy on his mysterious night adventure.

III

All Gaul, said my ninth-grade Latin teacher Mrs. Johnson, was divided into three parts. Apparently this was something Caesar had determined two thousand years ago. What I had discovered as more important was that my paper route, prized Fairfield number II, was also divided into three parts: 1) picking up my stack at the *Mirror* building off Main Street; 2) delivering papers over an eight or nine-block area of downtown businesses and a few nearby residences; and then 3) walking the three quarters of a mile home to my house on the Circle.

While picking up papers for profitable Route II of the *Fairfield Daily Mirror* and walking home from town involved challenges I had daily to face, the actual delivery of papers was generally as unthreatening as a walk through an Ozark meadow. Not all businesses were as nice as the ancient shop run by two old women, Brents' Store; but that cozy space stands out in my memory now as representative of the middle part of my paperboy's daily existence.

I guess you might call Brents' an early version of a department store or else a late instance of the general store. They carried clothes, fabrics, dishes, housecleaning equipment, small appliances, hardware items, and even a small selection of hardcover books.

The two proprietors, Miss and Mrs. Brent, worked the narrow, wooden floored shop alone, as they had for as long as anyone I knew could remember. Miss Suzanne Brent was the older, a slender, slightly stooped woman with a twinkle in her eye. She saw the humor in every situation, even the potentially tragic. Mrs. Jacqueline Brent, her sister-in-law, younger by only a few years, was taller and fuller, more womanly, if also ancient.

While Miss Suzanne Brent shrugged her shoulders and winked at the odd occurrences of life, Mrs. Jacqueline Brent wept and laughed more openly, for the history ascribed to her did not allow for the detachment of irony.

Jacqueline Delacroix, once belle of Fairfield, had married Henri Brent, of the Brents of historic St. Genevieve, Missouri, the week before he shipped to France during World War I. He left the oldest town in the state, the first settlement west of the Mississippi, to aid the old country from which his ancestors had emigrated a century and a half earlier.

Gassed at Argonne, he lived for forty years an invalid under the care of his wife and maiden sister in a stately old mansion two blocks west of the center of town. He could sometimes be seen on warm, sunny days sitting in a wooden wheelchair on the screened porch that swept around three sides of the two-story, white frame house. Even then, however, an Afghan would be draped across his knees, and a gray scarf kept the breeze off his neck. A wool cap was pulled down low, almost touching the dark glasses that covered his damaged, sun-sensitive eyes.

Brents' Store was an easy delivery for a paperboy, as the ladies in charge always greeted me by name and inquired after my needs as if they worked for me, rather than the other way around. Coming out of the dark corners of the store, they touched with their soft hands the familiar counters and tables, not for support, but reaffirming their world.

"Are you warm enough out there, Mark?" one would ask in winter and look around for a thick pair of gloves I could have "on loan." Often there would be no one else in the store. I wondered later, in fact, how they had stayed in business, so little business seemed to be conducted whenever I came by.

"You'd better rest in here for a minute," the other would insist in the heat of August. "Take a soda, Mark." Along the back wall sat a red, rectangular cooler in which drinks rested in a mixture of ice and water. And they had one rack of crackers, cookies, and chips kept, in theory, to occupy children while their parents shopped or gossiped. I seldom saw parents or children.

Both these ladies were perfect grandmothers, although, having had no children, they also had no grandchildren. Their soft, barely wrinkled faces, the fluttering way in which they moved around the shop trying to take care of or to please me, and their silver hair pulled up in buns made them grandmothers to me and the store their family home. It would be a long time before I understood that the house on Missouri Avenue, which occupied an entire city block, was their real home, that the store was, however many years they had kept it up, only a business.

Shaded by huge oaks and providing space around its four fireplace chimneys (no longer used) for a small flock of pigeons, the Brent house stood on the site of the old stage coach inn that had existed before Fairfield. Travelers of the last century stayed overnight at a frontier hotel on the top of this small rise before heading on toward new settlements as far away as Sante Fe or the gold rush towns of California.

Growing up in the state famous for containing the starting point of the Pony Express, my friends and I often got confused in relating legends about the old Brent house. Many times we told visitors from other regions of the country that Fairfield was the eastern terminal for that early mail system of the American West. Riders took off on fresh horses, we explained, from what was now 200 Missouri Avenue in clouds of dust. Exhausted carriers and mounts raced in from the prairies to our west on the final leg of their continent-crossing journeys. Local history was actually far less glamorous, though not without its curious subjects.

Jacqueline Delacroix's grandfather, for example, one of the town's principle bankers, had bought the stage coach property when the train came in and built its depot a quarter of a mile east. Though he never made use of this central piece of town real estate, his son, Phillip, a widower at the turn of the century, razed the old structures of inn and stables to build the grandest residence of his day. He retired to its splendor with an only daughter to look after him and his many possessions.

These two lived together for over ten years until Henri Brent asked for and won the hand of one of Fairfield's most desirable young ladies (herself not quite so young by then). Their marriage met tragedy on a battlefield of Europe, as her husband came home a shell, nearly blind and deaf, consumptive, confused.

I would see this victim of history often in the first year of my paper route. I passed the Brents' romantic dwelling every day on the way home from downtown to the Circle, that third part of my Gaul, prized *Mirror* route II. And once he even called out to me from his wheelchair on the west-facing porch.

When Henri Brent called out to me from the porch of the Delacroix family mansion on Missouri Avenue that fall afternoon, however, I did what many adolescent boys probably would have done under the circumstances: I pretended that I didn't see or hear him.

In defense of this uncharitable act, I might admit a typical teenager's shyness. Like most people my age, I did not generally seek contact with adults, unsure about what I should be doing or saying in their presence. Too, I could usually make the assumption that no one other than parents or teachers would be calling me or my friends. And, finally, I might point out that it wasn't absolutely clear the World War I veteran had spoken to me specifically, or, for that matter, that he had actually delivered an understandable message.

I had heard a sound, it's true, something that might have been "Zsst! Boy!" across a distance of perhaps fifty feet from the house to the sidewalk where I was walking. It was also possible that the crippled man, hunched over in a wheelchair, wrapped in a blanket or shawl, had simply cried out in pain, "Shhfft! Aii!" feeling a twinge from some part of his injured body. Or, it might also have been that he was calling, not out across the yard and over the black cast iron fence that surrounded the property to me, but back into the house to his wife or sister: "Jacki, Sue!"

The man was supposed to be incapacitated, wasted physically and mentally; so it wasn't likely that he would be reaching out from his isolation to a stranger passing by, to a boy, who, if all were told, at this age had no idea where Argonne was, who couldn't imagine being a soldier, and who understood not a bit the forces of history.

Whatever Henri Brent said or didn't say that first day he might have spoken to me, I just kept striding down the Seventh Street sidewalk, head up, eyes fixed forward, paper bag swinging against my hip. I was, remember, into the third phase of my paper route, walking home after my last delivery, McCorkle's Shoe Repair at the corner of Fairfield and Seventh Streets. And there were several reasons besides a basic fear of the unknown in Henri Brent that would have kept me moving steadily along toward Kingshighway, Valley Lane, and the Circle. The most powerful magnet drawing me on many nights was Sheila Knight.

Sheila Knight—or the idea of Sheila Knight—had taken her place in the continuation of my love life after my confused relationship with the Bells sisters. Still attracted to Susan, I could never relax in her presence after being kissed (and possibly examined) by her older sister Tricia. So you might say my sexual education had shifted into a fantasy mode.

Sheila Knight lived in the middle of Valley Lane. Now, perhaps, you will begin to understand at least in part why I often took this short cut, despite its fearful character. And you can speculate more accurately about what Billy had been doing the day he chased me from this spot.

Near the low point of Valley, right next to the tracks, was Sheila Knights' house. And Sheila Knight was—well—not beautiful, not gorgeous, but—what?—perhaps, something like luscious. At sixteen she was a little old for me to pursue openly, but her woman's body and thick auburn hair took a prominent place in my imagination. And, I now guessed, they were something to Billy Rhodes as well.

Sheila's parents lived in that house on Valley Lane too, though my awareness of them in that small structure was then and remains now rather fuzzy. There was a house; and, as far as I was concerned, Sheila filled it up.

Actually, the Knights' home was less of a house than the two-bedroom structures on the Circle. It had perhaps three small rooms in all, a sagging front porch, wooden siding that badly needed painting.

All of the houses on Valley and on a parallel street (Greek Lane) closer to 00 were similar, some with outer walls covered by tar paper made to look like brick. The children who lived here seldom became friends with Circle kids. They rode the same school bus and their mothers shopped at Tucker's grocery store, but we never seemed to know their names or speak when meeting. I had only realized that Sheila existed this fall, when the shortest route home from my paper route went by her house and I discovered that I wanted to see her ripe form hanging clothes out on the line or picking vegetables in the small field next to her house.

When Billy proposed I meet him at 8:00 one night, then, after I'd discovered him hiding in the shadows beside Sheila's house, I had a general idea about what he was proposing. But, as is often the case, the specific details making up the general pattern were slightly but interestingly different than I'd imagined.

IV

Did we have daylight savings time that particular year? I seem to recall that there was debate about the question throughout the decade. In some years we moved the clocks forward in the spring and back in the fall, but not in others.

There may even have been at times a local option. I think there were situations where a county or state went one way, but the smaller community within it another. I know that twin cities or towns divided by a county or state line sometimes ran on two different clocks, a fact that amused children but must surely have irritated adults trying to coordinate work, school, and shopping.

During the years of my paper route I do know that it was dark in the middle of winter if I walked home after 5:00 o'clock. And even in the fall I think of myself as arriving home often near or after sunset. My memory of summers during my growing up is of a long, long twilight. After I had made my round of downtown businesses and come back to the Circle, our games of Kick the Can continued in a prolonged dusk, stretching essentially to bedtime. And that would only have been possible with daylight savings time.

I raise the question of daylight savings time when trying to figure out how I could get out of the house so easily at 8:00 o'clock on a November school night after clocks had been set back an hour.

In my first year of high school, I didn't have much homework, so going out in the neighborhood might have been equivalent to staying in and watching television. I would have been allowed after dinner to play basketball on the dirt court we had set up in the front half of the Vacant Lot. It was not a cold night, I remember that specifically, so I might have just said I was going down to Billy's for a minute.

It's possible, now that I think about it, but unlikely, that I snuck out of the house. It would have been fairly easy to slip up the stairs from Charles' and my bedroom in the basement, cross the little landing by the kitchen, go out through the garage while the rest of the family was in the living room watching TV. I think, though, that I did my sneaking out of the house later, when I was a senior in high school and Charles away at college. At that time I had a bedroom in the attic and tiptoed down in my sock feet in the early morning to go out the front door.

At any rate, there I was, a few minutes before eight one cool night late in the fall, waiting for Billy in front of the Vacant Lot's basketball goal and wondering what craziness wilder than smoking grapevines this guy was going to get me into. I didn't have too long to consider the possibilities because Billy seemed to be working on some kind of schedule.

"Come on," he urged as soon as he found me and started down the street at a brisk walk. Near the bottom of the Circle, where I had made my famous goof in Kick the Can, Billy ducked between two cars and, breaking into a little run, went between two houses, down a row of hedges separating their backyards, and hopped a fence into the empty lot next to Dr. Masters' house.

The doctor owned that lot, but a row of small trees set it off from the manicured yard around his house. We stopped in the shadows of those trees.

"OK," said Billy, one hand on my elbow, as he looked up at the Masters' house. "OK." There were lights in several windows, but I didn't see anyone or anything of interest in the yard.

This house, remember, was the original residence for the farm that had once covered several hundred acres along Piney Ridge. Most of the homes in the Circle proper sat on what had been a pear orchard. Black Street had been the lane out to "Piney View," as the house was called. Built just before the turn of the century, this Victorian structure was a rival to the many fine homes along Missouri Avenue like the Brents'.

Dr. Masters had rescued the house on the edge of town from neglect, though he was unable to stop the subdivision of the surrounding property into small home lots. His two-story, five-bedroom structure anchored the neighborhood in its position at the base of the Circle.

From where Billy and I stood in the shadow of trees, the house looked to me bigger and grander than ever. There was a screened porch with white, wicker lawn furniture at one end, and a neat little balcony came off one of the upstairs bedrooms. I noticed, perhaps for the first time, the trellises on which roses climbed, a modest gazebo tucked into one corner of the yard, stone walkways running from garden to birdbath, from house to garage. Unlike the one-car units attached to each house in the circle, this garage was a separate, two-car structure with a little cupola topped by a rooster weather vane.

The Masters' home, I realized, was more like an estate than a house. But what were we doing here? I hoped we weren't planning a robbery!

Billy looked like a would-be thief in the dark as he raised a finger to his lips, motioned for me to follow him, and slipped out of the row of trees into the Masters' back yard. In a crouch, he ran to the huge pear tree by the north corner of the house. Then he began climbing up the trunk, which was at least three feet in diameter.

I didn't even see what he was holding onto until I tried to come after him: there were old knobs and bumps, where limbs had once been, which he used as hand- and footholds. I'm not sure I would have seen them even in the daylight unless I'd been told where to look.

At one point a notch, carved in the bark by some sharp instrument and big enough to hold the toe of a tennis shoe, allowed us to reach the first branch and pull ourselves up. From there the climb was easy. Billy went up the main trunk for perhaps ten feet, than horizontally out a large branch to a point several feet away from a small upstairs dormer window.

Lying on his belly in a fork, Billy peered through the leaves at the small, darkened square.

"Billy!" I whispered from the base of the limb he had climbed out. "What...?"

"Shh!" He turned his head and held up one hand, palm facing me, for silence. I couldn't see very well from where I was behind and below him, but I could tell there were curtains and a shade pulled halfway down in what I assumed was a bathroom window.

A light came on in the window, illuminating Billy's face among the leaves. I could see only a profile, but I felt his intensity, mouth slightly open, breathing heavy. He held up his hand to me again, one finger raised.

At this point I wasn't sure where I wanted to be. Dr. Masters had a son and a daughter; and I assumed we had not climbed up here in the dark to watch ten-year-old Gerry take a shower. His sister was a high school senior, the Homecoming Queen, captain of the cheerleading team. Not only was blonde Janet Masters as beautiful in her way as red-haired Cathy Williams, but she was also a local princess, the darling of Fairfield's country club set. We were going to peep on her?

Billy didn't move, and I realized that, from his vantage point, he could look not just into the room but right into the bathtub. I also saw that his finger was still pointing up in the air. Above him was another branch, smaller but still substantial enough to hold me. I got the picture.

Peeping was, I felt, a daring act. Sneaking into someone's yard, climbing his tree, and ending up barely an arm's length from his daughter's privacy went beyond any casual snooping or spying we might have done in the past. There would be no reasonable explanation for our present position, should we suddenly be required to deliver one by, say, Dr. Masters, standing below us and training a high-powered flashlight up into our faces.

Not only were we about to violate an established social rule and probably some civil law by peeping, but the object of our attack was a member of one of the town's elite families. Getting caught in this act would be about as damaging to our and our family's reputation as setting fire to the entire county . . . which Billy had, of course, almost done on our expedition to the Open Space of our woods several years earlier!

I began to feel very uncomfortable about what I was getting into. On the other hand, I made no effort to climb back down to the ground.

In fact, to the surprise of one part of me, the rest of me began to climb up to the high limb Billy had recommended. I inched forward on my stomach until I reached a position above Billy, though several feet farther from the house. And through the small bathroom window I saw Janet Masters, wearing a pink terry cloth robe, step across an elegant black and white tile floor toward a large, oval bathtub. She bent down out of my sight and turned on the water.

To Billy's regret (I heard a muffled complaint, "Sstt!"), the young lady pulled shut the shower curtain to take her bath. We had a mind-numbing view of her breasts as she dropped the robe off her shoulders and stepped into the tub; but immediately after that image burned itself into our memories forever her left hand slid the curtain over, blocking our view.

We had a second moment of excitement when a long arm reached around the curtain for a towel hung on a rack by the door. But when the whole woman emerged from the tub, her wet hair combed back behind her ears, she was discretely wrapped in fluffy pink from above her breasts to the middle of her thighs.

I was relieved and thrilled to reach the row of trees between the house and the empty lot next door. It was the first time I'd ever seen a woman without her clothes. But as I listened to Billy curse and stamp his feet at what had eluded us, a question rose to the surface of my mind: what had Billy been doing on the tracks down by Sheila

Knights' house that had inspired him to take me on this
nighttime adventure?

V

Billy would only say that, if I liked what I saw from the Dr. Masters' pear tree, I would find something even better on Valley Lane. I didn't know if I wanted to do any more of this sort of thing. I also didn't want to beg. So I took the position that, whatever I wanted to see in other people's windows, I could do my looking on my own.

"I know what you're doing," I claimed. "And I can take care of myself."

"Yeah! What, then?"

"Um-hm. Um-hm." I nodded, though he probably couldn't see me in the dark where we were, cutting through back yards to the Limestone side of the Circle.

"You wanna come with me down to Valley sometime?" He nudged me with an elbow.

"Maybe I've already been there."

"You were moving pretty fast this afternoon to see anything," he chuckled.

"I was late. I've been there other times." This was true, but I'd never lingered to see what might be visible inside the Knight house on a dark night. Reflections on the metal rails could spook me.

We were back at Billy's house now. He said, "I'll let you know next time things are right. You can come with me."

"And I'll let you know. I go by there every day on the way home."

"OK. But nobody else, right?"

"Right. Right. See you." He went around the side of his house to come in the back door. His absence from home might not even have been noticed. I came in the same way, through the garage. And, for this time at least, I made it back to my room without having to explain where I'd been or what I'd been doing.

I tried to finish some homework, I think, but it was pretty hard concentrating. I kept seeing a pink robe slide off Janet Masters' shoulders when I was supposed to be solving problems in plane geometry—"the sum of the squares of the sides . . . "

There was one other vision from the night that kept surfacing in my mind's eye too, something I saw just as Billy signaled me to start down the tree.

Janet must have shaved her legs in the bath. And finding a place on one calf still rough, she put a foot up on the edge of the tub, bent over, and drew her razor over the spot several times. I saw her in that position just before I hung from the lowest limb of the tree to reach the carved toehold in the trunk.

That raised leg in front of a straight one, the back arched, absolutely took my breath away. I think I must have been aware as well of the certainty that beneath her pink towel Janet was wearing nothing at all! Even remembering it that night, my breathing picked up, and I couldn't sit still.

I had a brief scare when Charles came down to bed. I was still at my desk.

"Where have you been?" he asked.

"Oh . . . uh . . . just doing homework."

"I looked in here earlier."

"Hmm."

"Anyway, what do you know about Brents' Store?"

"What do you mean, Brents' Store?"

"You deliver there, don't you?"

"Yeah, sure." I took them the paper every day, of course. And today, as usual, they fussed over me, worrying that I was late. Miss Brent was concerned that I would be walking home in the dark and told me to be careful. "Those old ladies are the same as ever."

"Well, I heard the store was closing. They say anything about that?" Dells' Printing company, where Charles worked, was in the same block as Brents' on Main Street. And Charles usually kept up with the downtown gossip.

"Closing? No. The store looked the same as ever. How could they close? They've been there forever." This would be a loss. Not only did they look out for me every day, giving me sodas and snacks, but they were regular tippers when I had to collect on Thursdays.

"Hmm," continued Charles. "Maybe it was just a rumor. Mom or Dad didn't know anything about it either." Sitting on the edge of his bed, he pulled his pajamas out from under the pillow.

"Why does it matter to you?" I didn't see how it would make much difference to Charles or Dells', for that matter, if Brents' folded or stayed. I cut off the light at my desk and pulled back the covers on my bed.

"It's the downtown storeowners. They're afraid that the new shopping center is hurting their business." A single line of stores had been built where the A & P had gone up on Kingshighway: a drug store, five- and ten-cent Ben Franklin, and a small clothes shop were connected to the grocery store, the largest unit.

"What do you mean?"

"There's talk of another shopping center, besides Paterson's." The mayor and his son had been the major developers of Fairfield's first shopping center. "That might leave shops on Main Street empty."

This didn't make a whole lot of sense to me—what was wrong with new stores in new places? I couldn't imagine downtown not being the place most people came to shop.

"Well, I'm sure the Brents aren't going anywhere," I concluded. I went through the door to the unfinished half of the basement, where we had a sink and a shower, to brush my teeth. I didn't see the point of Charles questions. But I was glad the conversation had drifted away from what I had been doing that night.

I had a hard time not thinking about the evening's events, however, once I got in bed and we cut the lights out. It must have been at least an hour before I went to sleep. Part of what troubled me, of course, was guilt. I knew that what I had done was a pretty outrageous invasion of someone's privacy.

I wouldn't have wanted our positions reversed, Janet Masters watching me take a shower and then examine myself with microscopic intensity, as growing boys do. I winced at the judgments she might pass on my physique, even as I realized it would have been ludicrous for someone of her high status to crouch down at a basement window of our little house in hopes of such a sight.

The excitement of the day—I had seen a girl's nude body!—even carried over into sleep, as I had for the first time an unsettling, recurring dream. It was in part a repeat of what Billy and I had done together and, in part, I guess, a projection of other ideas and worries occupying me at the time.

The dream began with me already in the pear tree behind the Masters' house. This time Billy was not even there; and I should have had the good limb reaching almost into the bathroom window. But I was up on the one above, just as before. The light was on in the bathroom, though at first I didn't see Janet Masters. And, as I waited for her to come through the door from the hall, I made an unhappy discovery about my own condition: I was naked!

Actually, I was not completely without clothes, for it seems that I had on shoes, a shirt, and a light jacket. But what I generally considered key items, pants and underwear, were definitely missing. There I was, balanced on a tree limb fifteen feet above the ground in the backyard of the largest house in my neighborhood, in sneakers and a coat, with bare legs.

Now, my consciousness of this bareness was, as is often the case in dreams, not synchronized with my actions: I should have noticed this absence of clothes earlier, before I started out on any adventure. I am angry in the dream that I've let myself get into this situation, and I try to recall the circumstances that would account for my not wearing pants. But I can't remember the past (my getting dressed) to this present (finding myself only partly clothed). I would like to go back in time, redress my grievance (so to speak), and then return to this point. But I'm allowed in the dream only to regret my mistake. I can only stay or leave the tree.

Now that I've gone so far in pursuit of a glimpse into this window, I seem to conclude that I might as well go through with my plan, trying to ignore or override the basic flaw in dress. I conclude for the time being that everyone who sneaks around at night does so without pants, so I am, in fact, appropriately dressed here.

Of course! Why was I worrying? I look around expecting to see Billy or the Baker brothers in the bushes wearing only jackets and shoes.

Then I think further that it's probably especially appropriate to wear no clothes in this particular situation: to peep when you yourself are partly nude is what the rules call for. My outfit is not simply satisfactory, then; it's just right.

Yes, that's it. No one would see anything odd about how I'm dressed, should they happen to see me, which is pretty unlikely, given that it's night. Not only that, I reason to myself, but no one would blame me for peeping since, if Janet looked out the window, she could just as easily see me. Fair is fair.

Then two things happen more or less simultaneously in my dream: Janet comes into the room wearing, not a bathrobe, but a cheerleader's outfit—white letter sweater, short skirt, boots with tassels; and the limb on which I have been lying gives way, dropping me through the window into the bathroom right at Janet's feet.

Well, I don't fall all the way, as my feet, tangled in branches, seem to get stuck somehow up on the window sill. I end up face down on that black-and-white tile, but my legs are reaching out into the night.

This, as you can tell, is not a flattering introduction of myself to Janet's world. Actually, as I lie there, I suddenly wonder if this isn't Marcia Terrell's house, not Janet Masters'. The figure wearing the snappy outfit might not be a belle of Fairfield but one of my oldest pals, that tomboy playfellow.

I do not look up or say anything. Perhaps my dream self thinks whoever this is won't notice me, or that it's perfectly normal for a half-clothed boy to fly through the window whenever some girl takes her bath.

This person's tone of voice, in fact, is quite calm. She seems to find my appearance not only something she can deal with, but something she has probably anticipated. "Hmm," she says thoughtfully.

I lie perfectly still.

"Hmm. A man. I've always wanted to shave a man." Then I hear the stropping of a razor.

Do I need to say that I wake from this dream in a cold sweat?

Part Six: Out on a Limb

Chapter VI

Let me sketch route II, downtown south, just a bit here so you can see where I marched each day after school. Although I am recalling my journey the day after Billy and I climbed Dr. Masters' giant pear tree, the places I went and the things I saw would have been very nearly identical on any day for a number of years. By the time I finish the route, perhaps I'll be able to tell you what else was inspiring those unsettling dreams of Janet Masters and her bathroom.

Picking up my papers on Fairfield between Seventh and Eighth Streets, I first went south past the Pin-Up Bowling Alley, Murdy's Furniture, and Phipps County Lumber. Of those early deliveries, the bowling alley stands out most sharply in detail several decades later. Since I arrived before most people got off work in the afternoon, there would seldom be anyone bowling. The parallel lanes (six? ten?) to the left of the entrance were darkened.

To the right of the lanes along the back wall stood a row of pinball machines where a boy or two who had no after-school job might be lingering. Several of these quarter-a-turn, nickle-a-ball games, I remember, featured flashing images of the female form: cowgirls in short skirts and jackets with fringed sleeves sat astride galloping ponies in a Wild West game; and interplanetary voyagers wearing skin tight space suits fired ray-guns in the Battle of the Galaxies.

There might have been several adult customers hunched over coffee at the establishment's snack bar. They always looked to me as if they had no regular occupation. I dropped the paper on the end stool by the cash register.

I loved the smells at Phipps Lumber Company of sawdust and paint being mixed. There were also wonderful drawers and bins full of every manner of construction device: bolts and hinges, screws and pulleys, pipe fittings, hoses, and belts, tools hanging on the wall. Ever since Billy and I had tried to turn Old Man Simpson's garage into the Circle's first kids' store, I looked for more and more challenging building projects. And this was where I came to get supplies. When I was delivering the paper, of course, I couldn't do more than taste the air, take brief inspiration from the sight of material, and watch lucky contractors loading flatbed trucks with banded stacks of bricks.

After the lumber store I turned west on Sixth (which marked the southern boundary of downtown) and went one block uphill to Main Street where the old A & P building stood (now a struggling independent grocery store). I then walked north past three well-established drug stores, one for each block: the Rexall's, Dixon's, and Ninth Street Drugs.

These were places where the high school's "good" crowd hung out. (There would be no rival fast food places in Fairfield, not even a McDonald's, for another decade.) Cheerleaders and band members, debate club and class officers, athletes whose parents were also churchgoers sipped ice-cream sodas at the fountain, then picked up prescriptions for their families from the friendly pharmacist at the back. I walked a little straighter and pushed the hair back out of my face in these stores. There were also two dime stores (Ozark Goods and a Woolworth's) along the way, favorite browsing stops on Saturdays for the younger high schoolers like myself. But I also knew that boys sometimes shoplifted candy and small items from both stores.

I had customers as far north as the First Missouri National Bank at Tenth and Main. My half of downtown went to the south side of Tenth Street; and Roger's route (number I) had from there north to the middle of South Central Missouri State's campus. After delivering at the bank (closed, of course, by the time I got there), I came south on Fairfield, returning to the office, with stops at the Uptowne Theatre, Ray's Racks (the pool hall), Ronald Keen's law office, and Davidson Jewelry.

Ray's teenage patrons, nearly all male, were at least one social level below the group congregating at the drug stores, but the pool hall was one step up from what we might have called in those days a "joint." The only females seen here were Ray's stout wife and several young, heavily made-up women who never stayed long and who did not play pool. I would end up here in high school more than I would have predicted at this time. I actually came to play three-rail billiards, a game for which I had some aptitude but greater appreciation. I love angles and lines of flight, the principles of contact and reaction, schemes for sequential play.

I could see all kinds of people at the office of Ronald Keen, attorney-at-law. Although he made his money with routine legal business—probating wills, filing deeds, establishing trusts—Keen was also known for defending clients who could not afford a lawyer. Uneducated country farmers came down from the hills when their electricity was cut off and asked his assistance. Sometimes he got indigent but generally harmless men out of jail into cheap lodgings and found them at least temporary employment. And young boys who got into scrapes a little more costly than their fellows often had Ronald Keen to thank that they would receive one more chance and that their records were kept clean.

I also had customers one block to the east and west of Main along the numbered streets. On Eighth Street, for instance, was Jerry's Barber Shop, the owner a good tipper (ten cents every week), but he always wanted to kid around with me. He made me uncomfortable by asking about my girlfriends, if they were all "hot" for me, if I was "getting any" (any what? I wondered).

On a few of those blocks off Main there were also houses in which older people lived or which had been divided into apartments for young couples. Although I passed probably a dozen churches, only Grace Episcopal received the *Mirror,* and I left it for the rector, Father Duncan, at the parish house next door. Nominal Baptists, the Landons had little genuine interest in religion. After Vietnam, however, I found the Anglican tradition represented by that little church on 9th Street an unexpected source of strength.

In all I had close to fifty customers.

I moved steadily through this circular route, but I often paused a few extra moments near the midpoint of my daily round, at the First Missouri National Bank. The building had closed at about the same time I left school (I dropped the paper through the night deposit slot), but I was still impressed by the clean, open space visible through the double front doors, the solemn columns standing on marble floors. In the back was the huge metal door to the safe, the dial to its combination lock as big as a pie plate. Here were stability and order, I always thought. Decency and responsibility were invested in this quiet building.

Not only did the bank represent present stability for this community, but it also fixed the town's past. On the wall behind the tellers' stations was a famous mural done in the style of Missouri artist Thomas Hart Benton and representing a history of Fairfield.

One had to inspect both foreground and background to understand how much was included. You had to scan along hillsides and look down by rivers, evaluate the large figures while paying attention to miniature scenes, link what was pictured in the woods on the left to action going on next to the river at the right; but there in a space perhaps twenty-five by five feet were all the elements that went into the first one hundred years of our town.

Today for the first time, I believe, I tried to find my neighborhood, the Circle, on that mural. I realize now that I was starting at the beginning of the town's life and tracing events to myself as its latest product.

In the top left corner was a famous incident in our history, Mrs. Betty Shields killing a bobcat on top of a one-room cabin. She and her husband had traveled from Tennessee in the middle of the last century to settle the Ozark wilderness. You can see Thomas Shields, one of the men credited with founding Fairfield, stepping into a clearing beside the cabin. He stands next to an Osage chief, Wetago, who points off to more open country in the west where his tribe will move in retreat from white settlers.

The Osage sold their land at what seemed foolishly low prices to people like the Shields, purchasing larger tracts in Oklahoma. However, when the Osage's new territory was found later in the century to hold vast oil reserves, they became the richest single Native American tribe in the country.

Beneath the wilderness scene of the Benton-esque mural a man is pictured nailing a sign, "Farfield," to a tree. This represents the official founding of the town. The incorrect spelling of the town's name reflects a number of legends about the origin of our frontier village: some say "Farfield" reveals an illiterate citizenry, unable to spell; others argue that our forefathers (and mothers) had cleared the land by fire (you know, "far'"); and still others think the sign was an effort to explain how far away from civilization this new territory was in 1857 (and perhaps in 1957). One story even had it that these pioneers were named Fields, not Shields; and they wanted to name the town "Fields."

Several portions of the mural represent the Civil War's impact on Fairfield. As the last railroad stop southwest of St. Louis, the town was a strategic military objective. Union troops are depicted setting up Fort Blank on high ground north of the town. A forge at Maramec Springs, thirty miles away, supplies metal works for war now and later, peace.

While the railroad's extension west reduced Fairfield's importance as a transportation center after the war, the founding of a land-grant college, the development of local agriculture, and the town's becoming a county seat spurred development into the twentieth century. While some local boys are marching off to war in Europe near the end of the mural, Miss and Mrs. Brent (although not pictured) are setting up shop in one of the new downtown buildings.

To the west of town, in the very last section of the mural on the right, new homes are being built after World War II. The growth of Fort Leonard Wood increased the demand for new homes in a number of nearby towns. And, now that I look closely, I can see the beginnings of the Circle, a string of wooden frames going up on concrete foundations stretching through an old pear orchard.

Studying those half a dozen structures to see if one could possibly be where I live now, I try to forget the sign I saw earlier today on the door of Brents' Store—"Closed."

VII

I was in a hurry to get home that afternoon for all sorts of reasons. I wanted to know why Brents' Store had a "Closed" sign posted on the door. And was this just for today, or were they going out of business permanently, as Charles had suggested?

I also planned to ask Billy what he had been doing when he chased me up from the tracks, although I doubted that I would go down there with him to find out. Had he seen more of Sheila Knight than we saw of Janet Masters? Or was something else going on in that house?

Since the paper had not been late today, I walked by the Knights' on Valley Lane when it was still light. Perhaps because it was colder, though, I didn't see her outside the little house next to the tracks.

(While I have a habit of thinking of the Circle as the only Route 66 neighborhood in Fairfield, by the way, this less prosperous group of houses on Valley should also be recognized as part of "America's Main Street.")

As I came onto Black Street from Valley, I once again spotted my pal Billy. He was just turning onto Limestone up ahead of me, and I recognized him at this distance by his slightly overweight form and the paper bag hanging on his right hip.

Now I asked myself a question that might have occurred to me yesterday: why wasn't he riding his bike and throwing papers, as nearly all paperboys did on residential routes? Then I realized that there was someone walking along with Billy. It was Marcia Terrell.

I jogged to catch up, calling out when I was pretty close. "Hey, Billy. Marcia. Wait up." They did. "You done?" I asked Billy, slapping his bag for papers as I fell in on the other side from Marcia.

"Got Limestone and half of Oak," he responded.

"Ah." I noticed that Marcia was carrying Billy's book.

"You showing her what it's like?" I asked Billy.

"Um, yeah. Something like that."

"Pretty dull," I suggested.

"Over there," Billy said to Marcia, pointing at the Blottners' house (a young couple with twin babies). He threw a paper skillfully right to their small front porch.

"Blottners'," said Marcia and flipped over a card in the book.

"You want to play some basketball tonight, if it's not too cold?" I asked Billy, trying to wink slyly to him.

"Hmm. Maybe. What time?"

"Oh, I don't know. Say, eight o'clock?" I tried not to look conspiratorial.

"OK. Yeah" he responded. Then he added to Marcia. "Fold one."

She pulled a paper out of his bag (why was Marcia's presence here starting to bother me?), folded it once side-to-side, then again. She tried to make the top third fold across the middle and reach the bottom third; but the paper, a thick one, splayed out, and she couldn't fit the ends together. She gnawed at her lower lip in concentration.

"Hold it by the sides," Billy advised. (I knew I didn't want Marcia to join us later for basketball; but there was something else troubling me about her walking this route.) Billy took the paper from her and with deft turns shaped it into a neat square. "You throw. The Webbs."

Marcia had never thrown like other girls, and now the paper, released sidearm, sailed neatly to the porch steps. "Close enough," admitted Billy. I wondered why Billy hadn't folded his papers at the *Mirror* building.

I found I had to ask Marcia. "You're not taking over his route?"

"Maybe."

"I'm not sure I'm giving it up yet," Billy offered. We were at his house now. "But I'm showing her the ropes, in case I do." To her he said again, "Fold one," handing her another paper.

He took one more copy out of his bag and, rather than folding it or handing to Marcia, gave it me. "I guess this is where you get off." We had passed the Vacant Lot and were at my house. "Landons," Billy informed Marcia, who flipped over another card in the book.

I stood frozen at the bottom of the sidewalk that led up to our front stoop. There were things going on here I hadn't anticipated, didn't understand. Billy and Marcia kept walking up the hill together, nearing the curve toward Ridgeview. "See you," I called to their backs weakly.

Surely he was pointing to customers, not putting his arm around her waist? She was leaning toward him only to get some explanation of what was written in the book, wasn't she? Did what he saw in Janet Masters' window inspire his interest in Marcia? I was getting a little confused.

Inside my house I was early for dinner, and Mom wanted to help me set the table. Before I remembered to ask her about Brents' Store, she wondered if I knew the Stanton house, on Ninth Street just off Missouri Avenue, introducing another factor into my puzzled thoughts.

"It's not on my route, if that's what you mean," I responded.

"I know. But I thought you might see it on your walk home. Do you know Catherine? She's in tenth grade, I think."

"I know who she is," I admitted. but I still didn't know where this conversation was headed. Perhaps harboring guilty thoughts about Janet Masters, I had to remind myself I had not looked in Catherine Stanton's window.

"Well, her father, who's in charge of the phone company, he's been transferred. The house is for sale."

"So?"

"It's a nice house. I want your father to go look at it."

"You mean, move out of the Circle?"

"It's a very nice neighborhood, beautiful homes. You can walk anywhere."

I did know both the house and the neighborhood, which I sometimes crossed going to the Uptowne Theatre. The neighborhood went as far south as the Brents' on Missouri Avenue. I only knew a few people in that area, and I suspected most residents there had children away at college or married with their own families.

Perhaps the oldest residential part of town, this section included the mayor and most anyone who was anyone. In the next few years, with a burst of growth in the second half of the 1960s recalling the post-war era, new subdivisions with large lots and fancy modern homes would spring up farther from the center of town, providing rival locations for Fairfield's elite. But right then, living close to the campus and downtown marked a family as well-to-do and well connected. The Circle was decidedly middleclass.

"What does Dad say?" I asked.

"Oh, I haven't asked him yet. He's been thinking again about building bedrooms upstairs for you boys. But it might be nice to have a bigger house."

Many of the families in the Circle were starting to expand their original two-bedroom structures. As their families, begun in the late 40s and early 50s, grew in number and size, some, like the Bells on Oak Street, had added an extension of family room and extra bedroom out the back. Others, like the Bakers up at the top of Limestone, had turned the garage into a den and, as we had, finished a room off in the basement. The Terrells had been perhaps the first to add dormers to their attic and put a bedroom for Marcia, a guest room, and a bath in the attic. The Martins outdid everyone by expanding in every direction possible, up, back, down, and to the side.

My Dad had taken measurements and drawn up a rough plan for what he wanted to do with our attic. We had a coat closet in the hall. where a narrow set of stairs could go. Then he planned to raise the entire back half of the roof and put bedrooms and bath over the master bedroom, downstairs bath, and Beth's room below. We would still have storage area over the garage and under the front roof. Although none of the rooms would be as large as those in a Missouri Avenue house, there would be privacy for everyone and some extra play space in the finished basement room. I was just learning, though, that Mom might have other ideas about our future.

"You know," she said, sitting down at the dining room table. Everything was set for dinner, but Dad wasn't home yet. "I sometimes feel too close to everyone else in this neighborhood."

"What do you mean?"

"Well, the houses are so close together. If I shook the dust mop out our living room window, it would practically reach the Morgans' garage next door." This was true, though the builders had at least used garages to block direct lines of sight from one living space into another. Sometimes, though, the bedrooms of two houses on the Circle did face each other.

"Another thing," my mother went on. "We're on the inside of the Circle, see. So out back we face the Terrells' backyard. There's not much privacy." Again, this was something I couldn't deny, though in the past I'd seen these relationships as more connecting than imposing.

My mother went on again. "Sometimes I feel that if we don't pull our shades down at night, half of Fairfield will be watching us do everything we do." Here was a line of thought I did not want my mother to follow!

"Well, I'm downstairs, so there isn't much of a view for us," I observed.

"I'll tell you what else," said Mom, turning the salt shaker around in one hand. "Have you ever noticed that there are really only about three or four different floor plans for all the houses in this area?"

"You mean the houses are similar?"

"They're identical, or at least our house is exactly like the Terrells', the Bakers' is just like the Petersons', the Williams' matches the Bells'."

"Hmm."

"They built this neighborhood so quickly, during the war, that they used just these few basic floor plans. So everyone knows what everyone else's house looks like, inside."

"Ahh."

"It's not the way it was where I grew up, in New Jersey." The Williams' family home was larger than this house, and it sat on a substantial lot with many trees. The stately three-story structure gave one a sense of isolation, even though there were houses on both sides.

"I can almost predict where Robert Terrell is sitting right now, since the houses are small and there are only a few ways to arrange furniture around doors and windows. At this time of day, he's home from work, having a drink in the easy chair in the southwest corner of the living room."

"Oh, I don't think you can say that. People do things differently."

"You watch, sometime." She pointed a spoon at me. "Sit out on the front stoop as it gets dark, watch lights go on in houses up and down the street. You can tell when people finish dinner and go into the living room to watch TV. When they get up to go to bed. Even when they use the bathroom."

"Come on!"

"It's true. Same thing in the morning, when everyone gets up. Who makes breakfast, who walks a dog, who takes a shower when—I know. And I think I want the Stanton house over on Ninth Street."

If she kept up this line of reasoning, I was going to want to move too!

VIII

Although I got no answers about what was happening with Brents' Store that night, I was sure I would find out the story the next day. Thursday was collecting day. Someone would be at Brents' Store when I came that afternoon, as they had always been among my most faithful and regular patrons.

Charles knew no more than I about Brents, although his boss, Mr. Dell, had also seen the sign on the door. My parents were more interested in discussing houses than pursuing gossip about downtown businesses. My Dad listened patiently to Mom explaining the advantages of living nearer town, and nearer the Survey; but it seemed clear, to me at least, that Dad liked being where he was.

To every shortcoming she found in our Limestone Drive house—the small rooms, the close neighbors, the plain style—he smiled with appreciation, noting that the family members stayed close, that we had good friends who had come here at the same time to raise children, and that everything around us was remarkably functional. There was concession (he would go see the other house tomorrow), but I wasn't planning on packing any time soon.

Claiming after dinner that this debate had included me long enough, I slipped out of the house, reportedly, to play basketball with Billy. Beneath the Vacant Lot Tree he informed me of his plans for the evening.

"I'm going up the pear tree," he said matter-of-factly and started off down the street.

"What for? You've seen what there is to see." I walked beside him.

"Naw. There's more. You haven't been there on the good nights."

"What do you mean?"

"And besides, tonight I'm going in."

"Going in? What are you talking about!" I grabbed his arm as he started over the fence to cut between houses and across the Circle toward the Masters' empty lot.

Billy turned to me, and, for the first time, I noticed a genuinely wild look in his eyes. He leaned forward and whispered. "I'm going in . . . while she's in the tub!"

"You're not!"

But Billy only chuckled and stepped up on the fence along the back of the Masters' empty lot. I didn't want to be a party to this scheme, but I couldn't seem to break away from Billy either. "How are you going to . . . ?" I asked, following him over the fence.

"Hey, I got it all worked out. I'll be in and out, and she won't even know."

"In and out of her bathroom while's taking a bath! And what do you want . . . why are you . . . what will it . . . ?"

Billy turned to me and said more calmly, "I just want to be there."

"Be there . . . ?"

"Shh!"

Now we were in the little stand of woods behind the Masters' house, and Billy was surveying the scene. As on the previous night, I could see a few lights, but none in the upstairs bathroom. Then that square brightened. Had Billy worked out the schedule of these other lives?

He darted forward to the base of the huge pear tree and went up the trunk as quickly as if it were a set of stairs. I hesitated only a second before running after him. I wanted to see what happened, but I decided to stop at foot of the tree and watch from there.

In order to describe Billy's plan, I have to explain something about storm and screen windows. In the 1950s construction companies were just beginning to use the single metal (or aluminum) window unit, which, once installed, allowed residents to change from storm to screen windows without removing or adding anything. A simple raising of one glass panel (and a lowering of another screen panel) changed a house window from storm to screen (and, of course, vice versa).

All of the houses on the Circle at this time, however, had separate storm and screen windows. Both were removable, wooden framed structures that hung in the casement outside the permanent window. Ours were painted a dark green to stand out against the white of our house. The storm window was divided into two panes, top and bottom, whereas the screen had no extra horizontal support piece. There were two metal support hooks screwed into the top of each window casement, and the storm/screen window hung from those supports on two upside down U-hooks fastened to the top of its frame. An eye-hook at the bottom was used to latch the window shut from the inside.

Although these removable screens and storm windows could never have been as tight as the installed single units, there must have been many fine carpenters building wooden frames in those days. As I remember it, each of those frames fit into its position with incredible precision. Thinking about it now, I can even hear a slow hiss of air (sfftt!) slipping from the sides of the casement as a storm window swings down into place.

There were no gaps, nor did we have to force a corner or a side. Each unit fit in its niche so exactly that you could not exchange the north living room window for the east living room window without becoming aware, when you tried to hang it from its metal supports, that you were making a mistake.

My father, of course, had long ago carefully labeled each window in two places with adhesive tape so there would be no such confusion. There was even an order to storage in the basement, as windows were stood on a two-by-four frame beginning with the north living room window and following a path around the house to end at the kitchen. His system was flawless.

To go from summer ventilation (screen) to winter insulation (storm)—and the reverse—were major operations. Such yearly events were loved by most fathers and hated by all sons. We devoted an entire Saturday to readying the house for its new season.

The first unpleasant phase in this task was the dusting off and hauling out into the sun of those units stored in the basement. Whether storm or screen, they needed a complete washing after their six months underground. We were usually allowed to spray the screens with a hose and let them drip dry; but the glass windows had to be soaped and wiped down with cloth to eliminate streaks. Next the old windows had to come down off the house, making room for the new, and carried to the basement for their six months' hibernation. The sills also had to be wiped clean of dust and dead insects and the glass panes of the fixed windows cleaned.

I guess spring was easier than fall because we were carrying down ladders and stairs the heavy glass windows and lifting up the lighter screens, but neither seemed easy at the time. In the fall even Charles got tired of picking up in the basement and hauling up the stairs and carrying around the yard and holding up on a ladder and latching in the windows our ten heavy storm windows (yes, I knew then and remember now exactly how many there were). For once my smaller stature helped me, as I was assigned the smaller windows in kitchen and bathroom, whereas Charles had primary responsibility for lifting the bigger frames.

My father, of course, had by this time promoted himself to an entirely supervisory capacity, checking that all hooks and supports were firm, seeing that window and windowsills were properly cleaned, confirming which window went with what room.

He added to our suffering, of course, by insisting repeatedly that this ancient rite of welcoming the new season was a fine one and recalling in detail the same operation (though, of course, much more arduous) as performed in his own Kansas boyhood. Mom helped by washing windows inside and by doing the Venetian blinds in living and dining rooms. After a while, too, Beth was big enough to help with the inside operation.

(Did we have storm doors as well as windows? Yes, we did, now that I think about it. My father handled that one task all by himself, taking the front screen door off its hinges and replacing it with an entirely different storm door. Both were wooden-framed like the windows, beautifully crafted. We must not have bothered with the back door, since it opened into the garage.)

Sometimes, with homeowners less thorough than my father, the little eye hook on the bottom of a frame, which secured the window, would be left loose in the annual task of installing and removing many storm and screen windows. Thus the screen or storm window hung in the casement but was unlatched at the bottom. If you could get it started from the outside, prying with a fingernail or perhaps a pocketknife, it would swing open on its two metal supports. Someone who had not bothered to latch a storm window might also fail to twist the lock shut on the inside window, which prevents the bottom half from being raised from the outside.

Up on his tree-limb perch Billy had seen that a Masters' upstairs storm window (probably recently taken from the basement and installed here for the winter) was unlatched; and the interior lock was also not turned shut. That window was to be his means of entry tonight.

I saw Billy scramble up the tree to the branch by the lighted window. Then he went past that branch to another higher one that actually went around the corner of the house, close to a darkened dormer window, probably a bedroom. To see what Billy was doing I had to climb halfway up the trunk on the little toe- and finger-holds he had established.

Billy's weight caused the limb he was on to bend down, some of the leaves brushing against the top of the dormer. He had been straddling the limb to this point, but now he swung underneath, hanging by hands and knees beside the darkened window. When he let go with his legs, his feet came neatly to rest on the roof beside the window. He let go of the branch and crouched on the roof. I could hear him breathing heavily from the effort.

I glanced over at the bathroom window and saw the pink terry cloth bathrobe moving around. Was she getting in the tub? Or getting out? Did she hear something? Would she go look? Would floodlights suddenly come on in the yard, throwing myself (halfway up the tree) and Billy (on the roof) into sudden view?

I looked again and saw Billy reach around the dormer with one hand and swing the screen away from the window. He pushed the inside window open. Then, holding onto the side of the window frame, he slipped headfirst into darkness.

IX

I had some pretty anxious moments halfway up the pear tree after Billy vanished into the darkened bedroom of Janet Masters that crisp November evening. I watched for the storm window to swing open again, the sign of Billy's escaping; and I looked to the lighted bathroom window to learn when Janet would finish her bath and start back to her room.

What could he be doing in there, I wondered?

I guess I was too young myself to create very fixed images for the possibilities. I knew there had to be in that room a bed (would he lie on it?), clothes (would he touch dresses hanging in the closet?), cosmetics (would he spray perfume?), mementos (would he cop her high school yearbook, a class ring, dried flowers pressed in books?). What other, unspeakable acts might a boy perform in a girl's private space?

Even more frightening to me were the things that would happen if we were caught. I supposed the least terrifying outcome was being accused of simple robbery, breaking and entering (though I didn't think Billy'd actually broken anything). Because of the age's reticence to admit to sexual activity, the word "rape" had not taken on the public connotations it carries today. When Jimmy Donaldson saw the word in a newspaper article and asked our ninth grade social studies teacher what it meant, we were told only that a woman had been "beaten up." How much more detailed and varied my children's understanding of that term and related terms of assault is today!

Before I had to attach a name to Billy's actions, however, events revealed that my companion had a more thorough plan than I had given him credit for. Just as Janet Masters' head and shoulders (everything below covered again by pink) showed in the square of bathroom light, the storm window in the next room swung out and Billy, lizard like, slid onto the roof. He got up on one knee, reached back with one hand and pulled the inside window down, then let the storm window swing shut at the very moment the light in the bathroom snapped off. By the time the light in the bedroom came on, Billy was up on the branch, hanging by his hands and knees and shinnying back toward the trunk.

Minutes later we were racing up Oak Street. I had started to cut through back yards in the direction we had come, but Billy said, "No! This way," and pulled me with him.

We ran to the new park, Westlook, just past where Oak comes into Limestone. There in the shadows by the swings, I tried to find out what had been the point of this adventure.

"What did you see?" Billy asked me.

"Nothing, or nothing much. I didn't go all the way up the tree."

"Ah, you should have. You had the good branch."

"I was also watching you. What did you do in there?"

"I was there, Mark; I was there."

"There?"

"In her room. In her house."

"So?"

"Well . . . . It's just doing it, don't you see?"

I guess I didn't. I understood the desire to peep, even though I was terrified of getting caught doing it. But I couldn't understand what drove Billy to sneak into that bedroom.

He would not tell me any more than this, however, and we both realized we should be getting home soon. With more hints that we might "do it again" or even "try Valley Lane," Billy left me at my house.

I was still puzzling about the night's events when I set out after school the next day to collect on my paper route. And I didn't make any particular progress in figuring out Billy in part because collecting proved difficult, as was often the case. Carrying the Thursday paper and taking in money required twice as long as a regular delivery even when things went smoothly. But since each *Mirror* route had its difficult customers who tried to delay or avoid paying, sometimes Thursday could last forever.

The transaction of collecting was, ideally, a fine thing. When there were no hitches, the power to procure came in exchange for advertised service: papers in subscribers' hands became money in my pocket. Each *Fairfield Mirror* customer awarded me 25 cents for the week's delivery, and, to record the transaction for history, I returned a little tab marked "Paid" from the appropriate card in my route's book.

This was how the adult world functioned, I believed. Goods and commodities traveled throughout society, transformed themselves with mathematical precision into service and satisfaction. Records were kept of promise and fulfillment (the "book"); and the order of the community stood out as clearly as streets on the town map.

Roger Peterson and I, having downtown routes, were again fortunate because stores and shops generally had to be open for business, nearly always had cash (even the correct change) on hand, and had to be concerned with their public image. Almost every other route, however, had its miser who hid from the sound of the doorbell, the house full of children with no parent ever at home, an old maid who fingered the depths of her black purse in vain for something other than the $20 bill you could not change.

These difficult customers were the carrier's responsibility. Paperboys had "bills" due at the *Mirror* office every Friday, a charge of twenty cents per customer for that week. A thin slip of newsprint with your name and the amount of your bill for the week would be tucked under the cord that bound together your Thursday stack of papers. When you paid your "bill" of something like $10.00 at the front office, you had, theoretically, a profit of a nickel for each subscriber (perhaps, then, $2.50 for the week).

But the family that moved to Nebraska without canceling their subscription, the woman who went to visit her sister and claimed to have left a note stopping delivery, the man who wouldn't pay because his neighbor's dog had eaten Tuesday's edition could reduce the paperboy's takehome pay.

Eventually, of course, Mr. Sweet, the *Mirror*'s owner, would review cases where a paperboy hadn't been able to collect; and usually the paper covered or split the loss of revenue. But when you were saving for a new bike, or when you just wanted enough money to buy popcorn at the Uptowne on Saturday, any shortfall in the week's collecting could be painful. Having watched Marcia walking with Billy on his route this week, I had developed a plan for the weekend that required successful recovery of all that was owed me.

The surprise hitch in collecting for me this time was Brents' Store: no one was there. I did not find an envelope (payment enclosed) with my name on it taped to the door; nor did a note direct me somewhere else for my money. There was only that same sign I'd seen the day before, "Closed." Then it occurred to me that, on the way home, I could stop at the Brents' house on Missouri Avenue.

It wasn't easy opening the iron gate by the street, walking up the long sidewalk to the broad front porch, raising the heavy knocker and hearing its rude thump sound down that ancient hallway. Through the small panes of the massive oak door and the sheer curtains on the inside I could see that everything inside was still and restful. But at my third knocking Miss Suzanne Brent did come softly down the stairs to the door. Smiling kindly, but raising a finger to her lips, she motioned me into the dark entryway.

"Shhh," she cautioned and pointed through a doorway to what, I guess, would have been a sitting room. In an easy chair in the far corner crossed by a bar of light from the window sat Henri Brent, wrapped in a dark, plaid blanket. His eyes focused far away or not at all, he was shuffling crudely what I took to be playing cards in his wrinkled, stiff hands. Miss Brent motioned for me to step across the hall into the dining room.

"You've come to collect," she said softly.

"Yes . . . I'm sorry to come here . . . I saw the sign on Main Street . . . what?"

"Ah," she sighed, taking a large, black pocketbook out of a drawer in the sideboard. Sitting down at the dining room table, she searched through the pocketbook for a smaller change purse.

"Yes, we're closed."

"But why?"

She looked up from her search with a puzzled expression on her face. "I . . . I don't seem to have any change. Wait just a minute." She went out of the room and down the hall. To find Mrs. Brent?

Watching her go, I caught sight of Henri in the other room. I saw that he had dropped his cards. They lay scattered on the carpet, as if he'd torn some newspaper to shreds.

Let me tell you the assumption I had made about those cards of Henri Brent. Something I had read, or a story overheard, or hints made in some movie led me to conclude that he had a pornographic deck brought back with him from Paris and the war. On the backs of the cards would be pictures of things American dough boys had been shocked to discover in the ancient capital of European civilization—naked girls, men and women, several women with one man, animals, extraordinary parts, forbidden acts. Henri Brent, the wreck of a Missourian who had seen the world, was, I thought, running those cards through his fingers in some war-blasted recollection of his own youthful fantasies.

Seeing and hearing no sign of the ladies of the house, I stepped over to pick them up for him. And I found they were pieces of paper with poems printed on them, pages from a book so worn with his shuffling that they felt like the thinnest of cloth. When I handed him a bundle, he tried to speak.

"Szz, szz. Snip-snip. Like scissors. Szz, szz," he said. I didn't know what he meant; his eyes still seemed vacant. But he felt the return of his poems, I think, and immediately began turning them over and over in his trembling fingers.

I stepped back into the hall in time to meet Suzanne Brent. She smiled and handed me my quarter—and a dollar!

"No, I . . . "

"We want to. You're a good boy." She pushed my hand closed around the money.

"No, no."

"Please."

"OK. OK. Thank you. But, the store . . . why?"

"There's the reason." She pointed at me, as if, somehow, I had caused the closing of this historic business.

"What do you mean?"

She reached out a hand and touched my paper bag, right near the base of the strap where a pocket held the route's book. "Look," she said.

X

In the darkened dining room of the house that stood on the spot of our town's earliest history, I followed the line of Miss Brent's finger to my paper bag.

"Here?" I asked, completely lost.

"The paper." And then I understood what she was saying. There was something in the paper about Brents' Store, some account of events that would explain her situation. I pulled out a copy of the *Fairfield Mirror*. It was, in fact, the one I would leave for her and her sister. I opened it up, but there was nothing about Brents' Store that I could see. I started to turn to the inside sections.

"No, there, there," Miss Brent said and pointed to a headline: "TOWN ADOPTS ZONING CHANGES."

"They've zoned us for business," she said. "We'll have to move."

"Move the store? Why? It's a business."

"Not the store. This house. This block has been zoned for business, II-A. The taxes will be so great we can't afford it, especially with Mr. Brent's illness." She looked across the hall, then whispered. "He's worse, you know."

"But this has been your family's home."

"Yes, I know. We can hardly think what it will be like to live somewhere else. Especially Jacqueline. She's been here since it was built."

"Do you know where you'll go?"

"Over to St. Stevens. Mr. Brent will be in the Old Soldiers' Home there. Mrs. Brent and I have rented a small apartment nearby."

"But then you'll have drive over for the store."

"Oh, it will have to stay closed, I'm afraid. Business has been very slow. And we haven't kept up, you know, with changes."

"Ahh." I paused, then asked, "And this house . . . ?"

"It will be sold."

"Oh."

"People tell us someone might want to restore it. It's such a grand house." She looked up, as if she could see workers already restoring a faded glory.

"I'm sorry." I really had no idea what to say.

"Oh, we'll be all right. Now, don't you worry." She rose from her chair and put a hand on my shoulder. "We'll all be close, even if we can't stay together." I could tell she didn't believe it even as she spoke, though she kept that kind smile on her face. "We can always get the *Mirror*."

And then I surprised myself by saying, "I'll come see you."

"Oh, no. We'll be fine. We'll hear about you. We still have friends in town."

I turned to go. She walked with me into the hall and to the large front door. Henri Brent was quiet in his corner, all his cards gathered into one pack. Had he been listening? Did he know what was about to happen to him? Or would he even recognize the difference? Somehow I got out of there.

In less than a year all three of the Brents were dead. I read it in the paper. The obituary recalled Jacqueline Brent's grandfather's contributions to town growth, Henri's service in the Great War, the sisters' many years running a popular downtown store. Since they had all been past seventy, no specific cause of death was listed. My mother heard none of the three could adjust to being away from their house on Missouri Avenue.

Sadly, that fine old structure was destroyed, leveled to make a new bank building, with drive-in facilities, and a municipal parking lot. While the house itself could have been renovated at a modest cost, the large lot (a square block) in a prime location (only two blocks from Main Street) proved too attractive to town planners and ambitious developers wielding political influence.

My mother took special interest in these events, I think, because we too had made some decisions at that time concerning houses and our future. We did not buy the Stanton house on Ninth Street; and the next summer workmen began raising our roof and building bedrooms for Charles and me in the attic.

That larger house in a stately part of town remained for many years a family landmark, representing an option not chosen at the time it was offered. My father's satisfaction with the Circle had overruled my mother's sense that her family past might lead to another neighborhood. And the children were never dissatisfied with the Circle. There were too many other kids there, too many things always for us to do to want anything else.

Although I occasionally walked by the Stanton house just for fun, my regular route home from Route II continued to follow Seventh Street, Kingshighway (business Route 66), Valley Lane, Black Street, Limestone Drive. It was within a week, I'm sure, of collecting from the Brents for the last time that I solved one mystery along that walk home, at last discovering what exactly had lured Billy Rhodes into the shadows beside the railroad tracks.

I had, by the way, at about the same time more formally declared myself a rival suitor to Billy for the attentions of Marcia Terrell. She did take over Billy's route, becoming the first papergirl in town history. With my last week's earnings, significantly augmented by the Brents' generous final tip, I had bought her a handsomely framed town map. On the glass were traced in broad red lines the borders of all *Mirror* paper routes, I through XIV. I told her to mark the way she delivered her own route, VI, with colored ink.

While Billy had impressed Marcia by recommending to Mr. Sweet that she get his route, I seemed to be at least an even competitor. I went with her into the paperboys' room when she picked up her first stack. And I tended to see her more regularly coming from school and on days when the paper was late.

Thinking, then, of the past (my many pleasant visits to Brents' Store) and my future (a meeting I had arranged for tonight with Marcia in Westlook Park), I walked in a kind of daydream down Valley Lane as the last glimmer of twilight was fading in the west. I was lost enough in fantasy that I did not really focus on where I was until I stepped over the Missouri Pacific's metal rails as they crossed Valley Lane.

Remembering the start Billy had given me earlier, I glanced to my left and saw what I almost expected to see, a form crouched on the tracks perhaps thirty feet away.

I should have, I suppose, broken into a run toward Black Street at this sight, but for some reason I felt I was seeing again the guy in my neighborhood who would do anything, and usually did. So, poised for flight but willing to find out what hunched on the railroad bed, I whispered a question, "Billy?"

The shadowy form raised a shadowy arm, "Past! Over here."

I squinted down the tracks. "Billy?"

"Yeah. Here." He probably waved again; but it had gotten even darker, and I couldn't see. I crunched down the gravel road bed.

"Shhh!"

I tiptoed up to the person I assumed was Billy. He took me by the elbow and hissed, "Look there! Look there!" I guess he pointed, but I couldn't see a finger. He squeezed my arm hard.

Then I looked and saw a small square of light in the side of the Knights' house. And in that square were the face and figure of any boy's dreams.

Standing in her slip before the *mirror* on a bathroom medicine cabinet, Sheila was brushing out her rich auburn hair. She stroked lush waves down each shoulder, back over her head. Billy's rapid breathing was audible beside me. He may even have been moaning. And I heard a strange scratching or rubbing in the dark beside me.

I, of course, was ready for more than this. Knowing Billy's ability to chart the nighttime activities of neighborhood households, I expected Sheila to disrobe soon.

There must have been, it had occurred to me before tonight, more than disrobing to generate Billy's enthusiasm, though I wasn't sure exactly what. Right now Billy seemed ready to explode, practically gasping for air beside me. Would she drop her slip and turn directly toward the window? Would we watch her soap and scrub that woman's body? Was Billy going in there, as he had Janet Masters' house?

None of these things happened.

This was the first time I began fully to understand how desire takes its individual focus in each of us. The usual way of saying it then was that So-and-so was a "leg-man," or a "breast-man" or a "fanny man." But it's also true that, for some, shoulders are the ultimate attraction. Still others go bananas over ear lobes or the nape of a neck, the backs of knees. The same is true, of course, for women who zero in on broad chests, tight rumps, bulging arm muscles.

This is a good thing, I suppose, keeping us all from chasing the same object, giving each of us a field of potential admirers. But viewing the same image along these different lines of sight can sometimes cause confusion, especially when an alternative path of desire has never occurred to you.

Billy loved hair. Janet Masters' wet blond hair tucked behind an ear had drawn him up that pear tree, not her long legs or ample bosom. And Sheila Knight's exceptional mass of curls lured him into the sometimes scary shadows beside Fairfield's railroad tracks. Either girl could have been wearing a formal gown, a flight jacket, or nothing at all, so long as she was washing or combing her hair.

When Sheila finished brushing her hair, flipped off the light beside the door, and disappeared into the rest of the house, the show, for Billy, was over. And it was all he had hoped. He rose from his hunched position and started down the tracks to Valley Lane and home.

I was stunned. This was it? This was all? We were through? Even when we came into the light up on Black Street and I got one more clue to Billy's psyche, I didn't put the pieces together to make a coherent whole.

Billy was carrying in one hand, I noticed, a woman's hair brush. His thumb swept over the bristles, back and forth, back and forth, making that scratching sound I had heard in the dark. It would be years before I realized that what he held in his hand was probably Janet Masters' brush.

And what, in the end, do you suppose I was looking for in those shadows by the tracks? To be honest, I don't think I could say yet. So innocent of the total female form, I suppose, I hadn't yet had time to specialize. I do know, however, that when Marcia Terrell and I sat across from each other at a picnic table in Westlook Park later than night, examining her framed map of the town, I was excited enough to find my hand touch hers as, chewing her lower lip, she traced the route she had walked that day.

Volume Four: Culture

Part Seven: In the Country

Chapter I.

Going steady? Was that what I was doing with Marcia Terrell after I began giving her presents and walking beside her to town after school? Perhaps. Perhaps I was even hoping to imitate the fabled Roger Peterson and Cathy Williams, whose actions on a walk through the woods had given me my first big clues about how sex is accomplished.

Because we were in different grades and had separate paper routes, mine on Main Street and hers in our own neighborhood of the Circle, Marcia and I couldn't spend all our time together. And many of the activities we shared seemed the product of coincidence as much as planning, since kids about the same age in any small town often end up side by side.

We were not really old enough to date (I was half a year away from getting my driver's license, for instance), so I don't think we can say that the relationship I established with my backyard neighbor had achieved any official, public character. Yet we saw each other almost every day, and we knew we were more than just friends.

To the daytime comradeship I should add our evening or nighttime association, which was more focused and intentional. Again, society's categories did not provide a precise term for what we did together in Westlook Park so many late afternoons of the first spring in my high school years. Perhaps "wrestling" comes closest to describing the physical aspect of our relationship

Not that we planted our feet wide apart and locked arms on shoulders and necks, twisting and pulling like collegiate opponents to bring each other to the ground. But we were both eager to touch and to be held, to feel and to respond; and we didn't know yet the approved procedures that satisfied these needs. We would learn one option, however, very soon.

Our tussles had to begin, or seem to begin innocently and spontaneously, but they would go on with sometimes intense concentration and fixed purposes. This late March evening, for instance, with night darkening and the temperature dropping, finds us about to begin a regular ritual in Westlook Park.

This park, by the way, has been put in by the town on the west side of Ridgeview Drive at just about the spot I lost my first kite. With the trees cleared, we have a grand view of the countryside, pretty much the same view we kids once gained in the Open Space. Route 66 is disappearing out there, as Eisenhower's interstate highway system is building I-44. But we can see the same route west.

I have stopped by one of the park's two see-saws or teeter-totters, those boards on fulcrums with seats at each end for riders. They are designed, of course, for children to rock up and down, but in our teenage recreation we'll put any equipment—swings, climbing bars, slide—to our own uses.

"Get on," I say, gesturing toward the far seat.

"You'll bounce me," she objects. The heavier individual, of course, controls a teeter-totter. Park etiquette calls for that person to sit closer in toward the center on his end, thus balancing the board. By scooting out and leaning back, he can lower his end to the ground and hold his partner high in the air. The bigger person can also take his partner up quickly, then stop suddenly. She'll fly off her end, and, when she comes back down, the board will spank her bottom. Marcia has ridden the see-saw with me before and knows my game.

"You have to sit here," she says, pushing me forward.

"Here's the seat," I claim, pointing to where the board has been narrowed for a rider to straddle it at the end. I grab her arm to pull her back with me.

"But you're heavier. You need to sit here." She puts a hand on my back to push me forward again. I wrap one arm around her waist to pull her back. Our hips bump and our shoulders rub.

If I could only get her in the right place for such tussles, I think. Maybe out in the woods on some mossy bank or in the middle of an open field of high grass. Then things could follow a natural course.

I have done considerable filling in, by the way, of that movie picture of lovers embracing. In close-ups of 1940s and 1950s pictures, remember, the bottom edge for images of kissers came generally at about the shoulders. Where the hands go, what part of whose middle lines up with another's, how legs lie—these are things I've added to the more innocent pictures of love from my childhood.

They would have us believe at the Uptowne Theatre that lips are everything, that from that center come shuddering and swooning; but there are other, more powerful sites of pleasure first revealed to me by Roger Peterson and Cathy Williams, who used to kiss and pet on her porch next to the Vacant Lot. Those places of excitement are outside the range of this decade's major media. But in the 60s the frame of desire will be dramatically expanded. And right now I'm interested in entering that larger picture.

Some months ago I began, late at night, to draw the human form on a Magic Slate, trying to visualize better what happens in sex. This is the appropriate medium for my teenage quasi-pornographic work, since I leave no permanent record for a parent or sibling to discover.

The Magic Slate has two plastic sheets over a soft dark board. Pressing with a wooden instrument (a pencil without lead) leaves behind a trail in which the dark base shows through the two plastic sheets. Your drawing is made up of lines where the bottom layer of the Magic Slate sticks to the base and appears dark. If you pull up those sheets, you erase what you've drawn.

I am, by the way, a pretty good drawer mechanically. That is, I can see and represent relationship with accurate lines and scale. The art teacher who came once a week into junior high classes said I lacked life, the vital ingredient of genius. That would turn out not to be completely true, but I was at this time overly concerned with the technique of drawing, with a strict but two-dimensional realism. So the nude females drawn on my Magic Slate looked a little more like mannequins than living beings. I draw enough, however—copying from individual figures in magazines and comic books—to get a much clearer picture than before of where all the parts of two people can go when they're making love.

Marcia has skipped away from me now at my end of the see-saw, laughing. She goes to the other end and waits for me to get on. I steady the seat at an appropriate height. She swings a leg over, but keeps the other foot solidly on the ground. "No bumping?"

"No bumping," I concede. We teeter-totter in a leisurely fashion for a while, me up her down, her up me down.

I am planning for my next series of leanings and touchings, holdings and squeezings, when over Marcia's shoulder (she is low, I am high) I spot an event I have wanted to see ever since Roger Peterson described its occurrence over a year ago. However, this is perhaps the worst possible time for me to witness it.

Beneath the tall metal swings, in the outer fringe of a streetlight's arc, two dogs are copulating.

Of course, that's what I assume they're doing. The Circle was not a farm, remember, so I did not grow up among barnyard animals reproducing their kind every spring. My total previous observation of animal sexual activity consisted of watching male dogs pursue female dogs without success. I observed once a tiny Dachshund trying to reach the back of a full grown cocker spaniel; and I had seen a German shepherd try to mount a much smaller beagle. I'd also been one of many neighborhood kids laughing at an excited male dog humping any boy's leg. But I'd never been present when the correct combination of size, height, and breed of any creature led to the act itself.

There is something else confusing me about what I see beneath Marcia (she is high now, and I am low). The dogs seem to be dragging each other along the gravel plot in which the swings are set. And they're attached back-to-back, not one behind and on top. What has happened here?

This scene sticks vividly in my memory afterwards because of what I later conclude to be an error in my father's second man-to-man lecture about sex. The first talk, now almost a decade back in my past, simply articulated the anatomical differences between the sexes and alluded to the necessity of both in families. His more recent presentation, actually rather thorough and organized, confirmed the general picture I'd developed from other sources. (My Magic Slate had by then recorded my progress beyond the notion that babies were produced by a man's poking a finger into the circle made by a woman's thumb and index finger.) But my father's account also was laced, I now believe, with several conservative principles designed to promote caution in any sexual experimentation I might undertake.

For example, the only position he described was the "missionary" one, and no two-person acts other than intercourse were ever mentioned. I also recall my father's telling me that, once begun, the sexual act cannot be stopped. If a man enters a woman, he cannot withdraw until after ejaculation, after fertilization, after conception has taken place. As I interpreted it, then, there was a physiological inevitability in copulation. Once initiated, the process continued until its end: reproduction.

The two dogs I saw together behind Marcia under the swings were, I concluded, snared in this biological trap. And they were, in fact, locked together; but coupling among humans can be interrupted.

I revised the impression created by my father and then reinforced by these two unfortunate dogs some months later when I tracked down the meaning of the Latin term *coitus interruptus.* Here at last Mrs. Johnson's labors to expand my vocabulary and to develop my understanding of classical culture came to fruition (so to speak). In less than an hour's work at our public library downtown, I achieved a graphic understanding of this phrase. (I probably made use of the Magic Slate somewhere in here as well.)

Still, at the time I was see-sawing with Marcia in Westlook Park, I believed unequivocally that, should I ever unlawfully enter into a sexual embrace with a girl or woman, I could expect no release until the inevitable conclusion. I would have to proceed through a series of necessary and connected steps—pregnancy, marriage, parenthood, grandparenthood, and so forth to eternity. The sight of the dogs and the correspondent thought of a possible future extending from a bump of my hip against Marcia's gave me, as you might guess, some pause.

That pause was translated from thought into action as I froze the tetter-totter with myself on the ground and Marcia high in the air. It is possible my mouth was open.

"Mark!" she said. She was so high on the see-saw that she was leaning forward, her hands gripping the sides of the board, her legs wiggling awkwardly below her.

"Marrkk!" Even in my dazed and wondering state, I recognized anger in this voice.

II

"Mark."

"Maarrkk!"

Now I was hearing two voices call me, one pleasant and familiar, another angry, almost a hiss.

"Mark, honey."

"Maarrkk!"

When my attention shifted away from the dogs I had been watching (who had finally pulled themselves off from the swings and, I hoped, from each other), and I saw Marcia scowling at me from high on the see-saw, I pushed up on the ground with my feet, bringing the board down to a level position. She hopped off her end immediately and walked toward me.

I was afraid she was going to slap me or something—she had sounded so mad. But as she passed the middle of the see-saw, her scowl evolved into a smile and she said "Hi!" brightly. The "Hi" was not for me, however, but for someone behind me, the owner of the second voice who had been calling me. I turned around and saw my mother.

As intently as I had been looking beneath Marcia toward a possible doggy symbol of my future, she had been looking over my head at my mother, who had been walking into the park from Limestone Drive. Now I was doubly glad those dogs had disappeared into the shrubbery!

"Mom!" I said nervously.

"Hello, Marcia," she said. "How are you. I was just looking for Mark."

"I'm fine, Mrs. Landon. We were, um, riding the see-saw."

"What did you need me for, Mom?"

"Your father just took a call from Joe Martin. He lives over by you on Oak, doesn't he, Marcia?"

"Yes, on the other side of the street."

"He has a Saturday job for you, Mark, if you're interested."

"At the tire shop?" Big Joe, as Mr. Martin was called in town, ran a very successful business putting new and recapped tires on this area's portion of America's growing fleet of automobiles. Especially as so many of us became two-car families during the economic expansion of the 1960s, well-run local enterprises like Joe Martin's Tires grew with the times. The job I was being offered, however, had to do, strangely, not with tires but with books.

I did not learn until later how Mr. Martin became involved with books in the first place, but for three or four years, the time I was in high school, he managed the distribution of paperback books for Fairfield and Phipps County.

He was stocking drug stores, gas stations, little country stores, dime stores, and the pool hall with inexpensive ($.25 or $.35 per copy) romance, detective, and Western fiction. He had nothing to do with hardbacks, trade books, or magazines, as there was no regular bookstore in town and the college operation dealt almost exclusively with textbooks.

Martin's network was strictly a pulp trade, leisure reading for bored housewives, night watchmen, and curious teenagers. As I learned in time, Mr. Martin was himself uninterested in what titles passed through his hands on the way to consumers. He simply fulfilled a contract to keep the cylindrical racks at several dozen area businesses stocked with Louis L'Amour, *Peyton Place* and its imitators, and the current who-done-its.

I assumed this was how small businesses survived sometimes, taking on extra operations when opportunities arose. It's diversification on a small-scale, though the yoking of one product (tires) with a totally unrelated one (books) often defies logic. I also remember seeing on my paper route that grocery stores occasionally sold clothes, hardware stores sometimes displayed cosmetics, and jewelry stores now and then had small pieces of furniture for sale.

When my Mom told me there was a job at Martin's, though, I was pretty sure I didn't want it. The tire operation was all I knew about, and it was hard work. My school pal Jimmy Donaldson had an older brother who was a fulltime employee there, so I'd heard quite a bit about what it was like.

The garage was a dark, smoky building, its few windows painted black on the outside like a factory's. A recapping operation kept the building hot, and exhaust fumes filled the interior space. Tires are inherently dirty and cars greasy, of course, so the overall-clad employees seemed marked by their work. And, because tire irons, air powered wrenches, wheels and hubcaps generate plenty of noise, no one bothered much with conversation during their long hours of physical labor.

Still, there was the possibility of money here, I realized later that night as I lay in bed before falling asleep. I might make more in a single day than I could all week with my paper route. My ideas about what Marcia and I could be doing together in the evenings took on added allure when prefaced by some kind of indulgence—ice cream, a movie, flowers.

Too, the prestige of having a second job, and not a typical one for my young teenage set, was attractive. I would lose my Saturdays perhaps, but I might gain Saturday night. By the time I fell asleep that night I had concluded that I would talk to Mr. Martin the next day. By the end of the same week Mark Landon was a young man boldly holding down two jobs, a *Fairfield Mirror* paper route Monday through Friday and warehouse inventory-er in a book delivery business on Saturdays.

What convinced me to take the second job was that it had nothing to do with tires, with the operation for which Martin's was best known. My work went on in a small back room off Joe Martin's Fairfield Street garage, where books returned unsold from the stores he serviced were stacked in boxes, divided into categories on a workbench, and arranged for future shipment on wooden shelves.

My assignment was fairly straightforward: to check all returning copies against a master inventory, prepare those titles for which we could receive credit to be mailed back to publishing houses, and slate for destruction copies that could not be returned.

It should be obvious from the start that this was not a particularly exciting job. I worked alone in a room with thousands of books and at least a dozen book supplier catalogs. There was no variety in what I did, as each Saturday I found my storeroom filled with new boxes of books brought in from our outlets. I filled eight-hour days classifying and stacking these books into simple categories.

But I liked this job for two tangential features of its situation: what I read in some of those unwanted books, and what I witnessed among those employees at Martin's whose days were filled with road dust where mine were marked by printers' ink.

I had to sneak my readings of daring gunfights in routine westerns and frantic embraces in conventional romances, for Big Joe managed to pass by the open door to my room about once an hour, expecting reports of progress or at least clear signs of activity. I learned to stash my current interest at the end of a shelf, where it could come and go among the stacks I was actually counting or organizing.

I always had one ear out and one eye open for the form and tread of my always vigilant boss, then. And, in an unexpected benefit for my future academic career, I learned to read fast, to find points of interest in works clearly written according to formula. I also learned that I was interested in the formulas themselves, in the building and satisfaction of desire along fixed, familiar principles.

The defeat of outlaw Bob Slug by U.S. Marshal Dick Keele was repeatedly satisfying for me, especially after the villain had humiliated several dirt farmers, insulted Miss Warmheart, the local school teacher, and cuffed a young boy too timid to ride with him on a rampage across the prairie. But I found more and more that I wanted instances of romantic as well as battlefield success.

Yet there was never enough in the passionate embraces of Nancy Fortune, Nurse, with Dr. Thomas Rich, Surgeon, to satisfy fully these adolescent longings. My mining in thousands of pulp novels was aimed at application in the case of one Marcia Terrell, papergirl extraordinaire and femme fatale at this time of my life. And in this project, I believed for a time, I was on the road to success: I felt I was discovering a model that could take me beyond incidental contact with the girl of my dreams to the delights of sexual fulfillment.

Well, not complete sexual fulfillment. Again, despite my father's good intentions, his explanation of sex had still left some gaps in my understanding. And I didn't know fully what I was trying to accomplish.

He had explained, that is, the coming together of egg and sperm; and I understood that in the act of sex I had the good fortune to provide the latter. But he gave no extended explanation of the sensations this process generated in me, in my body. It was all supposed to feel good, I knew that. But my father supplied no analog by which I might have anticipated the explosive intensity of orgasm. Thus, when it came, it came as quite a surprise.

This does not mean that I had not experienced orgasm. A healthy teenager, I had been having nocturnal emissions for some time. Until this second talk about sex with my father, I had begun to fear that the wet spots in my pajamas were a terrible sign I was reverting to an early childhood self, to a boy who couldn't stop wetting the bed. My father's explanation gave me great relief. But so far at least, orgasm was something that had occurred only when I was unconscious.

Again, my father was not at fault here. Somewhat advanced for his time, he did not even view masturbation as evil, a sin. Without endorsing it as a regular pastime, he talked about "the sound of one hand clapping" as an inevitable part in a boy's growing up. But, at least in my memory of his lecture, he was less thorough, less precise about the end point of all that rubbing, pumping, pressing.

Of course, there could have been technical weaknesses in my performance, a lack of knowledge about when to go hard, when to be gentle, where to squeeze, what to stroke. Perhaps, I simply lacked the necessary persistence.

At any rate, despite a lot of attention to erections and longing that year, I had not, at the moment I went to work at Joe Martin's Tire Shop, achieved expertise at the adolescent art of self-abuse. Thus, I could not anticipate fully where I wanted to go in my nudgings, bumpings, pressings with Marcia Terrell. This is where the men in the next room figured in: while preparing cars to return to the road, they also charted for me in some detail the land of desire.

III

I heard more than I saw what went on in the garage outside my workroom at Martin's. Since I was surrounded by books and constantly consulting catalogs, I only occasional had time to check on the next door operation in which cars arrived, rose up on power lifts, lost their wheels with old tires, and received the wheels back again with new tires. What I saw and heard was often fragmentary, bits and pieces of work getting done and conversation carried on that floated in and around the sound of steel tools banging against car parts, into mobile metal cabinets, and onto the concrete floor.

"Hey, Stick," I might hear, for instance, one Saturday morning. "Get this one." I would then note the sound of a heavy rubber tire rolling from one of the cars high up on a rack to a nearby workstation. Stick was the tallest and thinnest of Martin's workmen. He sported a scraggly, blonde moustache.

"Lemme get this old lady where I can work on her," Stick might call back. He lifted the tire waist-high and settled it horizontally on this machine that would separate it from its wheel. I heard the hub clang into place, its center transfixed by a metal spike the size of a car's axle.

"Be gentle now, Stick. You want her to like you after." The first worker went on to another wheel. With a power wrench at the end of a long orange cord he was removing the nuts from the second wheel.

Spinning a metal cap down on top of the spike to hold the wheel securely, Stick pushed a foot pedal at the base of his machine. I heard compressed air drive a circular arm at the base of the machine up against the side of the tire. With the grind of a mechanical lever, the rising arm broke the seal between rim and hub: "Phhmmp!"

"Turn her over, Stick, turn her over! You got her the wrong way." His companion laughed, and Stick must have lifted his foot off the pedal. With a hiss, the arm descended. He grabbed the wheel with two hands, raised it, flipped it over and back onto the machine. I could hear a grunt of effort.

"Now go back to work, Stick," called his friend. He had removed another tire and was now rolling it over to his work station.

Stick's foot hit the pedal again and the arm rose to the tire: "Phhmmp!" The other rim separated from the hub. Placing a blade-shaped metal tool on the machine's spike, Stick now pushed a second pedal with his foot. The spike rotated the tool, which, inserted beneath the rim, lifted the tire free of its wheel. Stick bowled the worn tire toward a stack of carcasses along the side wall, where it thumped against one pile.

"Aw, Stick. You ought not to just love 'em and leave 'em," said his companion. But the ever expanding automobile business in those days inspired just such a relationship between Americans and their cars. Shiny new vehicles replaced their predecessors before they had worn out or proven themselves unable to meet the demands of the present. And the stacks of discarded tires in Martin's garage were matched by acres of rusting automobiles in great countryside junkyards.

However, there were new cars to replace the old ones and new tires to keep everyone moving down old, two-lane Route 66 and new four-lane, limited access Interstate 44. Stick took one of four new tires that had been rolled out by an office salesman and threw it up on his machine. Car owner and shop owner, tire salesman and laborer were units in a consumer nation, enjoying apparently unlimited natural resources and unequaled productivity. It was no wonder we were in love with our place in the world and our way of life.

Stick and his friend provided for me at this time a model of happy indulgence in America's success. I saw their efficient installation of new tires and heard their chatter of pleasure as a continuation of my pulp fiction stories about the American West read in the back room of the same garage. Bad guys driven from town, six-gun wielding hero, with an arm around his girl, looks toward a prosperous future in a growing frontier town. And I wanted to step up my own participation in this glittering enterprise.

While my Saturday eavesdropping and reading at Martin's Tires shaped new fantasies of romantic entanglement, my weekday paper route carried me to real life meetings with Marcia Terrell. Especially in the late afternoons, after we had both finished our deliveries, or in the early evenings after dinner, we could spend time together at Westlook Park.

We told each other the unusual events of our days (she might have sailed a copy of the *Mirror* into the Johnsons' side yard fishpond; I could have seen from a distance a brief but decisive fistfight in the alley behind the pool hall). And we found ways to bump hips sitting down together on a bench, touch toes in the swings, overlap hands on the jungle gym.

Marcia's latest interest, however, seemed to reduce the opportunities I was trying to develop for ending up in each other's arms: she had become obsessed with basketball. And, unfortunately, in those days this was strictly a noncontact sport.

While the girls' game was just beginning to change from the fixed position mode of the 1930s and 1940s, even boys on defense kept a polite distance from their counterparts when they squared up for two-handed set shots. A slap on the arm or a foot in the way was invariably a foul. Always a good athlete and now with a woman's height (I was still painfully an inch shorter), Marcia was thinking seriously of trying out for the high school's junior varsity team next year.

"Let's shoot some," she said one Monday afternoon after I had been working at Martin's for several weeks. She had picked up her ball at home when she dropped off her paper bag.

"OK," I agreed, though I would have preferred some situation in which she stayed still. "But be careful you don't get hurt." I was also harboring attitudes appropriate to the time about women and exercise: too much wasn't good for them.

"Who won last time?" she pointed out with some warmth. It was true that she had beaten me, but I thought I had explained why: the court was not regulation. In fact, this court looked more like a motel swimming pool someone had filled in with sand.

Basically oval in shape, with the goal at one of the small ends, the court had been laid down in a narrow space among trees. It had also been constructed by the side of Ridgeview Road, at the top of a long slope down toward Springers' Pond. So one side had to be built up inside a rock wall nearly three feet tall, and the court itself was a heavy mixture of sand and clay, perhaps twenty feet long and no wider than twelve feet. (Since I was taking geometry that year, I understood that a complex algebraic formula was necessary to generate such a shape in place of the simpler and standard rectangle: "x times y.")

At the time, of course, I was astounded that responsible people had designed and installed such an irregular facility at such an inappropriate place. Because the court was at the highest point in the park, any missed rebound to the west rolled for hundreds of yards downhill before coming to rest in the creek bottom approaching the pond. Now I've come to realize that these mismatches occur frequently in our world.

Because of its odd shape, Westlook's oval basketball court inspired its own special game. It was difficult to dribble under the basket without bouncing the ball off the stone retainer at the court's edge. And there were no corners to shoot from, so most of the time one-on-one players just traded shots from about fifteen to eighteen feet in front of the basket. Marcia, however, was developing a style of play that was new to me at least.

Rather than facing the goal, Marcia turned away from it and, dribbling first to one side, then to the other, backed steadily in toward the basket. Unless she turned too far to one side, where I might have a chance to steal or knock the ball away, I was steadily forced to retreat. As she backed in, I could see a look of intense concentration on her face, the lower lip caught in her teeth.

When she got close enough—well inside the free-throw line—Marcia, in one continuous motion, turned, jumped, and shot over me. I felt pretty ineffectual as a defender, standing there with my hands up but unable really to affect her shot. She was getting better and better at making these turn around, short jumpers.

So, of course, I began to try the same strategy on her, facing away from the goal and backing in. But she had developed a defense for her own offensive move, although I wasn't sure it was was legal: she stood her ground behind me, sometimes slowing my approach with a subtle push from one hand in the small of my back, sometimes actually blocking me by slipping quickly to the spot into which I was trying to step.

"Foul!" I called at one of these little collisions.

"What?"

"You can't push me. I have the ball."

"I'm not pushing. I'm just standing here. You bumped into me."

"Well . . . I . . . just don't push."

There was a little grin on Marcia's face as she gestured for me to continue play. She bounced on her toes, light and quick.

I dribbled a few times, then turned again and started backing in. This time she seemed even more aggressive, anticipating my move and beating me to the spot. Now she seemed to be blocking me with her whole body. I felt that I was running into her with my shoulders, my thighs, my back. And she seemed to be meeting me with increasing force.

Then she slapped the ball, and it bounced off my knee out of bounds. Her possession.

She was much better than I at backing in, and soon she had scored with one of those little jump shots. I began to fear that I would lose again, so I became more forceful on offense too. I swatted at her hand if she tried to put it on my back. I leaned into her when I felt contact. On defense I pushed her in the small of the back. I leapt to stay between her and the basket, my hips meeting her backside. After a while she was having trouble getting to the position she wanted. And I was making as many turn around shots as she.

Then all of a sudden I realized I was interested in something besides winning this game of basketball.

IV

Why was I slow to see the reasons Marcia would bump into me in those one-on-one contests in Westlook Park? From my vantage point of nearly three decades later I can see she had found her own ways to initiate physical contact with a member of the opposite sex.

Part of my youthful blindness derived, I guess, from the fact that we were playing sports, an activity which I assumed was single-sex (all male) for anyone past puberty. While girls could participate ineptly in softball or kick ball, grown women stood on the sidelines to watch men in real athletic contests. Whenever she had a ball in her hands, Marcia would appear to me as simply another boy. She was an opponent, and my objective was to outscore her by making more baskets than she did.

Still, there were other factors that affected how I saw Marcia on a basketball court, factors determining even the parts of her I acknowledged as being there.

The framework for my appreciation of Marcia as female was provided by a favorite masculine pastime of that era, girl-watching. On street corners, in department stores, and at town parks males over the age of twelve regularly observed, appraised, and classified all members of the opposite sex. Length of leg, narrowness of waist, and amplitude of bosom were standard measures.

Sometimes, however, I had difficulty applying this known system of judgment in new contexts. A woman walking into the wind in a flowered sun dress against a background of blue sky possessed a sexual identity I had been trained to recognize. But a ball hawking, fast dribbling jump shooter contradicted rather than confirmed the model of femme fatale.

Fortunately, a special variety of ogling outside my high school during lunch one day about a week after Marcia beat me at basketball (21-18) led to an important breakthrough about women and sexual identity.

In those innocent days, by the way, we were not required to stay in the school building for the lunch hour, as is now apparently the universal practice of American secondary education. And we had a full sixty minutes to eat, not the squeezed twenty-five minutes my children are granted to bolt down their food before the next wave of students pushes into a crowded facility.

Many of my classmates did eat in the cafeteria in those days, but others who lived close walked home for a sandwich. Some patronized the little neighborhood grocery store, Match's, which had a sandwich counter; and a few of the older students ate bag lunches in their cars and then cruised the area ogling pedestrians and each other. There was a freedom there we should value today, especially now that it is gone.

I did not see Marcia at lunch generally because she was still in junior high school, a block and a half away. In fact, this separation of my life into a celibate school arena without Marcia and a love life in the neighborhood simplified things for me to some extent. I studied the biology of reproduction in the classroom and laced those essentials with spicy playground anecdote. Then I applied both kinds of knowledge in the laboratory of the Circle with Marcia as my primary subject. This may or may not have been such a good thing for Marcia, but at that age, like most of my friends driven by adolescent desire, I had very little conscience in such matters. I soon learned as well that Marcia had her own interest in these same matters.

The Marcia I pursued in the Circle was not, as I've said then, fully defined for me. From the waist up, the picture was pretty clear. Certainly I knew she had lips I had been able to kiss; there were breasts I wanted to hold; and I felt my arms belonged around her waist. But below that her form went kind of fuzzy in my mind.

It went out of focus on my Magic Slate too, now that I think about it, whenever I tried to draw the complete female body. I began to add detail, however, as I said, to the shape of things hidden by observing older girls in my high school, that is, by girl-watching.

I saw upperclass girls of Fairfield High School in automobiles as they circled the building during our unstructured lunch hours. Those cars contained Big Men on Campus and the sexiest women I knew, cheerleaders like the alluring Janet Masters; but the cars also concealed as much as they revealed.

Still, one girl had the full attention of the freshmen and sophomore boys who lingered around the school's front steps after eating and before classes resumed at 1:00: Susie Bodell, petite but curvaceous younger sister of Pete Bodell, Fairfield's only all-state athlete who had graduated two years earlier. Susie drove her brother's car while he was playing halfback for the University of Missouri's football Tigers. And in that 1949 Ford coupe Susie did something that inspired my imagination, fleshing out (so to speak) my understanding of basketball player Marcia Terrell.

One of the great thrills for those car-driving juniors and seniors was "getting rubber" at the bottom of the hill in front of the high school. Turning onto Maramec Springs Road from one of the side streets, drivers popped their clutches, with accelerators pressed to the floor, on the run up to and past the beige brick building. They threw loose gravel behind them, burned tire marks into the pavement, and sent the acrid aroma of hot metal and melting rubber drifting toward those younger students as a reminder of how insignificant they were in the grand scheme of things.

Most of these cocky youngsters doing the driving were, of course, male—athletes and pool hall denizens, angry young men who might soon be dropouts or enlisted men in America's armed forces. While nearly all the women in these cars were passengers, the best and the boldest of tire-screeching, gear-shifting, pedal-pushing hot rodders was the dazzling Susie Bodell. She could do something not all of the boys could: she got rubber in high gear.

To squeal tires in a manual transmission's third gear required a big engine (Pete had replaced the standard six-cylinder with a hefty V-8), a sturdy transmission (he'd moved the gear shift from the column to the flour to accommodate an overdrive), and considerable coordination. Not only did the car need the power to kick the back wheels up to a higher speed, but hand and foot had to work together on accelerator, clutch, and gear shift. To the whistles and cheers of an admiring student body, Susie got rubber in all three gears.

The first burst of acceleration was not as difficult as the second two. From a standing start, Susie floored the gas pedal and let out the clutch at the same time—wheels spun, getting rubber. But going from first to second, and from second to third, she had to double-clutch her brother's special transmission.

In double-clutching, a driver must first disengage the clutch (depress the pedal with the left foot), shift out of the lower gear (using the right hand), reengage the clutch in neutral (releasing the pedal) to synchronize the spinning gears, then depress the clutch again, shifting on to the higher gear. Finally the clutch is released another time, popped, to get rubber again (in second gear)—once more (in third). During this entire operation, the driver must vary the position of the gas pedal with the right foot (down during each acceleration phase, up for double clutching).

Such coordination was a masterful thing, suggesting a will to control, an intensity of focus, and a desire to achieve that in those days we usually associated with men.

Little of this thrill-inspiring operation, I must note again, was actually visible to us youngsters standing or sitting on the school steps. We could see Susie lean forward in her seat, eyes fixed on the road ahead, her lips slightly open as she worked a stick of chewing gum. And the puff of smoke beneath the rear wheels confirmed our ears' recording of the brief but decisive rip in the middle of that big engine's throaty roar. Ah, but what went on out of sight, behind the driver's door panel where Suzie's arm was rocking forward and back and those strong legs were making things happen was a mystery for me, a mystery and a wonder!

This picture, of Susie driving, is another one of those images of the past I have had to fill in from the future. It resembles the time Linda Roper bopped Martin Pruitt in the genitals at the rehearsal for our junior class play. I saw what happened, but I had no experience to interpret the more significant part of the event, Linda's reaction. Martin's doubling over I could understand, but how Linda would know so precisely the immediate and long term effect of that blow was beyond me for many years.

I see the rectangular frame provided by the driver's side window on a 1949 Ford, by the way, as symbolic of that era's circumscribed vision. Much as the 1950s movie screen showed the lovers' kiss only from the shoulders up, we could witness a woman's driving only in terms of arms and head seen from outside the car. And if I try to fill in that conventional picture of the past in more detail, I generally turn up a housewife in a woody station wagon with automatic transmission on her way to the grocery store.

However, in the one specific case of Pete Bodell's souped-up '49 Ford on Maramec Springs Road, I can now visualize the following things going on behind that driver side door panel. Susie sits in sweater and skirt on the sheepskin covered front seat. In order to get the mobility necessary to her effort, she must hike that skirt up from knees to alluring mid-thigh. Because the skirt is tight, she does this a leg at a time, rocking on her solid little bottom. She flexes her fingers on the steering wheel, glancing up at the rear-view mirror. (I seem to remember as well two large sponge dice swinging from that mirror.) She leans forward, reaching down for the gear shift with her right hand.

And suddenly, out on the steps of Fairfield High School (a good place to learn something, now that I think about it!), I connect the strength and purpose in Suzie's exhibition of skill with Marcia's basketball triumph, the backing in and scoring over a boy of similar size and ability. Clutch, shift, double-clutch and shift again, give it gas, pop! Dribble, step in, bump and turn, jump and shoot! I didn't understand it all; I couldn't really even imagine it; but I was as excited as I'd been several years earlier when Tricia Bell kissed me in the family bomb shelter during a hot summer game of Kick the Can.

I began immediately to think how I could change the field of Marcia's and my play to a place where the basketball and the hoop would no longer be necessary.

V

The new model for the physical capabilities of women inspired by Susie Bodell's energetic driving received an unexpected confirmation at Martin's Tires on the following Saturday. I had spent the morning working my way through an unusually large number of books returned from gas stations and little country stores across Phipps County. Coming back to my workroom after lunch (at the sandwich counter of Dixon's Drugstore,) I surprised Stick and his girl friend, Blossom, behind a mountain of tire carcasses in a corner of the garage.

"Blossom" was not, of course, Stick's girlfriend's real name, which I never learned; but since she appeared so consistently for months afterwards in my sexual fantasies, I decided she needed a name and christened her "Blossom."

A flamboyant dresser, she was a large women, tall and especially wide in the hips. Her hair was blonde and fanned out from her head, to my mind, like a large pale flower. She worked at a downtown beauty shop; and if Stick didn't meet her for lunch, she was often waiting for him in front of the store at 5:30 on Saturdays. They went bowling, I think, and out to eat; but he was rather tightlipped about their dates, especially when teased by his co-workers.

Though I had no Blossom to accompany me, lunch was still the most exciting event of my long weekend workday at Martin's. In fact, it was so much the high point that I generally went late, at 1:00, to keep the remainder of the day, when my energies flagged, short. That I left at an odd hour and that there was always so much noise in the garage perhaps accounts for the fact that I came up on Stick and Blossom that Saturday undetected. Although they never saw me, my vision of them added one more important piece for me to the puzzle of how men and women come together.

I had walked the two blocks (one west, one south) back from Dixon's to Martin's in a bit of a daze, reviewing a conversation I had had with Jimmy Donaldson, my easygoing classmate whose father worked in the Missouri Geological Survey's map department.

Jimmy's older brother, remember, was a full time employee at Martin's, though my conversations with him never went further than exchanged greetings. In part because they lived in the country, the two older Donaldson brothers had fallen behind in school and become quiet, even sullen young men, wondering how their contemporaries always got better jobs, more pay, greater opportunity. They had attended a small country school for the first seven grades, and heavy snow or bad weather usually meant their missing classes.

Helping Mr. Donaldson with the small family farm (several fields of corn, a chicken yard, and a pig pen) also kept their attention more than books. Jimmy, the youngest, came along after the consolidation of county schools and the expansion of bus routes into rural areas. So in his case a general family ability blossomed at school, and he was already planning for college and an engineering career.

Jimmy slipped onto the stool next to mine at Dixon's lunch counter. He often worked on the farm over weekends, but today he had come to town with his mother. "Did you hear about the hayride?" he asked. I was waiting for my order, the traditional hamburger and coke.

"What hayride?" Hayrides, of course, were fabled events in my circle, an occasion for significant advance in one's petting experiences. In theory, a hayride was only a sunset trip around a farm on a wagon pulled by a slow horse or tractor. But claims of and rumors about sexual achievement during a hayride mushroomed in the following week.

"Saturday night, on the Ropers' farm."

"Where's that?"

"Not too far from our place. Out Cemetary Road, maybe four miles."

Hayrides occurred both in the fall and the spring, sponsored in Fairfield by, of all things, church groups. I guess the theory was that, since teenagers would find ways to be together, it was better to offer them supervised opportunities for socializing than to leave them on their own.

A waitress set my hamburger in front of me. It came steaming hot inside a plastic wrapper puffed up like a balloon. I popped down on the plastic bubble with the palm of my hand, breaking open the seal at one end.

"So?" I asked Jimmy. Neither of us had yet summoned the courage to go on one of these hayrides.

"So, let's go."

"You mean, get dates?"

"Right. Who would you ask?"

"Who would you?"

"Well, I'm thinking about Susie Bodell." He grinned.

"Sure!" I was eating my sandwich as we talked, but I noticed that Jimmy was eying it curiously.

"You hungry?" I asked, afraid he might be without money for lunch. Not everyone had the income of two jobs, as I did.

"No, no." He looked around a bit distractedly.

"Well, who will you take, really?" I asked again.

"Well, maybe Donna Easley." She was in our class, a quiet but friendly girl. I knew he had thought about asking her out.

"OK. I could ask Marcia Terrell," I said hesitantly.

"Oh-oh, a junior-highschooler!" he teased. "She won't know what's coming."

"Hey, I'm going to behave. It'll be chaperoned, right? It's just a ride in the moonlight, seeing the countryside."

"Um-hm, um-hm. Hey, where did you get that hamburger? There's no grill here."

"I know. They have an oven. But the sandwiches are also precooked."

"Precooked? Why isn't that bag melted." He pointed beside my plate, where I had discarded the wrinkled plastic.

I realized I didn't know how this system worked, but I pointed to the small unit up on a shelf.

Dixon's featured the standard lunch counter arrangement: a long line of stools in front of a counter punctuated by napkin containers, ketchup and mustard holders, salt and pepper shakers. On the other side of the counter, where the soda jerks worked, were sinks, cabinets, a many-doored ice cream freezer, and storage areas.

Against the back wall was a long mirror in which customers saw themselves and the store behind them. Milk shake mixers, an ice-cream cone dispenser, fruit juice machines, and other small appliances sat up on a long shelf above more cabinets. At one end of that shelf sat a small oven, perhaps the size of a bread box.

"There," I said, pointing. "They put the sandwich, inside its bag, in that oven."

"And it doesn't melt?"

"Heats from the inside," I explained, though I wasn't even sure how I knew that. I suppose I had simply deduced the process from observation.

This was, of course, an early microwave oven, the first I ever knew about. Those who ate at Dixon's complained about the system (it didn't really taste fresh, the sandwiches weren't made locally, the bread tasted gummy); but it was undeniable quick and produced no greasy mess. Dixon's put chips beside their sandwiches and dispensed with French fries

"Inside the oven?" asked Jimmy.

"Umm, inside the burger." I was thinking about this myself.

"Little waves go through there," I added, remembering now a conversation overheard here on an earlier Saturday. "Yeah, radio waves heat up the stuff inside the oven, but not the oven itself."

"I don't get it," Jimmy admitted. "But I think I'll try it." And he ordered a hot ham-and-cheese sandwich for himself, studying the operation at every step.

This was one of the little signs of a larger national progress, of course, our small town affected by advances in technology. It was almost as if we were being heated up by the waves of new knowledge emanating from scientific centers across the country. We were being matured to a new state of more convenient living by forces originating perhaps with the space program, an astronaut's oven.

However interesting evidence of such a phenomenon might be to me now, at the time it was definitely only background noise. My primary focus was girls and how to warm them up. And whether I would follow through on a deal made with Jimmy to get a date, whether Marcia would accept, whether my parents would approve of the whole idea, and what might happen under the moonlight occupied my thoughts as I walked away from Dixon's microwave lunch counter.

I reached my workroom at Martin's by skirting the garage where cars went up on lifts and tires were repaired or replaced. Discarded tires made huge hills along the back and side wall of the building, until they were picked up perhaps once a month for recapping or disposal.

Today a virtual mountain of rejects obscured the door to my room, walling off the front corner of the garage at the same time. For some reason, when I got to my door, I hesitated, perhaps hearing something; and then I stepped around the side of that mountain. In that darkened front corner were Stick and Blossom.

What I saw in that screened-off section of the garage took some time to decipher. Amid several stacks of worn tires as tall as he was, Stick was standing, his back toward me, in front of the shop's front wall. On each side of his slim hips I could see two pale crescent moons.

I noticed that Slim was having an apparent effect on the two slim moons. His hips were thrusting forward rhythmically, and synchronized with the rocking of his pelvis was a waxing and waning of the moons. When he went farthest up, they bulged out, perhaps doubling their width. When he pulled back, they thinned and nearly disappeared.

How does he do that, I wondered? There was a sound produced there too, a low moan punctuated by almost gleeful, short shouts just audible at this distance over the garage's general din:

"Mmmmm—Yii!—Mmmm—Yii!—Mmmm—Yii!"

And then, glancing to a darkened window on the side wall, my eyes drawn by flickering, shadowy images, I saw, mirrored, the couple from another view. He was erect behind her, resting a hand on her hip. And she was bent forward at the waist with her arms stretched out, fingers splayed against the wall

Until then I hadn't even realized that Blossom was there, that those two moons were all of her not obscured by Stick. The reflection in the window was not as sharp as a mirror's, but I could see that Stick's pants hung loose on his hips, while Blossom's dress was hiked up onto her back. And I could see now a woman so energetically jumping back into a man that her blonde hair flew up at every "Yii" like a windblown puff of smoke.

I put the two pictures together—direct and mirrored, back and side, unified and separate figures. Shazzam!

Part Eight: In a State

Chapter VI

When, undetected, I backed away from Stick and Blossom at play behind the mountain of tire carcasses in Martin's garage, I turned immediately to installing a new method of book sorting in my workroom.

There was nothing terribly wrong with the system I had inherited. Unsold books were brought in from separate stores in cardboard boxes. I unpacked the boxes in my workroom, stacking books from the same distributors together in piles on a large table along the back wall so they could be checked against lists of returnable titles. I used crude wooden shelves on the two side walls for books to be pulped, works from unfamiliar publishers, and books whose status would change with the next month and thus required immediate attention. (I also had a place for books I wanted to read myself, a little at a time, as I worked.) But at some point in recent weeks it had occurred to me that I might devise a more efficient sorting system.

I began suddenly that Saturday afternoon by emptying the shelves of all books, almost wildly stuffing volumes into boxes and shoving cartons into corners and outside the door. I flung empty boxes into a pile in another corner. I yanked the table out into the middle of the room, and, dragging a discarded metal magazine rack in from the trash, I used it to hold distributors' lists, catalogs, and industry guides. This made a tidy reference area along the back wall.

Taking the flaps of cardboard boxes that were torn or coming apart, I made large signs for the eight or ten major distributors we worked with. I posted them at the top of shelf sections and then subdivided each section to accommodate individual publishers. The table was left empty so that I could heave a load of books up on one end, organize its contents into small piles over the rest of the table top, then transfer them to the correct shelves.

This concentrated organizational effort reminds me of the time Billy Rhodes and I had set up a kids' buy-and-sell shop in Old Man Simpson's garage on the Circle. Billy had left me in charge of arranging floor and wall space as he roamed the town in search of stock. And I spent many long hours considering possible patterns, constructing special displays, hanging containers from the rafters. Eventually, of course, the whole effort was doomed, as Simpson had a plan for the store we kids never even dreamed of.

By working furiously and taking no breaks, I completed the change to my new operation at Martin's Tires that same Saturday. In the end I felt confident I would be able to process books far more quickly than I had in the past. I walked home, in fact, with a new sense of accomplishment. I was inspired to believe I might be a person bold and confident enough to ask Marcia Terrell to nestle down with me on a slow moving hay wagon drenched in moonlight.

Before I reached the Circle and could put my new confidence into play, however, I found my attention drawn to a black VW beetle stopped at the intersection of Route 66 and state road 00. Though there was no other traffic, the beetle continued to idle before the stop sign, and it brought my own thoughts of myself and Marcia, Blossom and Stick to a pause as well.

This intersection, by the way, was the major crossing point at that time for north-south and east-west traffic in south-central Missouri. It lay just west of the downtown area because Kingshighway, built as an early bypass for Route 66, lay about four blocks from Main Street. When the population grew in the next decade, and when a second by-pass for Route 66 (the first section of what was to become Interstate 44) was built further west, the town would expand around this point, making it more central to the larger community. An indication of how unhurried those days before the four-lane by-pass were is the fact that no stop-light controlled drivers here. This was a four-way stop.

It was not the sight of a beetle at this intersection that brought me to a confused halt on the way home that afternoon. The downsized, four-passenger Volkswagen was one of the most common cars of that era. Those VW beetles were (are!) long lived, economical, and functional, favorite first cars for young drivers and second cars for families. They looked from the outside too small for grown people (that's why some owners put toy wind-up keys on the back), but they were so well designed inside that all four riders sat comfortably, at least for regular in-town driving.

Because this particular bug seemed to hesitate at the intersection, I looked at it more closely. I was standing beside the easternmost stop sign waiting for my chance to cross. Right in front of me was, I realized, the classic couple of my high school, Linda Roper and Martin Pruitt.

He, the driver, was a student leader, class officer and talented musician. Linda, smart and sexy, was Latin Club President. Her tall slender body forecast fashion trends to come. Where I saw them side-by-side in the two front bucket seats of the VW, and when I overheard just one phrase in their conversation as they pulled away at last from the stop sign, I knew I had to try to become half of a similar couple.

Even in the simple act of sitting together in a Volkswagen, Linda and Martin seemed to exude a fine romantic glow. In public places they were even more startling in their representation of the ideal relationship. Part of their secret, I know now, is that, when talking to others, they seldom looked directly at each other; yet they functioned as a perfectly coordinated unit. Both spoke to their partners, each asked questions of the other, the second finished sentences begun by the first; but their attention was always turned toward their listeners.

Though they didn't glance at each other, they did touch: arm around the waist, hand in hand, a chaste kiss at greeting or parting. Their motions were connected, related, synchronized, though Martin never had to say a word as he stepped aside for Linda to go past the door he held open or when she reached to take the jacket he had found too warm for the moment. They seemed to possess a physical intimacy granted couples many years married; but coming from solid middle class families and pursuing professional careers (he aimed for medical school, she to teach), respectability eliminated any hint of coarseness in their relationship.

The phrase I overheard Martin offering to Linda was simple but evocative, then and now: "In the backseat," he said.

I knew enough about the fabled place of teenage lovemaking to extrapolate from these three words a much longer and more intriguing conversation. Although I could not see Martin's face as he spoke, I deduced from Linda's expression that he had answered a question she had posed. They were going to "do it" in the backseat of that beetle, I concluded.

Immediately, I wondered how this were possible, the backseat of the humpbacked Volkswagen being so much shorter than those of the traditional vehicles for teenage coupling, the Ford and Chevy. Though neither Martin nor Linda was heavy, together they stretched out to six feet at least. How would they fit under that tiny dome? I needed my Magic Slate to evaluate the alternatives.

Still, where else but in cars did illicit love occur for the American smalltown middle class of the 1950s? There were few motels whose managers would overlook a lack of luggage, but there were plenty of dead-end streets, quiet alleys, and county roads with little traffic where privacy could be expected. Since few mothers worked, staying home with young children, they took away opportunities for trysts in a boy's or girl's own house. Parties were relentlessly chaperoned. Only in the automobile did my generation have the chance to slip away from the vigilant eyes and the supervised space of our elders.

Walking now out Kingshighway toward Valley Lane (the shortcut over to Black Street and the Circle), I let my mind entertain a series of rather silly variations on how Linda and Martin could fit in a Volkswagen. Could this thing be done with knees bent, legs all crumpled up? Wouldn't that be like trying to squeeze a small plant, roots, leaves, and stem, back into a tiny seed? Billy Rhodes might be one to create such a human pretzel, but I could not really see two such elegant lovers as Linda and Martin knotted up in that way.

Would it be possible to have legs out the window? I imagined four bare feet in the open air—two up, two down, toes wiggling. But wouldn't this draw the attention of Lovers' Lane's passersby? Maybe it would work with legs reaching up into the front seat? But then I saw an accidental kick releasing the emergency brake and the car's rolling from a dark driveway into a busy street. Or a pants leg hooked over the gear shift, a toe punching the cigarette lighter, hips wedged between the two front seats—all too risky.

The Stick/Blossom method could be ruled out here, couldn't it? There was no sunroof in this beetle, but I still pictured for a moment Martin's torso rising out of the curved top of the bug. But this was so silly my imagination transformed him into an Ozark hillbilly, a Lil' Abner standing behind Daisy Mae. He was chewing a piece of straw and gave a cry that would bring pigs from across the country. Impossible, I concluded.

Even as I turned such possibilities (and figures) over in my mind, I realized that in some sense the question of how you could do it in a bug was for me academic. They probably could do it somehow. The real question was, what was I going to do, presumably with Marcia Terrell, at the hayride next Saturday?

I have since wondered, by the way, if I even heard Martin and Linda's conversation correctly. After all, what

I remember is only the three-word phrase, "in the backseat." Many things could go in the backseat besides lovers—groceries, sports equipment, school books.

It's also possible that I had mistaken Martin's words. He might have been talking, say, about fruit he had picked up for his elderly grandmother, which he was bringing to her "in a basket." Perhaps Linda had asked a simple question about the VW's motor, which, unlike those in American cars, was not under the hood. He could have said, "It's in the back. See?" Or he might have been responding to her story of an uncle, who was in an "income tax fix." There's no evidence to conclude that what I heard was said at all. Given my frame of mind at the time, I might well have put words from my own dark psyche directly into Martin's mouth.

Whatever the truth, however, when I reached the Circle, I was ready to put my proposal directly to Marcia.

VII

Marcia surprised me by accepting my invitation to the hayride immediately. It was Sunday afternoon, and we were in Westlook Park at the top of the Circle. Sitting in side-by-side swings, we scuffed our feet in the gray dust generated by younger playground visitors. I would have volunteered to stand behind Marcia and push, but she had gotten mad the last time I'd tried it. My hands strayed just a bit more with each push, and she went too far, too fast.

"Where is it?" was the only question Marcia posed about the hayride.

"At the Ropers', down Cemetary Road."

"Ah. I think I know where that is. Linda Roper? she dates Martin Pruitt, doesn't she?"

"Yes." There was an awkward silence. She gave herself a little push in the swing.

"I've never been on a hayride before," I offered. "You?"

"No. They say it's fun. You sing songs, watch the fireflies."

"Yeah. Tell ghost stories, get scared." I was leading up to how she might need a comforting arm around her shoulder, a strong man to lean against; but she changed the subject.

"How's your job at Martin's going?"

"Oh, it's pretty boring actually. I just sort books." I lifted my feet up, pulling the swing forward as I leaned back on the chains.

"Is it better than a paper route?"

"Um, I guess so. I get more money." Kicking my feet in the dust as I came through the low point of the swing's arc, I sent myself sideways, taking on a small, elliptical orbit that came close to Marcia.

"My route may get bigger," observed Marcia. "They're building out Hill Road, past Ridgeview." She watched the wooden seat of my swing as it came over next to hers.

"Any dogs out that way?" I asked.

"There's one, a beagle. But he's chained." This time my swing seat gently tapped hers as it came by. "Stop that," she said, putting a hand on my shoulder and sending me back toward a regular path; but she didn't sound angry.

"Whoops!" I pretended surprise. I let the swing arch out away from her, then come back over to her side. "At the hayride," I wondered. "Do they go down roads or out in the fields?"

She watched my swing come back again and bump hers, this time a little harder. "I don't know. What time does it start?" She slapped my hand where it held the swing's chain, then pushed my shoulder again.

"Jimmy said 6:00. I wonder if we get back before dark." I swung back again. "Ouch!"

This time Marcia had pinched me, reaching under my arm and catching me on the chest. It was not so hard, but she was sending a message. "You're bumping me," she explained.

I grinned. "It was an accident." I let my swing slow down, still circling but not touching hers. But now something new was troubling me: that pinch.

A pinch had always been a favorite weapon for the women I knew, my mother, my sister Elizabeth, girls in the Circle and at school. When I didn't move quickly enough to clear the table, Mom would take my ear between her thumb and forefinger to get me out of my chair. Elizabeth would kick, bite, and pinch in any fight with her older and bigger brothers. And in our wrestling contests Marcia had used a pinch on the back of the arm or in the side to draw the line I should not cross. But something I had read recently affected the meaning of this last pinch.

It would be nice if I could claim reading in school as the place for this new knowledge. Then that central, historical feature of democracy, public education, could be credited with one aspect of my continuing development. Or if those Westerns or detective novels I had squirreled away to read at Martin's Tires were broadening my horizon in this way, it might show that a free-enterprise entertainment industry was having a conscious effect on the world's future. But I was learning about adult behavior this time from an underground source unrecognized by most adults.

Billy Rhodes had made the discovery near the Cut, that half-mile channel dug in Piney Ridge through which trains moved east and west on the Missouri Pacific railroad tracks. There was always a lot of trash in the brush which covered the slopes of the Cut. Especially at the back of the Vacant Lot, where a bridge across the Cut had been projected by town planners but never built, kids in the Circle would find discarded cans and bottles, worn and dirty articles of dress, crumpled magazines and newspapers.

I didn't know if strangers used this spot to dump their junk, or if our own friends and neighbors secretly slipped over here to get rid of things they had not put in the garbage. Perhaps tramps and passing hoboes went through the town's waste, saving what they could use and dropping what they didn't want in this handy location on their way out of the area. Whatever the causes, exciting finds were always being made in this unkept edge to our neighborhood.

One of the most famous of such discoveries was the only work of pornography I was to able to scrutinize in detail before I went away to college: one copy of a pulp magazine entitled *Flames of Passion*. It is quite likely that this was part of Old Man Simpson's stock, having circulated in and out of his one-car garage many times before it was dropped or discarded here. *Flames* was what we would now call "soft porn," containing short stories built upon lengthy tease situations that culminated in furious bouts of sexual intercourse.

Sometimes these stories had suggestive black-and-white drawings, though the crucial areas to me were always darkly shadowed (almost, it occurs to me now, as if they had been done on a Magic Slate!).

A letter-to-the-editor section inspired unrealistic conclusions on my part about the size of most male genitalia and the number of nymphomaniacs in any small town. There were also a few feature articles about such things as nudist colonies. In accompanying photographs black boxes covered the eyes and private parts of overweight, gray figures. Despite its frayed and smudged condition, this single volume brought to the imagination of Circle boys a whole universe of characters and events that suggested daily life in Fairfield was a sadly uneventful affair.

A single tale from *Flames of Passion* created an unsettling context surrounding our current romance when Marcia pinched my arm that Saturday before the hayride. The specific story was entitled "Ransomed," and its "moral" (*Flames of Passion* did offer a philosophy of sorts) was that we should never deny the power of desire.

In "Ransomed" a successful American businessman is vacationing with his wife in a Middle Eastern country. At a crowded bazaar, Mrs. Whatever is snatched from her husband's side by a gang of masked men. Although Whatever throws himself heroically on the assailants, he is overwhelmed by numbers, falling with a blow to the head as his horrified wife looks on. Then she blacks out when the fiendish villains cover her face with a handkerchief soaked in chloroform.

When she recovers consciousness, Mrs. Whatever finds herself in the plush boudoir of an Oriental palace. Here she stays a prisoner for several months, provided with every luxury and petted by servants. There is only one awful feature to her captivity, twice weekly visits from a huge bearded man who forces himself upon her.

Naturally this proper American wife resists the giant, but her slim frame and pampered flesh are no match for his great strength. His technique is diabolic and efficient: forcing her down on her back, he places a pillow over her face until she almost blacks out. When she can breathe again, he begins to have sex. If she resumes her struggles at that point, he smothers her again. Only when she gives up resistance and lets him have his way does he stop the suffocation.

There is one other strange feature in the assailant's bedroom behavior: the first step in his attack is always a pinch on his victim's left breast. More precisely, squeezing her nipple between his forefinger and thumb, he twists it one half-turn counterclockwise, then a half-turn clockwise.

He does this so methodically and consistently that, according to the story, eventually she gives in to this control. At the moment she feels his fingers on her breast, her breathing accelerates, her hips begin to heave, and desire races through her body like a wildfire. After a few months the pillow is no longer necessary.

You can probably guess the end of the story. Now broken in will and spirit, the abducted woman receives new freedoms. She discovers she is a member of a harem, over a dozen women, mostly dark-skinned, owned by an Arabian prince. And she has the privileges of the most recently obtained wife.

She is given a new name and taught to sing ancient folks songs set to a stringed instrument with a mellow, mournful sound. Wearing a veil and traditional Arab dress, she is eventually allowed to go shopping at the village market, accompanied by a single servant. Although she has only faint memories of her earlier life and little hope of rescue, her personality is not totally destroyed.

When, one day at the market, a strangely familiar white man speaks to her in English, she freezes in front of the fruit stand. Calling out the name of her husband, she begins to fall toward the ground. With a bound he is at her side. A single blow fells the servant; a car appears magically from a side street; and they race away across the desert clinging to each other. She is rescued.

Only later that night, when she is safe at an American hotel in a nearby large city, does Mrs. Whatever come to the full truth.

Despite the strain of long captivity and the excitement of sudden rescue, she believes she has recovered her former identity. After a soothing hot bath she dresses once again in European clothes and enjoys a fabulous meal with her husband at the hotel's chic restaurant. Back in their room she welcomes his embrace with a warmth uncharacteristic of her behavior before the ordeal. She does not resist his passionate kisses nor his hand slipping purposefully beneath her blouse. But understanding flashes through her mind as powerfully as desire rips into her body when he takes the nipple of her left breast, turns it once counter-clockwise, once clockwise.

VIII

Because our two Westlook Park swings were still moving when Marcia reached over to pinch me, her fingers caught me on the chest, almost exactly at the spot identified by the story. I did not conclude, of course, that Marcia Terrell had learned some tricks from *Flames of Passion*. What did occur to me was that perhaps I, like the wife in the story, had been suppressing my desire too long.

Had Mrs. Whatever been responding appropriately to her husband throughout their marriage, said the story to me, his complex scheme of fake abduction, prolonged captivity, and staged rescue would not have been necessary. Wouldn't I be avoiding a similar fate by releasing the passion I had been channeling into playground activities and basketball games? Wasn't a night hayride on the Roper farm the occasion to get down to the real business of physical intimacy?

Even if Marcia had not read "Ransomed" (and surely she hadn't!), wasn't her aggressive pinch a sign to me that I was not moving fast enough, that our relationship had matured to the point where leaning, pressing, kneading were inadequate to the fulfillment of our desire?

The site for the Third Annual Spring Hayride sponsored by the Fairfield Youth Fellowship (FYF) was, in fact, a favorable one for the kind of advanced necking I now had in mind. As soon as we stepped off the church bus into the open space between the Roper house and the large barn where they stored their farm equipment, I felt that this was the opportunity I had been seeking for some time—perhaps, now that I think about it, since, at the beginning of the Great Expedition, I had seen Mrs. Van Meer watering flowers in her front yard.

The Ropers' land was mostly open meadow, broken by tall poplar windbreaks and low, hedged fence rows. Two-lane cart tracks crisscrossed the lush fields, rising from creeks dry except during rain and cresting on small hills which provided scenic views of rolling Phipps

County countryside. As I gazed at this picturesque scene, I felt I had found the romantic background necessary to overcome any feminine reserve.

Although I didn't know it at the time, this farm's romantic appeal derived from the fact that it was more a model than a working farm. Mr. Roper, like a number of other small landowners in these years, had found it was more profitable to leave ground fallow than to plant, tend, and market a crop. According to my parents at any rate, government subsidies paid the Ropers for keeping land out of cultivation.

Taking advantage of special tax laws and commerce regulations, Fred Roper was busy not planting corn or raising hogs, not buying feed and spreading fertilizer, not seeding or using pesticides, not harvesting and shipping a product. Agricultural research companies, families living in the country but working in town, and the first agribusiness conglomerates were all making money off a system most citizens in the same communities knew little or nothing about.

This network of support gave Mr. Roper time to mow grass, repair fences, and clear lanes on his hundred acres, after he had put in eight hours every weekday supervising the grounds crew at South-Central Missouri State College. For all I know, he had his barn painted bright red, the pond stocked with perch, and his one stand of mostly oak trees thinned at government expense. Over the years the Ropers' farm became so well manicured it began to resemble a theme park.

I knew most of the kids milling around the well landscaped sideyard of the Ropers' house that spring evening because, like Jimmy Donaldson and Donna Easley, they were from my grade. Although we differed in size (some still had their growing to do while others had gotten that adolescent spurt), we looked very similar. The boys had short hair, and most of the girls' was at shoulder length and turned up. Our dress was nearly uniform: the girls in short skirts and sweaters; the boys with khaki slacks and plaid dress shirts, the short sleeves rolled up one thin turn.

There was one invisible dividing line at work here, though, separating this group from others in their class: those old enough to drive had split off from those not yet sixteen. Boys with birthdays late in their sophomore year or in the first months of their junior year could now pick up girls, go to the movies, and then stop by the drive-in for something to eat on their own. To go out on an official date at my age I had to accept rides from parents or attend organized, chaperoned events like this hayride.

There were two wagons on the hayride—flatbed affairs, perhaps eight feet wide and about twice as long—pulled by a pair of Missouri mules appropriate to Ropers' typical-farm effect. The tongue of the second was yoked to a hitch on the back of the first, making the wagons like cars in a train. Hay bales covered the floors, stacked highest (perhaps up to five feet) in the middle.

I was angry at first that Marcia and I ended up on the front of the lead wagon, thinking our position there too conspicuous. But most riders ended up looking (when they were looking at all) out to the sides or back at farmland unrolling behind them. Leaning against a wall of hay bales, Marcia and I had far more privacy than I at first had anticipated.

Too, the focus of attention for the younger set and first-time hay riders was the beautiful couple of Linda Roper and Martin Pruitt. Since she had offered the family farm to the Fairfield Youth Fellowship, she felt a duty to participate in this event, though both she and Martin could drive.

Letting all the others get on first, she and her "steady" sat high up in the front of the back wagon, a central location. Many times throughout our ride I saw their graceful forms outlined by moonlight against the sky. In my opinion, of course, Linda was only attending for show since, whenever she and her beau really wanted to be romantic, they always had their "backseat."

"Comfortable?" I asked Marcia once the ride had started.

"Um-hmm." She snuggled up against me, allowing my arm to come around her shoulder. The wagons began a gentle descent from the barn area toward a grove of trees across the creek bed. Linda's father, wearing overalls and a broad brimmed, cone-shaped straw hat, was our mule driver.

"Do you suppose they're a couple?" I asked Marcia, pointing to the two animals before us.

"They are carrying the yoke," she said with a giggle. She didn't seem to mind my getting close.

I squeezed her shoulder, trying to encourage her to turn toward me. I was ready to try for a first kiss when we entered the stand of trees down by the creek.

"What do you think their reward is for pulling us on this hayride?" This was my feeble attempt to be risque, to match the topic of conversation with my intent.

Marcia shifted her body, turning her face up at me with a smile. "Doing what comes naturally?"

She seemed ready, so I leaned over and planted a light kiss on that lower lip she caught with her teeth when she was worried.

She returned my gentle kiss. But then she asked, quite illogically, I thought, "Did you hear the one about Betty and Johnny out on a date?"

"Uh . . . um . . . no," I conceded. Of course, I knew the "date joke," but this genre was generally the province of boys. Girls, especially girls I knew like Marcia, did not hear or tell this kind of story.

"Well," she continued softly in my ear. "Johnny picked Betty up to go to a show."

"Um-hm." I brought one hand from Marcia's waist up and forward beneath her sweatshirt.

Marcia pushed her body closer to mine but continued to whisper. "Then he turned down Lovers' Lane and parked. Betty looked at him and said, 'Hey, this isn't the movies!'"

I learned later that the other hayride couples were as active as we were. Jimmy would not give particulars, but this date with Donna Easley began what I viewed as a torrid romance lasting nearly a year.

Marcia pulled away from our kiss, looked at me and said: "Then Johnny answered, pointing to other couples in other cars, 'They're not movie stars either.'"

Of course, some couples sat too close to the official chaperons, a minister on each of the wagons. His cough or a word of conversation interrupted their embraces. But up at the front, Marcia and I were close only to other couples wrapped in each other's arms. We must have seemed to them, as they to us, single shadows shifting with the wagon's bumpy ride.

But I was getting distracted by Marcia's continuing joke. "'Want some Coke,' Johnny asked Betty. He had a little flask. 'It's even a cherry coke,' he claimed."

Impatiently, I closed for another kiss. "Come 'ere," I said gruffly, and rather stupidly since she was "'ere."

All these hay riders had agreed upon petting limits, of course, things that in ordinary circumstances could or could not be attempted. I had never touched or been touched below the belt; clothes were never removed; and we had always been vertical. The exciting part was now that these same limits were under special assault; and no one knew what might be achieved or conceded.

Marcia wouldn't give up her joke, though. "Then Betty said, 'Hey, that's not Coca-Cola!'"

The wagons rolled out from under the branches of the creekside oak trees, moonlight spilling across the fields. Above us floated Linda and Martin, the ideal lovers. They were not kissing, however, but rode side by side, his right hand closed over her left, resting on one knee.

This time Marcia pulled me to her, whispering, "And Johnny answered, 'That's not cherry in there either!'"

Tired of her talk, I pushed her gently down on the wagon bed. She did not resist. One of her slim arms went around my neck. I put a hand on her knee and then slowly slid it up.

Still, Marcia whispered, almost fiercely: "Then Johnny said, 'Can I put my finger in your bellybutton?'"

I started to draw back at that, but she held me close. My hand had reached point I never thought it would.

"'Hey, that's not my bellybutton!'"

"'That's not my finger either.'"

And then we rolled off the wagon.

IX

Here is what had happened: one of Mr. Roper's mules, in a moment characteristic of that animal, decided that the last step he had taken was the last he ever wanted to take. This recalcitrant creature stopped dead in his tracks at the top of the little rise on the other side of the creek we had just crossed.

Our other mule, asserting an analogous stubbornness, not only kept walking at this point but leaned into the yoke and harness with new intensity. These contrary motions applied torque to the front wagon's shaft, which was then conveyed by whip action back to the second. And the little train was first jolted back, then yanked forward, and finally brought to a shaking halt.

While our Missouri mules had come to the top of this small hill, the wagons behind were still at two different lower levels. The first was above a small crest in the middle of the hill's slope, the second coming off that hump. Thus, when the mules rocked up and back, the hitched wagons behind them swayed to opposite sides of the path and then converged into the hill's trough, buckling up the train carrying two dozen members of the Fairfield Youth Fellowship in varying degrees of passionate embrace.

The saving grace in this accident, as far as I was concerned, was that Marcia and I were not the only pair of lovers thrown from the hay onto the ground. Nearly half the party ended up either off the wagon or sufficiently bounced about among the hay bales that, though no one was hurt and all of us were laughing at our own embarrassment, the whole ride had to be reorganized.

Flashlights appeared out of nowhere (Mr. Roper apparently had them in the giant pockets of his pressed overalls). And an inspection for injuries by the hayride's organizers (including Linda and Martin) revealed too clearly that our activities had not been limited to viewing the scenery. Shirts that should have been tucked in were pulled out or had suffered strange dislocations. Carefully applied lipstick and layered make-up now sported blurred edges and a smudged quality. And hair once perfectly in place stood oddly on end, pulled loose from ribbons and clips. So when we were all loaded onto the wagons once more, and the mules were convinced to work in concert again, Marcia and I found ourselves almost in the lap of the lead wagon's minister chaperon. My exploration in the land of desire was over for this night.

Oh, the hayride was still fun, as Marcia and I rode nestled together. And there were songs to sing, stars to wish upon, something actually approaching youthful fellowship overcoming shyness and disappointment. But later, while my Dad was idling our car in front of the Terrell house on the Circle's Oak Street after driving us home, I had to leave Marcia with only a promise to take her out again soon, probably the very next Saturday.

"I had a great time," claimed Marcia, standing under her porch light.

"Me too. You're not hurt or anything?"

She laughed. "You're the one who's been rubbing his elbow."

"Well, it's sore from throwing papers. So . . . um . . . can we, uh, go somewhere again, maybe next weekend?"

"Another hayride?"

"No, I don't think there is one. But maybe we could see the movie."

"I'll have to ask. But I'd like to." She was chewing her lower lip. The way she looked at me, I was sure it would be all right to kiss her again. But there sat my father in his car, waiting.

"OK. I'll see what's on at the Uptowne. And talk to you later."

For a moment I thought I would give her a good night kiss after all. But I couldn't seem to make myself lean forward to do it. Then, recalling similar moments of uncertainty in my past, I wondered if I could shake hands instead? Make a bow? Salute? Finally I just turned, stumbled down the stoop, waved, and ran out to the car.

I did not see Marcia during the next week, even at the office of the *Fairfield Mirror*, where we both picked up papers for our routes. I knew she was coming to school and following her regular delivery route through the neighborhood, but our schedules were out of phase. I finally had to call her on the telephone.

She said she couldn't go out but would meet me in Westlook Park at dusk Saturday. Dusk sounded like a good time for me, so I didn't argue for more. After our hayride I had gotten my Magic Slate out again. And, recalling what Marcia and I had done on a wagon, as well as what I thought I had seen around me, I had some new ideas about what could be done on a merry-go-round.

I was determined to pave the way of my evil intentions, however, by bringing another gift to that someone I was ready now to offer a more binding relationship: we should become officially boy and girlfriend, I concluded.

All girls wanted to go steady, I had been told. And with such formal ties in place, I concluded, certain pleasures were more likely to follow. Of course, I had to do this right—that is, find something appropriate to offer her. That task would be the goal of my lunch hour on Saturday, the one break in my day at Martin's Tires. On my way out of the garage on this mission (flowers? candy? jewelry?), I gained a new understanding of the book distribution business run by Big Joe.

Joe Martin was not in the book trade for profit, at least not cash profit. (Of course, I had known from the beginning that he had not accepted this delivery operation in order to educate the masses!) He had taken on the job to make new contacts for his tire business, especially in more remote areas of the county. I began to figure this out after overhearing a brief conversation between Big and Little Joe on the sidewalk in front of the store.

"Just get names and acreage for now," said Big Joe.

"Not equipment?" asked his son.

"That will follow"

"OK. We still don't show much gain on the paperbacks."

"Fine, fine. I never hoped to do more than break even."

"Volume's never gone up. I mainly move them around on the shelves."

"That's great. Just keep showing up at each shop. We're in this for the tires, like always."

When I went over this odd conversation with my father and brother later that afternoon, we put together a rationale to explain why this tire company had expanded into the book trade.

Martin's reputation for quality products and reliable service had already won him the lion's share of the automobile tire market in town, but rural car owners did not routinely come to him. His business had succeeded in town because of the personal touch he developed through established church, social, and business connections. The countryside needed another kind of organization, and becoming a paperback book wholesaler turned out to be an effective strategy to canvas this new territory.

By sending his son and other employees out to little rural stores and back country filling stations, Martin built a network of associations in a new class of clientele. The books were entirely incidental. He could have been selling ice cream or vacuum cleaners.

What mattered to the business was the time Little Joe spent chatting with store owners and lingering customers while he plucked books from racks, added new titles, and straightened his display. Throughout he was massaging a new group of potential purchasers. The Martin's tire company trucks even served this ulterior purpose on their supply runs: the painted panels were effective advertisement.

While the automobile tire was the initial product for sale, Big Joe was also getting ready to add another important line: farm equipment tires. As agriculture evolved in those years away from small, one-family farms, the equipment for running larger operations inspired the development of bigger, sturdier, lightweight tires. And Big Joe, attending tire distributors' conventions as far away as Denver, had foreseen the need for change. He contracted with the right manufacturers to have what Phipps County farmers wanted before they knew it themselves.

As good as Big Joe and son were in capturing a great part of this expanding rural market (while not losing any ground to competitors in town), he did later miss out on a major industry advance: the radial tire. A chief competitor, the Firestone dealer, was the first to see the attraction of this new design.

Envisioning greater speed and longer trips brought about by the expanding interstate highway system, he discontinued earlier models and gambled on the new tire. By the time two-lane and winding Route 66 was replaced all across Phipps County by four-lane, limited-access Interstate 44, the highest percentage of cars speeding past Fairfield and using our streets featured radial tires, many of them coming from the local Firestone dealer.

While these men had successful strategies for their business interests, I, still a boy, found myself a little unsure about how to proceed with Marcia. I felt that bringing the right thing to her this evening was the key to success, but I couldn't seem to come up with anything as good as the framed town map I'd given her months before.

What I would have liked to do was visit Brents' Store on Main Street. They had such a variety of odd things there that I was sure I would have found the perfect gift. And the two older women who ran the store were always ready to help their paperboy. They would have hummed and chirped sympathetically about young men growing up and making their first calls upon young ladies. And that would have inspired sentimental recollections about the old days when Henri Brent came from St. Genevieve to court Jacqueline Delacroix. But the grandmotherly Brent sisters were gone by then and the store converted to a drive-in bank. I would have to do this shopping on my own.

I had thought Dixon's might be the place to look, especially since I was already there to eat (another microwave hamburger, I'm sure). But while a lot of their stock seemed to belong to the world of romance, nothing suited my idea of Marcia. Cosmetics, decorative candles, inexpensive earrings and bracelets, even boxes of candy I could afford were perfectly appropriate. Yet when I imagined each one presented to the girl I had grown up with on the Circle, it didn't seem right. In the end I found what I wanted at, of all places, the hardware store.

X

The merry-go-round at Westlook Park, where I was to meet Marcia that night, was simple but functional, a wheel perhaps ten feet in diameter mounted horizontally on a sturdy metal post so that it could spin above a sandy pit. An enthusiastic child rider would kneel on one knee, the other foot kicking off in the sand to keep the wheel in motion. Eight spokes reached from the center to the circumference of the merry-go-round, an octagonal wooden bench on which riders sat. There was also a backrest on the inside of the riders' bench, perhaps two feet high, though the centrifical force of the merry-go-round in motion made those boards more something to hold onto than lean against.

What I had in mind this Saturday evening was not a spinning merry-go-round but a stopped one. The riders, however, might be in motion. Two teenage romantics could, I thought, stretch out on one section of its circular rim as easily as on a wagon bed. The merry-go-round might also rock up and down on its base a bit, but this motion was seen as complimentary not contradictory to my intentions.

On the way to the park with this plan in mind, I began to think of myself as having arrived at last in a new country. I was no longer an innocent young boy shaped by his environment and directed by others. With new stature and will, I was asserting my own demands on the universe. I would have what I wanted. And what I wanted was Marcia Terrell.

That very Marcia was waiting for me by the larger of Westlook Park's two slides. I think I had been a little delayed by the conversation I'd had with my family about Martin's tire business. And Marcia had been held up herself leaving home, but I was to learn why only later in the evening.

"Here," I said, holding out the gift I had finally selected. "Something for you."

Marcia seemed surprised, and impressed.

"For me? You got this for me?" She held up in her hands the orange hoop of a basketball goal.

I had not been able to afford the entire set of steel post, wooden backboard, rim and net; but I think I pleased her with the idea of a gift. She looked at me now, framed in the circle of metal.

"Sure. The park's goal," I gestured toward the court, "is not regulation. You need to get your dad to build you one in the driveway. Put this goal up on the garage. And, so, this is a start."

"I've been thinking about it," she admitted, turning the hoop in her hands. "I like basketball."

"Well, I like you," I blurted out, my first effort to put something of purpose into words.

Marcia gave me a funny little smile. She was embarrassed, I assumed, perhaps a bit intimidated. "Oh," she said, chewing her lower lip and leaning back against the side of the slide's ladder.

"Let me see what it would look like," I offered, suddenly inspired. I pointed to the top of the ladder, which might have been close to ten feet high, the standard for a basketball goal.

Marcia turned and looked up. "OK. But I don't have my ball."

"That's OK, that's OK."

I stepped around her and took the steps two at a time. Sitting on the top, I held the hoop out in both hands. "Try an imaginary ball."

She made a two-handed shooting motion, but she seemed to be forcing herself to be enthusiastic. I called out "Two points!" She turned and stood looking across Ridgeview toward the Circle's houses.

"You don't like it?" I called.

"It's fine. It's good," she said, but she didn't turn around to face me.

I climbed down, resting the hoop against the slide's base. I walked over to her and, in my second bold move of the evening, wrapped my arms around her from behind. I was thrilled to find that she leaned back into me. I smelled her clean hair, and my body, pressed against her, grew taut with anticipation.

It was a beautiful, moonlit night, by the way; so, even though dusk had nearly passed, everything was still lit up for romance. A warm breeze drifted out of the woods surrounding Springers' Pond. In the middle distance cars thrummed down old business Route 66 out of town and into the countryside. We could hear from the other direction reassuring sounds of mothers calling their younger children in for the night. "Hey," I whispered. She turned and we kissed.

We kissed for a quite a while, I would say, leaning and swaying together. "I'm doing it," I thought to myself proudly. "Lips to lips. A boy with two jobs is wooing the pretty girl in his neighborhood. He brings a gift and then smothers her with kisses. Not bad, not bad."

Finally, in one of our pauses for breath, I put an arm around Marcia's waist and ushered her toward the moonlit merry-go-round. My heart raced.

I don't know which of us wanted more to be horizontal, but we were immediately stretched out on our sides down one section of the seat as if it had been made for this purpose. Since we were about the same size, we were fitted up against each other as well: mouth to mouth, belly to belly, toe to toe, this to that.

And let me tell you, we went to work on that playground ride, kissing and gasping, holding and reaching, pulling and straining, pushing and pushing back.

Would I get some clothes off, I wondered, or could I reach beneath them? That had always been a problem for my imagination of sex, the covers we all wore in public. I wanted to get down to the real stuff, even if I wasn't at all sure how far I would go once I got there.

Following a path charted on my Magic Slate, I had a hand beneath her sweatshirt for a time, then squeezed between us where I had reached on the night of the hayride. Marcia went beyond her limits as well, pulling shirt and undershirt out of my pants and digging one hand down into my belly.

I was more excited than I had ever been. And she was positively shaking, wriggling and squeaking, pushing me up against the back of the bench. All of a sudden she froze, and I could see her eyes go wide in a kind of wonder under the moon.

"You OK?" I whispered, a little nervous, my head pulled back.

"Oh? Oh?" It was as if her eyes were not in focus. Then they snapped back.

"I have . . . I have to . . . have to go. I have to go. We can't do this." Even as she spoke, though, she was holding me, pressing against me, shivering.

"What?"

I was still riding a wave of desire whose crest I did not know (remember my failure to anticipate the full nature of climax, despite my father's effort to explain it). We can't do this?

Then someone called out from several houses away, "Marcia. Marcia." Instinctively, I tried to block out the sound. Marcia, startled, clutched me where my desire was fullest.

I would like to think Marcia's own need directed that sudden grab, but I think a kind of fear or panic or confusion was involved as well. Still, she grabbed me, squeezed, and moaned. "I have got to go."

Later I would know why she had to go, that her mother, always fearful of the world outside her home, had been pulling her one child back toward the nest. The hayride would turn out to have been her last date for some time. Our casual meetings in the future, unlike those of the luckier Jimmy Donaldson and Donna Easley, would have to be stolen from beneath Mrs. Terrell's nervous watching. In the next weeks Marcia would even give up the paper route she had handled so well that the *Mirror* was expanding it to include new streets off Ridgeview.

I suppose I should admit that a middleclass, middle-American morality of fear related to Mrs. Terrell's anxiety lay in the background of my own thoughts when Marcia and I first lay down on the merry-go-round. The closest I felt to guilt for what I was doing, however, was to be confronted for a moment with a recollection of Linda Roper and Martin Pruitt as they had been silhouetted against the night sky of the hayride.

I felt that these idyllic lovers never gave in to such frantic passion as drove the writhing couples in the hay or Marcia and me on the merry-go-round; so I must have been pursuing the wrong impulses.

Once again, of course, I was wide of the mark, for Linda surely felt the same shakings as Marcia: she became pregnant the next summer. The Pruitt and Roperfamilies did a remarkable job of keeping it all quiet. And the couple never did marry, or at least they didn't marry each other. The last I heard, they were living comfortable lives with small families, he a doctor in Oklahoma, she a retired Michigan school teacher home with her young children. But all this wisdom was to come to me long after Marcia and I lay shuddering on the merry-go-round bench.

When her mother's voice startled Marcia out of her trance and into holding me, I felt something I had not known about take possession of me: a pounding explosion that suddenly added one more key event to my understanding of the process my father had described for me in his second birds-and-the-bees talk.

"Oh, ho!," I would think later when it was all over; "Ah, ha!"

Before it was over, however, I seemed to be trying to break free of Marcia's grasp, my hips banging into the backrest behind me. But she, apparently quite interested in what was happening, did not let go of me. And, if I had looked puzzlingly at Marcia a few moments earlier, she now saw enough in my face, an open book, to inspire a response: she laughed.

She held on to me; she looked down; she looked up; and she whooped.

I wasn't exactly sure how I was supposed to feel about all this, so I laughed too, adding to my body's shaking bits and pieces of giggle, little shouts of surprise, gasps of relief, hisses of wonder, and a tiny little gulp of worry: "Who! Ha! Foo! Swp! Ho!"

"Hee! Whoa! Ssst! Hmm!" sang Marcia back to me. We were having a great time. Maybe it was the greatest time.

It wouldn't be so easy to have great times in the months ahead, as both our own understanding of what was happening and our parents' concern complicated such easy, first-time pursuit of passion. But we seemed to know that, in wrapping ourselves together on the edge of the Circle, we had moved into a new field of experience.

This land was not fully charted, it contained dangers and rewards we could not anticipate, and lots of other people would have plans for how we should travel in it. But each of us had found this new territory, and the knowledge was exhilarating to both of us. I was out of the Circle at last, beyond the limits of innocence if not fully arrived at understanding. I was older, bigger, wiser, and more ready. And the road before me was open.

Epilogue: Direction

A train from New Jersey to Missouri one summer of my growing up has provided yet another landmark in my childhood. The Landon family was returning from a visit with the maternal grandmother near Paterson. When the westbound train made its way around the famous "Horseshoe Curve" in Pennsylvania, I recognized the end of one phase and the beginning of another.

In order to go east or west across a deep valley in the Alleghenies, trains have to take at one point a giant U-turn along the sides of mountains. With a long train, like the one we were riding that August, you can look out a window and see the other end, engine or caboose, snaking along in front of or behind you.

And if, as happened to us on this particular journey, another train is coming from the opposite direction, you might look out across a great reach of space and see a train apparently running parallel to you but actually headed toward the cities you had left. It would be going into the horseshoe at the other end of the "U." As we rode west on *The Pioneer*, then, we saw moving in the same direction on the other rim of the valley our double, The *Martha Washington*, whose destination was the East Coast.

"Look at this," said my father, pointing out the window of the dining car as we were having lunch. "An east-bound train that looks as if it's following us." And then he explained the phenomenon.

"Aren't we going home?" asked Beth, who hadn't taken all this in.

"Oh, yes," said Mom. "Let me draw you a picture." She took one of the postcards she had bought on the train and, with a pencil, drew a little map to show the horseshoe curve. Arrows represented the two trains.

"That's the same as us," said Beth after a minute.

"What do you mean?" I asked.

"We're going this way," she said, showing where the arrow of the train pointed. Then she added, "And Mom and Dad are going that way." She drew another arrow next to the train, directed backwards. After another pause, we figured it out: sitting in the dining car's booth, the children were facing forward; our parents were looking toward the rear of the train.

Even Charles embarked on an explanation of this situation, that we were not necessarily traveling where we were looking, as you do in a car. But eventually we realized Beth had made a joke. We all laughed with her then. And we made jokes about where we were going throughout the rest of the trip.

And, as I've said, I felt I understood then where I was going in my life: back to the Midwest, where I would live out the rest of my childhood. During this vacation I had taken in my parents' satisfaction at the life they had created there, their own opportunities and those of their children.

This sense of being settled deepened on the train ride home because the Landon family stepped up to more satisfactory accommodations. Unhappy with the crowding we had endured coming east in a single sleeping compartment, my father booked additional space on the return trip, an upper and lower berth for my brother and me. Now Mom and Dad had the lower bunk in the bedroom compartment, with Beth sleeping on the fold-down upper bunk. Charles and I were in the next car forward, me in a top berth, Charles below.

This meant hopping over metal platforms between cars, an act I have always felt queasy performing. The rush of air from the doors and the harsh sound of wheels spinning and linkage straining inspire the thought that, should that metal plate you're standing on give way, you would drop beneath the cars and be instantly cut in two.

Our extra sleeping space took the general tension out of our traveling, though. And we enjoyed the train and each other all the way to St. Louis. In a certain sense, then, the Landons, on the way back home aboard *The Pioneer* felt that they had already arrived.

In another sense, of course, none of us ever arrives at a stationary place in life's journey. We are always moving; and the world around us changes constantly.

I should admit here, for instance, that on the Texas-bound *Desert Wind* out of St. Louis I must have ridden past a lost landmark of my childhood without recognizing it. And had I realized more fully where I was at that moment, I would have had a different understanding of myself and my world.

Out the train window west of St. Louis, I might have seen, had I looked in the right direction at the appropriate moment, those large openings in the limestone cliffs I had once assumed were carved by a river, perhaps the Meramec on its way to the Mississippi. (Of course, those openings turned out to be man-made, not natural: a gravel company was dynamiting rock out of the hills.)

If I had been alert, I might have corrected several misapprehensions about the nature of my universe half a dozen years earlier than I did. I had thought, remember, that these huge caves were near Jefferson City and that I saw them whenever we rode from Fairfield to visit my father's parents in the state capitol.

Although the path of our great highway, Route 66, had been moved several miles north of these bluffs since I had last crossed the Chain of Rocks Bridge on the way to New Jersey, the Missouri Pacific tracks still lay next to the old two-lane road, both parallel to the Ozark riverbed and running right along the foot of the limestone cliffs

I must have been involved with other things when the train rolled down the old trail to the West, perhaps talking sports with my dad or playing cards with my mother. It could even have been nighttime, too dark outside for me to see if I had been looking.

Apparently, I was destined to recover this element in my sense of place a few years later, when another mission (working for the state geological survey) carried me into this territory. We all endure such confusions along the pathways of our lives. And I still believe we should be grateful when any misplaced piece of our story is recovered, however belatedly.

Most of us have a hard enough time dealing with things that we see change over time right in front of us. Such elusive phenomena as images that slip loose from their moorings in memory are probably best left to travel wherever they will.

Returning to Fairfield and the Circle on this very trip, I had immediately to come to terms with a significant alteration in my old neighborhood. At the top of our hill, where Limestone ended as a paved road, the town had created a new street and a municipal park. This was the Westlook Park whose many facilities I would later use with Marcia Terrell for purposes town officials had not foreseen.

The thing about this park that struck me immediately, however, was the fact that, with its creation, the very location of my childhood had been revised.

You might think all of us kids welcomed this park, an official place to play. The town had put in the swing set, see-saws, slide, and basketball court. It's true that we made use of all these new facilities, but in clearing five acres of woods for this park, the town had opened up a view west that reached toward the Gasconade.

"Geez, that's our view," complained Dennis Baker when he and his brother Archie took me up to see what had happened the day after I got home from our trip. "We invented it."

"I bet that's the Open Space, over there," added Marcia Terrell, who had come with us. She pointed toward a distant north-south ridge on the other side of which might have been our special discovery.

It wasn't, of course, the complete view we enjoyed from our spot well beyond Springers' Pond, beyond where the High and Low Trails came back together. The prospect from beside Ridgeview Road was narrowed by intervening hills. And even this view would not be available at all times, as trees at the far end of the park sometimes grew to restrict that line of sight.

"I'm still traveling out there one day," observed Marcia, who has picked up some ideas from Cathy Williams, our neighborhood beauty, over the summer. I thought they were an unlikely pair, Marcia the tomboy and Cathy the future movie star, but they were developing common interests of which I was unaware.

"Roger's there now," observed Archie, who was pleased his chief rival was on vacation. It moved him up the Circle hierarchy. Roger Peterson was with his uncle in the Navy stationed at San Diego, on a visit that would inspire his decision to enlist after high school. Then he traveled even farther west, all the way to Vietnam, as did many others in my generation.

"How did you like the big city," Marcia asked me, as we turned away from the park and started walking back into the Circle proper. She didn't know that my grandmother's house was really in the country.

"I think I like it here better. There, it's crowded." I was thinking of big city traffic circles and places like St. Louis's Union Station.

"You didn't meet anyone you liked?" How was I to know she was thinking already in romantic terms? We passed the lane going down to the Springers' house.

"I had fun swimming with some guys."

"It's been pretty dull while you've been gone."

"It's too hot in August," I admitted. We were passing Mrs. Van Meer's house, but this time she was not out watering her flowers.

"We haven't even been playing Kick the Can."

"Let's play tonight."

"OK. Billy probably will." I hadn't seen him yet. There was another prospect of my return to the Midwest, teaming up with the guy who would do anything. I knew we wouldn't start another business together, but I did have some stories to tell about my travels.

So we did play Kick the Can that night, if I remember correctly, continuing a fine Circle tradition. I will leave us now in a hazy twilight spreading out to our individual hiding spots away from the base as I conclude this portion of our story of growing up in the Midwest of the 1950s. It's a good time to rest, I think, with events ongoing but repeating key patterns. Perhaps at another time I will bring these characters together again and trace their adventures through another cycle. Until then, gentle reader, fare thee well.

Books from Science & Humanities Press:

◆ **HOW TO TRAVEL**—A Guidebook for Persons with a Disability – Fred Rosen (1997) ISBN 1-888725-05-2, 5½ X 8½, 120 pp., $9.95 **18 point large print edition** (1998) ISBN 1-888725-17-6 8½X11, 120 pp. $19.95

◆ **HOW TO TRAVEL in Canada**—A Guidebook for A Visitor with a Disability – Fred Rosen (2000) ISBN 1-888725-26-5, 5½ X 8½, 180 pp., $14.95 **MacroPrintBook**™ edition (2000) ISBN 1-888725-30-3 8½X11, 180 pp. $24.95

◆ **AVOIDING Attendants from HELL: A Practical Guide to Finding, Hiring & Keeping Personal Care Attendants**—June Price, (1998), ISBN 1-888725-18-4 (accessible plastic spiral bind), 8½ X 11, 110 pp., $16.95, ISBN 1-888725-19-2 (Trade Paperback) 8½ X 11, 110 pp, $16.95

◆ **If Blindness Comes** – K. Jernigan, Ed. (1996) 18 point Large type Edition with accessible plastic spiral bind, 8½ X 11, 110 pp. Strategies for living with visual impairment. $7 (distributed at cost with permission of the National Federation of the Blind)

◆ **Paul the Peddler or The Fortunes of a Young Street Merchant**—Horatio Alger, jr (1998 MacroPrintBook™ reprint in 24-point type) ISBN 1-888725-02-8, 8½ X 11, 276 pp, A Classic reprinted in accessible large type-a great gift! $16.95

◆ **The Wisdom of Father Brown**—G.K. Chesterton (2000) A MacroPrintBook™ reprint in 24-point type ISBN 1-888725-27-3, 8½ X 11, 276 pp, A Classic collection of detective stories reprinted in accessible large type-a great gift! $18.95

◆ **24-point Gospel—The Big News for Today**—The Gospel according to Matthew, Mark, Luke & John (KJV) in 24 point type – ISBN 1-888725-11-7. Type is about 1/3 inch high. Now, people with visual disabilities like macular degeneration can still use this important reference. "Giant print" books are usually 18 pt. or less . 8½ X 11, 512 pp. paperback $38.95

◆ **Nursing Home** – Ira Eaton, PhD, (1997) ISBN 1-888725-01-X, 5½ X 8½, 300 pp., You will be moved and disturbed by this novel. $12.95 **MacroPrintBooks edition** (1999) ISBN 1-888725-23-0,8½ X 11, 330 pp. paper $18.95

◆ **Behind the Desk Workout** – Joan Guccione, OTR/C, CHT (1997) ISBN 1-888725-00-1, 8½ X 11, 120 pp, Reduce risk of injury. Over 200 photos and illustrations $34.95

◆ **Sexually Transmitted Diseases—A Practical Guide** – Assembled and Edited by R.J.Banis, PhD, (1997) ISBN 1-888725-06-0, 5½ X 8½, Illustrated, 150 pp. $16.95

◆ **Copyright Issues for Librarians, Teachers & Authors**–R.J. Banis, PhD, (Ed). (1998) ISBN 1-888725-21-4, 5½ X 8½, 60 pp. booklet. Information condensed from the Library of Congress, copyright registration forms. $4.95 postpaid

◆ **Inaugural Addresses: Presidents of the United States from George Washington to 2004** – Robert J. Banis, PhD, CMA, Ed. (1998) ISBN 1-888725-07-9, 5½ X 8½, 260 pp., extensively illustrated, includes election statistics, Vice-presidents, principal opponents, coupons for update supplements for the upcoming elections $16.95

◆ **Financial Planning for Common Folk** Finding Financial Happiness – Wayne Kuppler (1997) ISBN 1-888725-04-4 8½ X 11, 140 pp., workbook $49.95

◆ *The Essential* **Simply Speaking Gold** – Susan Fulton, (May, 1998), ISBN 1-888725-08-7, 8½ X8, 124 pp., How to use IBM's popular speech recognition package for dictation rather than keyboarding. Dozens of screen shots and illustrations. $18.95

◆ **Begin Dictation** *Using ViaVoice Gold* **-2nd Edition**– Susan Fulton, (1999), ISBN 1-888725-22-2, 8½ X8, 260 pp., Now covers ViaVoice 98 and other versions of IBM's popular continuous speech recognition package for dictation rather than keyboarding. Over a hundred screen shots and illustrations. $28.95

◆ **The Bridge Never Crossed—A Survivor's Search for Meaning**. Captain George A. Burk (1999) ISBN 1-888725-16-8 (Trade paperback) 5½ X 8½, 170 pp., illustrated. The inspiring story of George Burk, lone survivor of a military plane crash, who overcame extensive burn injuries to become an honored civil servant and a successful motivational speaker. $16.95 **MacroPrintBooks™ Edition** (1999) ISBN 1-888725-28-1 $24.95)

◆ **The Stress Myth** -Serge Doublet, PhD (2000) ISBN 1-888725-36-2 (Trade paperback) 5½ X 8½, 280 pp.. A thorough examination of the concept that 'stress' is the source of unexplained afflictions. Debunking the mysticism, psychologist Serge Doublet reviews the history of other concepts such as 'demons', 'humors' and 'hysteria' that had been placed in this role in the past, and provides an alternative approach for more success in coping with life's challenges. $24.95

◆ **Eudora Light™ v 3.0 Manual** (Qualcomm) ISBN 1-888725-20-6, 135 pp., 5½ X 8½, extensively illustrated. $9.95

◆ **Perfect Love**-A Novel by Mary Harvatich (BeachHouse Books, 2000) ISBN 1-888725-29-X 5½ X 8½, 200 pp. $12.95 **MacroPrintBooks™** Edition, ISBN 1888725-15-X 8½,X11 200 pp. paperback $18.95

◆ **Buttered Side Down** - Short Stories by Edna Ferber (2000) Edna Ferber ISBN 1-888725-40-0 A MacroPrintBooks™ reprint of a classic collection of short stories by the beloved author of *Showboat, Giant, and Cimarron*. 7 X 8½, 240 pp $18.95 Regular Print Edition (2000) ISBN 1-888725-43-5 , 5½ X 8½, 190 pp.. $12.95

◆ **Tales from the Woods of Wisdom** - (book I) - Richard Tichenor (2000) ISBN 1-888725-37-0 In a spirit someplace between *The Wizard of Oz* and *The Celestine Prophecy*, this is more than a childrens' fable of life in the deep woods. 5½ X 8½, 185 pp.. $16.95

◆ **Me and My Shadows- Shadow Puppet Fun for Kids of All Ages** - Elizabeth Adams, Revised Edition by Dr. Bud Banis (2000) ISBN 1-888725-44-3 A thoroughly illustrated guide to the art of shadow puppet entertainment using tools that are always at hand where ever you go. A perfect gift for children and adults who watch them. (Trade paperback) 7 X 8½, 67 pp. BeachHouse Books. 12.95

◆ **Growing Up on Route 66** —Michael Lund (2000) ISBN1-888725-31-1 Novel evoking fond memories of what it was like to grow up alongside "America's Highway" in 20th Century Missouri. (Trade paperback) 5½ X 8½, 260 pp., BeachHouse Books $14.95

◆ **To Norma Jeane With Love, Jimmie** -Jim Dougherty as told to LC VanSavage (2000) ISBN 1-888725-51-6 The sensitive and touching story of the young bride of Jim Dougherty before her Hollywood transformation. Dozens of photographs. 5½ X 8½, 200 pp.. $16.95

◆ **The Best Years of My Life- The Autobiography of Virginia Mayo** as told to LC VanSavage (2000) ISBN 1-888725-53-2. The captivating story of actress Virginia Mayo, from the Muny in St Louis to Hollywood. Dozens of photographs. 5½ X 8½, 200 pp.. $16.95

Watch for new books from BeachHouse Books

at www.beachhousebooks.com

- ◆ **Perfect Love**-A Novel by Mary Harvatich

- ◆ **Buttered Side Down** - Short Stories by Edna Ferber

- ◆ **Tales from the Woods of Wisdom**- (book I) -Richard Tichenor

- ◆ **Me and My Shadows- Shadow Puppet Fun for Kids of All Ages** - Elizabeth Adams, Revised Edition by Dr. Bud Banis

- ◆ **Growing Up on Route 66** —Michael Lund

- ◆ **To Norma Jeane With Love, Jimmie** -Jim Dougherty as told to LC VanSavage (2000)

- ◆ **The Best Years of My Life- The Autobiography of Virginia Mayo** as told to LC VanSavage (2000)

BeachHouse
Books

An imprint of

Science & Humanities Press
PO Box 7151
Chesterfield, MO 63006-7151
(636) 394-4950
www.beachhousebooks.com
E-mail: editor@beachhousebooks.com

Item	Each	Quantit	Amount
Missouri (only) sales tax 5.975%			
Shipping per order)			$3.20
	Total		

Ship to Name:

Address:

City State Zip: